Grim Tidings

Nancy K. Wallace lives in Western Pennsylvania with her husband in a 140-year-old farmhouse. The author of 13 children's books, she works as a Youth Services Librarian, and reviews young adult literature for VOYA magazine. She has two daughters, a collection of cats, and one Arabian mare. Find Nancy online on Twitter @FairySockmother and her blog http://fairysockmother.com/

For more information on The Wolves of Llisé series, check out www.AmongWolves.net

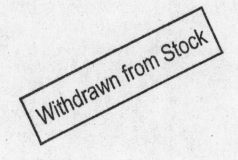

Also by Nancy K. Wallace

Among Wolves

Grim Tidings

NANCY K. WALLACE

Book Two of The Wolves of Llisé

HARPER
Voyager

Harper*Voyager*
An imprint of HarperCollins*Publisher*s Ltd
1 London Bridge Street,
London SE1 9GF

www.harpervoyagerbooks.co.uk

This Paperback Original 2016

First published in Great Britain in ebook format by Harper*Voyager* 2016

A catalogue record for this book
is available from the British Library

ISBN: 978-0-00-816023-4

This novel is entirely a work of fiction. The names, characters and
incidents portrayed in it are the work of the author's imagination.
Any resemblance to actual persons, living or dead, events or
localities is entirely coincidental.

Typeset in Sabon by Palimpsest Book Production Limited,
Falkirk, Stirlingshire

Printed and bound in Great Britain

MIX
Paper from
responsible sources
FSC www.fsc.org   **FSC™ C007454**

FSC™ is a non-profit international organisation established to promote
the responsible management of the world's forests. Products carrying the
FSC label are independently certified to assure consumers that they come
from forests that are managed to meet the social, economic and
ecological needs of present and future generations,
and other controlled sources.

Find out more about HarperCollins and the environment at
www.harpercollins.co.uk/green

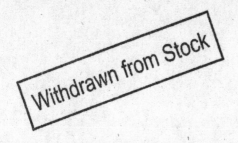

I would like to dedicate this book to my mother, Ann Kennedy, who made my childhood magical and instilled in me an early love of books and writing. As a wordsmith herself and a constant believer in my ability to succeed, I wish she could have been here to see these books in print.

CHAPTER 1

The Valley of the Shadow

At sunrise, they found the first body. They might have missed it entirely had the wolves not been searching off the trail. It lay hidden by brush in a small ravine; the left hand clawed the ground, fingers half buried in earth. The wolves whined and pawed before lifting their muzzles to seek their master's guidance.

Comte Richard Chastel clambered down the slope, small stones and dirt cascading from under his boots. Ombria's Master Bard, Armand, followed cautiously, grabbing tree trunks and branches to slow his descent and wielding his cane like a sword.

When Devin started after him, his bodyguard, Marcus, restrained him. "You stay here," he growled. "It may be a trap."

"What if it's Jeanette?" Devin objected, his first thought for the girl he loved with all his heart.

"If that's the case, they will tell you," Marcus responded grimly.

1

The body lay face down. Chastel and Armand turned it over gently. "It's Picoté!" Chastel shouted.

Devin released the breath he'd been holding. Thank God it wasn't any of his friends, Jeanette, Gaspard, or Adrian! As long as there was no tangible evidence of their deaths, there was still hope. He should have felt some small grief for the demise of the little *shérif* of Lac Dupré but he was overwhelmed by relief that he hadn't lost anyone he cared deeply about. Not yet, anyway.

Chastel bent over the body. "God," he muttered.

Devin edged closer to the incline trying to see what they were looking at.

Chastel stood up and wiped his hands on his pants. "Picoté's been beaten," he answered. "Very methodically, as though whoever did it was trying to extract information. All his fingers have been broken." He rolled the body back to its former position, allowing it to sprawl forlornly in the bushes.

Beside him, Armand averted his eyes. Ignoring his brother's outstretched hand, he turned to struggle painfully up the slope by himself.

Devin tried not to imagine what the *shérif* had gone through before he died. "What could they have wanted from Picoté?" he asked when they reached the top.

"I think they were looking for someone in particular," Chastel replied, "someone who was missing when they evacuated the village."

Devin shifted uneasily. "Me?" he asked.

Chastel shook his head. "Not this time, Monsieur Roché. I'm sure that you are on their list, too, but they knew you were at the chateau. Obviously, someone else who was important to their plan escaped their purge."

Relief flooded Armand's face. "Perhaps Jeanette and Adrian!"

Devin's hands clenched. Of course, poor Armand would think first of his daughter and his apprentice.

"I was thinking of you, Armand," Chastel replied gently. "You are the Master Bard of Ombria. With three of Llisé's Master Bards already murdered and one in hiding, can't you see that you are a primary target?"

"But Adrian was my apprentice," Armand protested, his voice strained. "Surely he was targeted as well!"

Chastel rested a hand on Armand's shoulder. "I'm sure he was, Armand."

Armand shook off his brother's hand, his face haggard. "What information could Picoté possess that would be of interest?" he demanded.

"I have no way of knowing that," Chastel replied.

"We need to leave this place," Marcus said. "I know we've traveled all night but we can't stop to rest anywhere near here. Let's get moving."

Only Devin hung back. "Surely, even Picoté deserves a decent burial."

Marcus shook his head. "Any attempt at burial would only alert them to our route. We leave things just as they are."

Already the carrion crows were circling. Devin looked at them with revulsion and followed Marcus. Armand trudged ahead, tight-lipped and grim.

Devin's chest hurt as though he carried a great stone over his heart. How could his trip to the provinces have turned so deadly? He began it with one goal in mind, to preserve the oral chronicles of Llisé by memorizing them. The quest became more urgent following the murders of several of

Llisé's bards. The information they'd carried was lost forever now and Devin had vowed not to allow any more of those stories to vanish from the history of Llisé. His best friend Gaspard had willingly followed him here, along with Marcus, a bodyguard his father had insisted on sending. Since then, someone had tried to kill Devin and the entire population of the village of Lac Dupré had disappeared overnight. The same evening, Gaspard had been kidnapped right from Chastel's estate. Jeanette had gone missing, too, perhaps because Ombria's Master Bard was her father and Devin's teacher or simply because she was in the village at the wrong time. It seemed particularly cruel that on the very night Devin had declared his love for Jeanette, she had been whisked away without a trace. If something had happened to Jeanette or Gaspard – the two people he cared for the most – he would never forgive himself.

Armand had sunk so deep in grief over his missing daughter, it was a full day before Devin dared to disturb his brooding silence. Not that Armand was the only one grieving over the current situation. They all sat mutely, watching the summer dusk transform into darkness, before they could leave the grove of trees where they had taken refuge during the day.

"Armand, what truly happened to the people of Rameau?" Devin asked, his voice hushed. The Ombrian legend recounted the tale of a town much like Lac Dupré, in which every single villager disappeared mysteriously overnight. It had happened years ago but the situation was chillingly similar to the deserted village they had searched only days before. Perhaps that story held some clue as to what was happening now.

Armand turned his head to look at him, his face shadowed

in the June twilight. "What do you think happened to them, Monsieur Roché?"

Devin shifted uncomfortably under his stare. "I don't know," he replied. "That's why I asked."

When Armand remained silent a moment, Marcus shook his head in warning at Devin. The bard ran a hand across his face before answering. "The general assumption is that they were all killed. It would be impossible to hide an entire village full of people for any length of time."

"But surely a mass grave would be difficult to hide, too," Devin persisted.

Armand turned his head away. "One would think so, Monsieur Roché," he replied wearily. "One would think so."

"I'm not familiar with the story, Monsieur Roché," Chastel said. "Until very recently, the Master Bard of Ombria was never a guest in my house." His attempt at levity was lost on Armand, who continued to stare out over the Ombrian countryside, so deceptively quiet and serene in the fading light. The fact that Armand and Chastel were half-brothers was still a matter of contention between the two men. Armand, in a particular, refused to admit to their relationship or accept Chastel's help.

Devin looked to Armand for permission. A bard always acquiesced if a Master Bard was present.

Armand waved a hand. "By all means, Monsieur Roché, enlighten him. I have no desire to."

Devin wasn't certain he wanted to tell the story either, especially this tale in particular, which intimated that the government was at fault. The joy of storytelling had lost its luster after last week's events. He cleared his throat and began.

"Gaêtan was born in the village of Rameau, the only son

*of a blacksmith. By the time he was eight, he manned the
bellows for his father's forge and quenched the red-hot iron
in cold water. As he grew, so did his responsibilities and his
understanding of the people of Rameau. Men gathered in
his father's shop to share their joys and air their complaints.
When a rise in taxes caused a furor, Gaêtan listened as the
men complained of their inability to pay and the hardship
the taxes brought on their families. As tempers flared, a
meeting was planned to bring their concerns before the
District Magistrate on his next visit to Rameau.*

*"Gaêtan's father, Edvard, made arrangements to send his
son to visit relatives for the summer in another village. He
feared violence because of the planned protest and wanted
his son to be safe. Gaêtan didn't want to leave and pleaded
with his father to let him stay. Edvard explained that he
was too young to engage in a debate about politics. Before
Gaêtan left, his father told him to remember that when he
grew to be a man it was important to stand up for what
he believed in, no matter what the cost.*

*"Gaêtan spent the summer with his aunt and uncle. The
date of the District Magistrate's visit came and went and
still there was no news from Rameau. Finally in late summer,
they walked Gaêtan home and found the village completely
deserted. Gaêtan ran from house to house calling first for
his father and then for his friends and neighbors. There was
no response. His father's last words echoed in his ears: 'Stand
up for what you believe in, no matter what the cost.'*

*"And so, Gaêtan stood alone in the village square. All
around him the windows of the cottages were dark and
shuttered. The chimneys stood stark against the forest; not
a puff of smoke emerged from their tops. He realized then
that the people of Rameau were gone. Not one man, woman,*

*or child remained to welcome him home. He fell to his knees
in the overgrown gardens and wept."*

Armand got up and left them, walking into the shadows
of the trees. Chastel raised an eyebrow. "Well, that was
rough. I'm sorry I asked to hear it. I'm sure it only intensified Armand's worry. No doubt, he has little hope that this
will turn out well."

"I share that sentiment as well," Marcus muttered. "I
cannot imagine that we will find those people alive."

"I hope you are wrong," Devin replied, refusing to believe
that he would never hold Jeanette again or hear Gaspard's
teasing voice.

"As do I," Chastel echoed.

The conversation trailed off awkwardly. Fireflies rose over
the surrounding fields, their tiny lights blinking in the dark.
An owl called from the trees and the sweet scent of flowering
summer grass permeated the air.

A whine disturbed the silence. Beneath the sheltering
branches of the trees that circled them, Chastel's wolves lay
gathered in the darkness, waiting. Chastel rose. "I'll leave
you. We'll check the route ahead," he murmured, "but we
will be within earshot should you need us."

Devin watched the Comte fade into the shadows. Chastel
never transformed in front of them. A perverse part of him
wanted to watch. He was still uncomfortable with the concept
that Chastel seemed to be able to change from wolf to man
at will. He glanced at Marcus. His bodyguard's eyes were
also fixed on the spot where Chastel had disappeared. Armand
emerged from the trees and slumped down beside them.

Devin apologized. "I'm sorry that I told that story. I didn't
mean to add to your burden."

Armand avoided his eyes. "Chastel asked to hear it – you

are obligated to comply. Most of these stories are close to the hearts and emotions of the people of Ombria. I wish that you had more time to get to know us better and understand why we fear your government in Coreé so much."

"I realize that the story of Rameau doesn't come out and blame the government but it is certainly implied. It must be terrifying not to know what the consequences of your actions may be."

"You are beginning to sound like a provincial," Marcus said.

Devin shrugged. "Perhaps I'm beginning to think like one." He gestured at Armand. "I have you to thank for that. I honestly never realized the inequities that existed in the provinces before I came here. Living in the Chancellor's mansion, having anything I could possibly want and servants to wait on me, I couldn't imagine how people in the other fourteen provinces lived. Everything Coreé needs conveniently arrives by ship, either down the Dantzig or around the southern cape."

"All those materials are made by the sweat of some provincial man's brow," Armand added.

"I know that now," Devin replied. His mind went back unwillingly to the village of Lac Dupré. "When they were searching for the villagers, Armand, Chastel's wolves would have found a mass grave."

Armand nodded grimly. "And that, Monsieur Roché, is the only thing that gives me hope."

Devin sighed. Hope was in short supply these days. His friend, Gaspard, was gone. He had disappeared just as surely as the people of Lac Dupré and Devin had no idea whether he was alive or dead. At first, Marcus and Chastel had assumed that they were being followed by the same men who had abducted him. But obviously someone was also preceding them down the road ahead, someone who had beaten Picoté to death in hopes of extracting information.

A movement in the bushes brought Marcus to his feet, his pistol in his hand. A huge wolf with reddish fur and deep, intelligent eyes emerged from the brush and whined.

Armand rose. "Chastel wants me to follow him," he murmured and disappeared silently into the darkness.

"How could he possibly know ...?" Devin began.

"Hush," Marcus told him.

Devin and Marcus sat in silence. Even the insects seemed to have dampened their chorus to an occasional unenthusiastic chirp. Both man and wolf were gone a long time. When Armand returned his face was ashen, his steps unsteady. He would have been unable to walk if Chastel hadn't supported him.

Devin felt a chill run up his spine. "Not Jeanette," he prayed silently. "Please, God, don't let it be Jeanette."

Chastel settled Armand on a tree stump. "Adrian is dead," he announced.

"What about Jeanette?" Devin's voice choked on her name. His mind was racing. "Adrian surely wouldn't have left her alone! They would have stayed together. He would have protected her!"

"There's no sign of Jeanette or anyone else," Chastel said quietly. "Adrian was beaten, too, before he died."

"I don't understand," Devin said finally. "The bodies have been placed directly in our path. These men seem to know where we're headed!"

"Only because we have been assuming that we were being followed," Marcus suggested. "Perhaps the reverse is true and we are following them."

"But you said they are still looking for Armand," Devin pointed out.

Chastel glanced at his brother. "Or they believe they know where he is going."

"But our choice of route was random," Devin reminded him.

"Was it?" Marcus asked. "I think Armand suggested Arcadia."

Armand wiped a hand across his eyes. "Only because Arcadia's bard has been murdered," he replied. "I hoped to establish a new apprentice while we were there."

"Armand, with Adrian's death, Ombria is without an apprentice, too. You are more valuable here than ever," Devin pointed out.

"If need be," Armand replied. "You will have to act as my apprentice, Monsieur Roché."

"But I am not a native of Ombria," Devin protested. "I cannot be an apprentice bard."

Armand shook his head. "These are dangerous times, Monsieur Roché; we can hardly expect things to proceed as they normally should. As long as you remember and repeat my Chronicle to the people of my province, you will serve my purposes."

Marcus stood up. "The Chronicles are none of my concern! I'll not have the Chancellor's son murdered on some back road in Ombria! We must find somewhere safe. Devin needs to disappear for a few weeks or months, if necessary. I thought by deviating from his original itinerary, we might elude our pursuers, but now I'm not so sure. I don't know Ombria as well as you do, Chastel. Where can we go?"

Chastel stabbed a finger into the night. "There are caves

to the north. I would never have known they were there except for my wolves. They go back into the mountains reaching from Ombria, clear into the northern reaches of Arcadia."

"Then I suggest we go there as quickly as possible," Marcus said.

"It is rough country," Chastel warned, "and hard walking. The land's rocky and only good for pasture; there are very few roads. We'll only have the wolves as guides."

"All the better!" Marcus said. "There will be less chance of our being tracked."

"We can only go a mile or so tonight and then continue in the morning. Traveling a road at night is hazardous enough, but one of us could break a leg navigating a rocky field."

"But there may be other villagers on the road ahead!" Armand protested. "Perhaps they are being moved somewhere. We will never know who is alive and who is dead if we don't continue this way!"

There was an awkward silence, as Chastel and Marcus avoided the stricken look on his face.

"Armand," Chastel replied softly, "perhaps that's for the best."

CHAPTER 2

Revelations

Every rock and tree seemed to hide possible assassins as they worked their way along the bushy hedgerows. Every twig that snapped or bird that took flight put them all on alert and they were edgy and tense as the midsummer sun beat down on their backs. The sweat that trickled down Devin's back was bred more of fear than heat. He prayed the Chastel's wolves would alert them to danger before it was too late.

They passed through a procession of standing stones, marching inevitably off to the west. Two tilted drunkenly, as though the very earth had shifted under them. One had fallen and was covered in a tangle of bramble and dead grass. It was mortally wounded. Even had someone attempted to resurrect it, a split ran diagonally, breaking the toppled giant in half. The Chronicles claimed that the concentric circles that had been chiseled into each stone represented Terre Sainté, the ancestral home of the first settlers of Llisé. Hundreds of the carved monoliths traversed the Northern provinces from this side of the Dantzig to the ocean on

Llisé's western shore, effectively dividing the empire horizontally, just as the Dantzig's wide waters split Llisé in half vertically. It was water as much as culture that separated Llisé's provinces from its capital, Coreé.

Devin extricated his boot from a loop of bramble. The fields were covered with blackberry bushes, concealing rocks and holes from unwary travelers. Devin's hands were shredded from deflecting them, his palms stained with the purple juice from the berries he had popped into his mouth. "Just so you know," he announced to Marcus, after Chastel and Armand took the lead, "I agree with Armand! If the villagers are still alive it's our obligation to try to save them."

"The four of us?" Marcus scoffed. "Against enough soldiers to hold 800 villagers captive? What's your plan, Devin? I'd be interested to know."

"I don't have a plan," he snapped. "You're the one with the military training. Why don't you come up with a plan? It's better than doing nothing."

"I have one responsibility," Marcus reminded him quietly, "to get you home safely to your father. What happens to the villagers of Lac Dupré is not my concern."

Devin intentionally let a bramble snap back in Marcus's face. "Don't you even care about Jeanette?"

Marcus deftly avoided it. "They don't have Jeanette," he said.

Devin swung around to face him. "What? How can you be sure?"

"Hush," Marcus replied, his voice low enough that only Devin could hear him. "If their captors were interested in Armand's whereabouts, Jeanette would have been questioned first. If nothing else, the threat of seeing her hurt would have prompted Adrian to reveal anything he knew."

"My God, Marcus, why haven't you told Armand?" Devin asked.

"Because I might be wrong and I don't want to get his hopes up."

Devin grunted. "So you do have a heart. I'd begun to doubt that."

"You know very little about me, Devin," Marcus replied. "Now hurry up! Can't you keep up with a man twice your age and a cripple?"

Travel at night on the road had been slow but now traveling during the day, Devin felt they had regressed to a snail's pace. Chastel kept them close to the hedgerows and trees at the edges of the fields where they were less visible. But the walking was most difficult there. Greying grass covered a maze of rotting branches as the June sun climbed higher in the sky. Armand would have fallen more than once except for Chastel's quick intervention. He no longer avoided his brother's hand. Perhaps the loss of everyone else he held most dear made him cherish this one family member he had left.

The wolves moved like grey shadows through the dappled sunlight. Devin never heard them, but occasionally a movement caught his eye and a slender shape would glide among the trees only to disappear into the brush a second later. He couldn't control his innate fear of them; even knowing that they obeyed Chastel did nothing to relieve his anxiety. Surely, there were other wolves in Ombria that owed no alliance to Chastel. Even the revolver that Marcus had stuffed in his pocket before they left did nothing to allay his fear.

Chastel called a halt shortly after noon, one finger to his lips. He motioned the men down flat in a clump of bushes. Devin lay with his heart thumping, his cheek pressed against sticks. The pungent fragrance of dry leaves filled the air. When Marcus laid a hand gently on his shoulder, Devin jumped. Marcus, too, motioned for quiet but pointed out toward the center of the field where two women and a little girl bent to pick blackberries, filling a bucket that they placed on the ground.

A moment later, Devin heard a snarl and a lone wolf darted out across the meadow. The screams that followed brought Devin to his feet, fumbling for his gun.

Marcus's hand struck him in the small of the back bringing him down with his full weight behind it. Devin fell face forward, tasting dirt and blood. Marcus pressed him against the ground with an iron hand. "Leave it," he hissed. "He is only frightening them away."

The screams and snarls faded, leaving the afternoon unnaturally still, as though the wolf had threatened even the insects themselves. Gradually, a few *cigale* began whirring, one bird broke into song, and a lone gray wolf slunk back through the trees, his tongue lolling from his mouth. Marcus stood up.

Devin scrambled to his feet, wiping a quick hand across his split lip. He clenched his fists, torn between anger and embarrassment, and avoided Marcus's eyes.

"Do what you're told!" Marcus snapped. "Even if Chastel's wolves had killed those women and that child – it's no concern of yours. We are dealing with much bigger stakes here than the death of a few peasants!"

There was a strained silence as Armand's gaze met Devin's. Armand's voice was steely when he addressed Marcus: "These are my people. If you do not recognize their value then perhaps I am traveling in the wrong company."

Chastel intervened. "I'm certain Monsieur Berringer

meant no disrespect. He is only concerned with Monsieur Roché's safety."

"Surely, these women and children are worthy of your protection, too, Marcus," Devin protested, dusting dirt from his trousers. "My life is worth no more than any other man's."

"You are a political commodity," Marcus replied coldly. "Your life or death could tip scales in Viénne that will have repercussions that will reach every province in Llisé."

Devin held his eyes for a moment and then turned his back. "Thank you," he murmured, tight-lipped. "I'm glad you've made my position perfectly clear."

As they moved on, Devin felt chilled in spite of the summer heat shimmering across the fields. He was irrevocably stuck with Marcus. His father had sent his most trusted bodyguard with him on this journey, and yet Devin remained unsure of what his orders were. And Marcus had no intention of telling him.

CHAPTER 3

Sacred Wells

Devin longed for firelight; sleeping night after night in the darkened forest left his senses jarred and raw. Until they had veered north, they had slept during the day. There had been something comforting about those languid afternoons when even the wolves had rested, their shaggy forms deceptively doglike in the warmth of the sun.

When they had traveled at night, at least there had been the road laid out before them. There had been reference points, a destination. Now he felt lost – both figuratively and literally. He was amazed that so much of Ombria remained uninhabited. Sometimes they traveled for an entire day without sight of another human being or a house.

Every day, the wolves found fresh water but they were running short of food. The end of the cheese and dried fruit had been consumed yesterday, leaving only the remains of the last loaf of moldy bread for dinner. He shouldn't have been surprised when Chastel gleefully dragged a deer carcass into camp. Marcus immediately set to skinning it, tossing

17

the least desirable parts to the wolves who had gathered around him.

Devin gathered a few branches. "Shall I make a fire?" he asked, feeling relieved he'd be useless at butchery.

"No!" Marcus barked. "Do you want to signal our position to half of Ombria?"

Devin hesitated, a sinking feeling in his stomach. "Then how will we eat it?"

Armand avoided his eyes. "We'll eat it raw, Devin."

Devin's response was immediate. "I can't."

"Then you'll go hungry," Marcus replied. He finished his gruesome task silently and then laid the raw meat on leaves in front of them. Chastel and Marcus picked up their portions without hesitation. Armand hung back for a moment and delicately selected the smallest piece.

In the deep shadows of an old walnut tree, Devin watched them eat, their mouths smeared with fresh blood, their hands dark and sticky. Glittering fireflies twinkled in the woods around them, their innocent, fragile beauty juxtaposed against a scene resembling some nightmarish fairytale. Devin closed his eyes and leaned back against the oak's massive trunk. He had never been so certain that Llisé existed as two completely disparate worlds – and yet each held secrets that men would die to protect.

He thought of Chastel's chateau and the night that Gaspard had told him he was going home. Devin had understood his friend finally giving in to his father's pressure to return to Coreé but he'd still felt betrayed. The prospect of a journey of over a year with no one but Marcus for a traveling companion seemed overwhelming. Gaspard might be irresponsible and careless but he was extremely good company. They had been friends since they were children;

Gaspard had always been cocky, irreverent, and funny in direct opposition to Devin's restraint. Perhaps it was their differences that had brought them together.

Devin's descent into nightmare came quickly.

He sat with Armand and Marcus in the coach racing back from Lac Dupré to the chateau. Soldiers had been seen in the village asking for Gaspard. Adrian had sent them to the chateau and yet, as the coach careened down the road, there was no sign of them. When the coach finally stopped at Chastel's, there were no horses standing in the yard, no sign that anyone but the household staff were about. Marcus knocked and the door was opened by Chastel himself.

"What's going on?" Chastel asked. "What's happened?" He had removed his jacket. He stood with his vest unbuttoned, his shirt loosened at the throat.

"Did some men come here from Coreé?" Marcus demanded.

Chastel nodded. "They're with Gaspard in the study, right now."

"Who are they?" Devin asked.

"I don't know," Chastel replied. "Gaspard seemed to know them. He called one of them by name."

"Who sent them?" Devin asked.

Chastel shook his head. "I have no idea. Is there a problem?"

A sudden feeling of dread overwhelmed Devin. He turned and ran, ignoring Marcus's shouts to stop. He yanked open the study door and then crashed head-first onto the floor as Marcus flattened him from behind.

Armand and Chastel halted behind them. "There's no one here," Chastel said in surprise.

Marcus rolled off Devin and staggered to his feet. "God,

will you never listen to me, Devin?" he growled angrily. *"If there had been a man with a pistol in this room, you might be dead right now!"*

Devin dragged himself to his knees. The room was empty!

Chastel circled the walls in disbelief.

"You saw no one leave?" Marcus demanded of Chastel.

Chastel shook his head. "Mareschal and I were in the hall the entire time. I assumed Gaspard would tell me what was going on when he had finished talking with them."

Devin pulled himself upright, an awful realization suddenly shaping itself in his mind. "You assumed they were his father's men, didn't you, Chastel?" he asked, his voice shaking.

"God, yes," Chastel replied. He stood with his hands clenched. "I think I may have left Gaspard alone with assassins in my study."

Devin woke to soft rain. The overcast sky stretched gray and ominous toward the horizon, promising a long wet day. He sat a moment trying to shake off the dregs of his nightmare. At least he had wakened no one and managed to escape Marcus's wrath. He straightened stiffly, sure that an impression of the old tree's ragged bark marked his back. Marcus watched him silently, his gun casually laid against his thigh. The ground still reeked of blood but the rest of the flesh had been consumed by the wolves; only bare bones littered the perimeter of their camp. Chastel and his pack had disappeared. Armand still slept, one arm beneath his head, his cane beside him.

Devin walked to the spring nearby and cupped the cool sweet water in his hands to drink. Although he hadn't participated in last night's grisly meal, he felt tainted by it.

20

He let the water rush over his wrists and sluiced it over his face. The icy water left him chilled and lonely. He missed Gaspard, who could find humor in anything – even eating raw meat and traveling among wolves. He was startled as Marcus approached.

"Here." His bodyguard extended a chunk of moldy bread. "I saved this for you last night."

"Thank you," Devin said, looking up in surprise.

"It was your portion," Marcus clarified gruffly. "You fell asleep before we divided it up." He turned and walked away before Devin could reply.

Devin shook his head and smiled sheepishly. "I see," he murmured. For just a moment, he'd been foolish enough to think that Marcus had given him his own piece of bread.

He ate the bread where he sat, listening to the ripple and gurgle of the little spring beside him. The sound was soothing and hypnotic. He closed his eyes.

"Etienne?" the voice was far away, mingled with water over stone. "Etienne?" the second call was louder, more insistent.

Devin jumped to his feet but Marcus was already running toward him. "What is it?" he demanded, his gun in his hand.

Devin waved a hand at the spring. "Voices," he said. "Didn't you hear them?"

Marcus shook his head. "I heard nothing."

Armand was on his feet too, stiffly walking to join them.

"There were voices coming out of the water," Devin explained.

Marcus glanced at Armand and then back at Devin. "I was watching you. Your eyes were closed. Did you fall asleep?"

"I wasn't sleeping," Devin protested. "I was listening to the sound of the water."

Armand quoted:

> *"When water flows,*
> *From sacred springs,*
> *Its blessed song*
> *Sweet comfort brings.*
> *Those gone before us*
> *Speak again,*
> *To calm our dreams*
> *And soothe our pain."*

"What's that from?" Devin asked.

"'Saint Gwenneg's Well'," Armand replied. "It's part of Arcadia's Chronicle."

"Will you teach it to me?" he asked.

"If you like," Armand answered. "Llisé is full of stories of voices coming from wells and springs but very few have made it into its Chronicles. I've never been blessed to hear the voices myself but I don't doubt that you did."

Marcus snorted in annoyance. "Well, I do. When did you last take any valerian, Devin?" he growled.

"Not since we left Chastel's," he replied. "I didn't bring it with me."

"Then I will see that you have some more," Marcus snapped. "I'll not deal with your waking dreams in a world that threatens to kill us at any moment!"

Devin's penchant for waking dreams had been a constant issue on their journey. Sometimes, unbelievably, a nightmare seemed to twist into reality, causing him to mistrust the very people he needed to rely on. Only valerian allowed him a restful night's sleep and he had left it at Chastel's chateau because of their hurried escape.

As the land became steeper, the moss-colored mountains grew closer. Every day brought new experiences. Devin realized he had never been truly hungry before. His childhood complaints of "I'm starving!" took on an entirely different meaning as his stomach gnawed and growled with constant hunger. The other men dined nightly on raw rabbit and venison, but Devin couldn't bring himself to try it.

The berries were a blessing and he took time to gather them even when it meant incurring Marcus's anger for falling behind. The hard green apples with their sour tang tasted heavenly. He found a cluster of mushrooms near a rotting stump and bent to examine those as a potential source of food.

"If you eat those," Marcus remarked coolly, "I may as well go home right now."

Devin stood and dusted his knees off. Marcus seemed intent on making him feel foolish and immature. He clenched his jaw and said nothing. Marcus had also kept him alive – no small feat in this strange new province.

They crossed field after field of wild flowers and brambles. Occasional wild apple trees hung heavy with small misshapen green fruits, their twisted branches and trunks so unlike the meticulously pruned trees Devin was used to in Viénne. The sloping fields gave way to steeper grazing land where fluffy sheep lazily consumed wild flowers and grass with equal pleasure. Even though the wolves had disappeared into the wooded hedgerows moments before, the sheep dogs raised their heads and started a strange keening bark. They rounded the sheep up and chased them, terrified and stumbling, down toward the lower pastures.

They stopped to rest for the night when an evening shower brought a sudden downpour. Cool mist floated up from the ravines. Devin filled his stomach with a few blackberries and curled up under a massive oak. He slept almost immediately, taking the swirling mist with him into a chaotic dream of Lac Dupré.

Adrian and Jeanette stood at the door of the Bardic Hall watching as soldiers lined the streets, herding people like animals toward the open doors of the church. Adrian, Picoté, and the fat little baker who made the best croissants in the village tried to resist and were ridden down and trampled by the horsemen, and then the village was set afire by the torches the soldiers carried. Jeanette was scooped up by one of the horsemen and Devin ran into the midst of it all but no one saw or heard him screaming.

A hand came down firmly over his mouth and jerked him into an upright position, his back against the unforgiving bark of the oak. "Stop it!" Marcus growled.

"They've taken Jeanette and the village is burning!" Devin protested, the smell of smoke and ash still in his nostrils.

"You're dreaming!" Marcus snapped. But suddenly, his hold on Devin loosened.

"I smell it, too," Chastel murmured, standing up.

Armand was on his feet, too. "Over there!" he said, pointing.

Flames glittered red through the trees to the west and smoke swirled up, a ghostly grayish rose against the sky. The faint cries of voices reached them even at this distance.

"It's Beaulieu," Chastel said. "The village lies to the west of here."

"What possible reason could they have to burn Beaulieu?" Armand whispered. "There are only a few hundred people who live there."

"The magistrate lives in Beaulieu," Chastel said. "If he

is dead then no one will be left to tell the tale of what happened in Lac Dupré, or here either."

"Except for us," Devin said, rising shakily. "We're the only ones left and they probably intend to kill us, too."

CHAPTER 4

Speculation

"Let's stop for a few minutes," Chastel announced after a particularly hard climb. They scattered wearily on the rocky ledges to catch their breath. The air was cooler here, the constant breeze refreshing, lifting their hair off sweaty brows. From their vantage point, the foothills below them spread out like a miniature patchwork quilt, pastures and cultivated fields bordered by hedgerows and woods. It all looked so peaceful and serene.

For the past few days they had climbed steadily upward, leaving the last remnants of civilization behind them. They hadn't seen another person for several days and the terrain grew more rugged with each hour. Devin's harp strap had been chafing his shoulder all morning. He carefully laid the harp on the ground and stretched out on the sun-warmed stone to rest. The harp, his cloak, and one set of clothes were all he had left of his belongings. Thankfully, Chastel had provided him with some essentials to take with him.

Marcus pulled a small telescope from his jacket. They waited in silence while he scanned the countryside, moving methodically over the hills and ridges Devin had found so beautiful and innocent a moment before. Marcus viewed everything as a threat. He never dropped his vigilance for an instant. Whatever his father paid him, Devin decided in that moment, it would never be enough. He waited until Marcus sheathed the telescope and slid it into his pocket before he spoke. "Are we safe, then?"

Marcus's laugh held no warmth. "You are never safe, Devin. Don't ever forget that, but I don't see anyone following us now. It doesn't mean that they aren't there – being as careful as we are not to be seen – but I don't believe they know where we've gone."

"That's a blessing then," Armand replied, rubbing his knee. "I'm sick of death."

"Loss seems to be part of life in Ombria," Devin said. "I realize now how unaccustomed to death I was in Coreé. I occasionally heard of an older friend of my father's who had passed away or a sudden accident that claimed a life. But death didn't seem to be a relentless specter lurking at the door the way it is here."

"Death is a very prominent part of life in all of the provinces," Armand replied. "It isn't just Ombria. Sorrento has access to better medical care because of your father's intervention but in the remaining provinces, people simply struggle to stay alive, to put food on the table, and care for their families. Death is never more than a moment away for any of us."

Devin batted a fly away from his face. "I think that's why my father agreed to let me come on this trip, to see all of this first-hand so that I can, in turn, tell him what life is really like here. A Chancellor pays only one official visit to each provincial capital in his entire term of office. His reports come from landholders in each region. Obviously, he can't depend on Councilmen like René Forneaux to paint an accurate picture of what is going on."

"It isn't only René," Chastel said. "You haven't seen the worst yet. The northernmost provinces are the poorest. Their growing season is the shortest so they have less time to grow the foods they produce. Some export part of their goods to Viénne and part is considered tax in kind to the landholder himself. For those that rely solely on their crops for a living, there often isn't enough left to feed their own families over the winter. Then the taxes are entirely too high for the services that most people receive. Roads are only maintained in the capitals and there is only one provincial school, which is never well attended due to the whole sponsorship issue. If a young man can't receive sponsorship from a nobleman in his province, he can't attend school. And even if he can, he can only be trained to take over his father's position as he ages. There is no way to better yourself in the provinces."

"It makes me wonder if it is even possible to restructure this into an equitable system," Devin said. "On one hand, we have the very rich and on the other, the very poor. Are there any small landholders at all?"

"A few," Chastel replied. "In some of the towns, the shops are owned by individuals. Every estate employs a blacksmith, a baker, a dressmaker, and so forth. Their services are available to the landowner's tenants, as well – at a price, of course. In some provinces, the town itself is owned by an estate, and all its residents are tenants of it. The system is designed to keep everyone neatly in their places."

"Where do you stand in all this?" Devin asked.

Chastel laughed. "Do you mean: am I part of the problem or part of the solution?"

"Part of the problem," Armand declared, swinging his cane playfully at his brother.

"A bit of both, I'm afraid," Chastel answered truthfully. "My family has owned our land for centuries. I grew up believing that I was entitled to more than my neighbors because I was rich and well educated. And then there has always been an unhealthy relationship between the villagers and the Chastels because of this ..." He hesitated a moment, waving his hand at one of his wolves who sprawled at his feet. "... this whole wolf business. Which has no actual basis in fact, at all," he finished with a smile.

They all laughed, even Marcus, who persisted in inspecting the slopes below them for pursuers.

"My father did make certain that the village always had a midwife, although a physician would have been better," Chastel continued. "He did pay his servants an equitable wage but I sometimes wonder if that was only to bribe people to work at the estate. With the eerie reputation that the Chastels have acquired, it hasn't always been easy to maintain a staff. Most of our employees are still from families that have worked for us for several generations. New employees are very hard to come by."

"You have sponsored many young men's educations," Armand pointed out.

Chastel inclined his head. "I've tried, but it isn't enough. It is unfortunate, but there is a great amount of provincial talent that is wasted."

"I have often thought that Jeanette would make a superb physician," Devin said. "She has a natural touch for healing and empathy for both physical and emotional pain."

"Well, that's not possible!" Armand replied, withdrawing into his shell again. "There is no use discussing what can never be."

"But instituting education for everyone might allow some other young woman to become a physician," Devin said. "In Coreé women are educated but the purpose isn't for employment. My mother can discuss literature, music, and art but only to make her entertaining company at parties. I've often thought she would have made a wonderful teacher herself, if she had only been given the chance. Instead, she spends her days planning parties and receptions when she might have had the chance to help develop growing minds."

"You are proposing massive reforms, Devin," Marcus said. "If the changes come from the top – in Coreé – they must be a series of tiny steps toward an ultimate goal. The Llisé you are envisioning is very far in the future. It won't happen in your father's lifetime and possibly not in your own. We need a Council that can set changes in motion but allow time for people to become accustomed to each step along the way before something new is added."

Devin propped himself on an elbow. "But there is so much inequality – so much that needs to be fixed now. People are angry and hurting. I wish I could just create some plan that would allow everyone to have a fair chance."

"Your father has made education available to everyone in his home province of Sorrento and you see where that has gotten him – a sharpshooter trying to kill him from the upper gallery while he spoke in Council Chambers," Marcus pointed out. "When the opposition resorts to assassination our very political system is at risk."

"There are those who have no desire to give everyone a

fair chance, Devin," Chastel said. "What you are proposing would be catastrophic."

Devin sat up. "For whom?"

"For everyone," Marcus agreed. "You are advocating revolution."

CHAPTER 5

Misconceptions

Both days and nights were cooler in the mountains, filled with the constant chatter of insects and redolent with the fragrance of pine. Layers of evergreen needles muffled their footsteps as they followed forest paths mapped out for decades by deer herds. Sometimes the rocky slopes hid sheltered valleys, with fields of vibrant wildflowers and tumbling streams. Each upward climb brought new land-scapes, some so beautiful that Devin could only gape in wonder that such places existed. How many residents of Coreé had ever glimpsed these wildly gorgeous scenes? He wished that he were an artist so that he could carry back proof of the incredible beauty he had the good fortune to experience daily. What an amazing addition it would be to his beloved Archives to include paintings from all fourteen provinces! Viénne had already been well documented because it contained the capitol city of Coreé but there were no paintings of any of the other provinces, as though they had no value in the compendium of material that the Archives contained. Here again was another inequality to add to the list he planned to present to his father if he ever arrived home safely!

The wolves began to range farther afield, slinking toward the shadowy shelter of the trees when a valley provided grass and forage for the deer. They killed only to eat, not for sport and while Devin didn't care to watch their tactics, he began to recognize some of them as individuals which stood apart from the pack. There were eight in all and they varied in color from lightest gray to dark charcoal, but their personalities and mannerisms were different. When they gathered with the men in the evenings, Devin saw the intelligence in their eyes and their utmost respect for Chastel. The relationship between this man and his wolves was fascinating and Devin began to record his observations like one of Armand's stories in his head.

Late one afternoon, they reached a valley of barren land that stretched desolate and dusty to the hazy horizon. Across its surface a few withered weeds had sprouted, twisting out of the dry and crusted earth. Insects scrambled across the dirt, hurrying to the greener fields and cooler forests beyond.

Devin stopped, one boot scraping at the parched field. "What happened here?"

Armand leaned heavily on his cane, his face smudged with dust and sweat. "Did you never learn about Comte Aucoin at the *Université*?"

"Yes, of course," Devin replied. "François Aucoin treated his servants like slaves until one day his people rose up against him. While he was on the way to Viénne, they waylaid him on the road with his bodyguards and killed them all. Then they returned to the chateau and slaughtered his wife and small children. They salted all of the land around the chateau so that nothing would grow there, hoping it would serve as a warning to other property owners of the power of the provincial masses."

"Good God!" Armand yelled, pounding his cane against the dusty ground. "Is that what they taught you in school?"

"That's what the official report states," Devin replied. "It's all I have ever read. I assume it's not true, then?"

"Not a word," Armand responded. "Comte Aucoin was the kindest man to walk this earth. In fact, he was referred to as The Gentle Comte. He treated his servants like valued employees and paid them fair wages. When he was killed, he was on his way to Viénne to lobby for education for all provincial children. He and his bodyguards were murdered on the road; his family was slaughtered along with every single servant in his household." Armand drummed with his cane again on the soil. "This land was poisoned by the *militaire* – not salted – which would only have provided a temporary disruption to agriculture. The warning here, Monsieur Roché, was to other landowners who might share his sentiments and views on education." Armand gestured with his cane at Chastel. "Do you see now why my brother, Jean, is so reluctant to involve himself in Llisé's politics?"

"But this was fairly recent," Devin objected.

"He was killed twelve years ago," Chastel replied, his face grim.

Devin nodded. "So it happened in my lifetime."

"You were still in diapers," Marcus snorted.

"That's not true and it's hardly the point," Devin protested. "The point is that my father was Chancellor Elite when it happened." He swallowed convulsively, his eyes on Marcus.

"He was," Marcus confirmed.

"Surely, he didn't condone this? He wouldn't have ordered

the deaths of Aucoin's wife and children …?" Devin's voice faltered.

Marcus's face was hard. "He has ordered the deaths of innocent people in the past, Devin – don't delude yourself that he hasn't." He paused for breath as all eyes remained on him. "But in this, you are right, Devin. Chancellor Roché did not order this. As far as I know, he was given the same report that appears in your precious history books."

"Then who did order it?" Armand demanded.

Marcus shrugged. "I have no idea. I knew nothing about it except the official record until you just told us your version."

"It's not a version!" Armand growled.

Chastel put a hand on his brother's arm. "Armand's telling the truth," he confirmed. "Aucoin and I were friends."

Devin threw a hand up in disgust. "Who would do such a thing?"

"I doubt you need to look much further than the same men who kidnapped Gaspard and emptied the village of Lac Dupré," Armand suggested.

Chastel sighed. "About six months before all of this happened, René Forneaux visited Ombria. I had invited him to stay at the chateau for a few weeks in the fall to do some hunting. François Aucoin was part of the hunting party. He and René discussed provincial politics over dinner several times. René was well aware of the man's sympathies and deplored them. René came back again the following spring. He stayed with me but I know he wasn't here when Aucoin was killed."

"But surely even if Forneaux were responsible, he can't have acted alone," Devin said.

"Devin, you know there are other men who support

René's views," Marcus said. "All it takes is a few who band together to accomplish their own purposes."

"I believe it is more than a few men," Chastel replied quietly.

"God," Devin muttered under his breath. "If all of this happens without my father's knowledge or approval, who is actually running the country, then?"

"That is the real question," Marcus replied. "And I can't give you an answer."

"Do you know?" Chastel asked.

Marcus shook his head. "No, and unfortunately, neither does Chancellor Roché."

CHAPTER 6

The Ghosts of Aucoin

Comte Aucoin's chateau still stood – a compact, stone structure with conical towers silhouetted against the sunset. The barren land reached within an arm's length of the walls where a welter of brambles and ivy competed quite successfully to conceal the lower story of the building from sight. Ivy curtained the windows and thorns barred the door.

"It's like something out of a fairytale," Devin murmured.

"More like *une fable d'horreur*," Armand commented, spreading his cloak across his shoulders. The air had chilled with the setting sun. A stiff wind stirred the dust around them into tiny whirling cyclones. To the north, thunder rumbled beneath darkening clouds.

"Do you think it's wise to spend the night here?" Devin asked uneasily.

"I think it is the last place anyone would look," Chastel assured him. "The place is reputed to be haunted. None of the local residents will come anywhere near it. They believe the land is cursed and so is anyone who walks on it."

Devin glanced at his dusty boots. "Well that's reassuring,"

he said dryly. "Surely Comte Aucoin's story belongs in Ombria's Chronicle, Armand. Why didn't you ever tell it to me?"

"We're not in Ombria anymore," Armand replied. "Comte Aucoin's land marks the boundary between Ombria and Arcadia."

"But you said the caves were in Ombria," Devin protested.

"They begin in Ombria," Chastel explained. "They certainly run under its borders but I couldn't tell you where the entrances are. We still have another day's climb to the openings my wolves use."

"If we are staying here, I suggest we find a way into the chateau before this storm hits," said Marcus. "Try to do so without disturbing any of the ivy growth on the outside. That might alert our pursuers to where we have gone."

"We've left a great many footprints," Devin pointed out.

Armand gestured at the sky with his cane. "The rain will take care of that. I think we're in for a downpour very soon."

The arched front door was completely obscured by brambles and hacking their way in would only serve to announce their presence should someone decide to look for them here. Chastel guided them around to the back where a curtain of ivy masked the kitchen door but fell aside at the touch of a hand. A small garden, nestled close to the walls, seemed almost intact. Among the scrawny ornamental plants grew a few herbs and vegetables.

Marcus halted and withdrew his pistol from his pocket. "Those aren't left from Comte Aucoin's garden. Someone's tending this," he said. "I imagine they are living here, too."

A bolt of lightning zapped across the dusty field above

them, thunder followed immediately. Marcus paused undecided but Chastel gave a low whistle. Devin smelled the wolves before he saw them – a heavy, wild, musky scent permeated the air as they gathered around the men – their hackles raised, lips curled over vicious front teeth. "We outnumber them," Chastel said. "Of that I'm certain."

Marcus nodded and cocked his pistol, slowly turning the knob on the door. It swung open effortlessly, revealing the dim interior of a kitchen. While a loaf of freshly baked bread lay on the table with a round of cheese and a bottle of wine, the floor lay littered with dust and leaves. Cobwebs clung to the beams as thick as curtains. Marcus put his finger to his lips and motioned for Devin to stay back. The wolves swarmed around the table, sniffing the air, and then padding off down a hallway.

"You'll have your mysterious resident shortly," Chastel remarked, his gun in hand.

Scratching and whining echoed from the hall and Chastel left to investigate. He returned a few seconds later. "There is a heavy oak door just around the corner that leads to the wine cellar. It's locked from the inside."

Marcus frowned. "So, someone is hiding," he said. "We can break the door down or post a few of the wolves to guard it and avail ourselves of our host's hospitality."

"That hardly seems right," Devin protested from the back door.

"There are a great many things on this earth that are not right, Monsieur Roché. This one is not of much consequence," Armand remarked. "Whoever is living here has already laid claim to another's dwelling and made it his home. We are no more at fault than he. Though, I'm sorry to lose access to that wine cellar."

"I'd feel safer securing that door with a lock on this side," Marcus said.

Devin lifted a ring of keys from a nail inside the door. "Perhaps you'll find one here."

The original lock for the wine cellar was still intact and Marcus found the key with little trouble. With both a lock and the wolves guarding the door, they sat down and shared their absent host's supper of bread and cheese around a single candle flame.

The pool of light barely touched the shadows gathered around them. Even the wolves' scent couldn't mask the odor of abandonment and decay that seeped from every corner of this once proud chateau. The wind whipped eerily around the corners of the building and the rain battered the tiles of the roof. And yet, the shadowed kitchen held a certain comfortable warmth and security even though an unknown intruder hid only a few feet away behind a locked door.

"This storm is nasty," Armand remarked. "I'm glad we found shelter when we did."

"Would you tell me the story of Comte Aucoin?" Devin asked. "It seems appropriate since we are making use of the poor man's kitchen. You are authorized to tell Arcadia's Chronicle, aren't you?"

Armand sighed and took the last sip of his wine. "I am, although my enthusiasm for storytelling has waned in the last few days. So much of our history has to do with death and fighting a government that may never recognize us as equal citizens."

"But without your storytelling," Chastel pointed out, "many would never have known what truly happened here."

Armand nodded. He took his time and tamped his pipe.

Drawing several times on the stem, he allowed the sweet smoke to fill the kitchen.

"Comte Aucoin came from an ancient family. Their roots were nurtured in Arcadian soil. Down through the generations they were known for their fairness, their kind treatment of their servants, and the equitable way they dealt with their neighbors. The last Comte, François, became a confrontational member of Council. He advocated schooling for his people, access to medical care, and payment for services rendered by provincials. His views were well known and he was targeted by the government in Viénne."

"Armand ..." Devin objected.

"Wait!" Armand held up a hand. "This is the official version in Arcadia's Chronicle. If you choose to dispute it, you may, but I can only tell you the story as I know it."

"I understand," Devin replied in frustration.

"François drafted a detailed proposal to present to Council expressing his beliefs and left his house and his family one morning in June, heading toward Pirée to take a ship to Viénne. His body was found along the road later that same evening. He and his bodyguards had been struck down by swordsmen. The next day the District Magistrate himself made the journey to inform François' wife and children of his death. He found the fields ablaze from one end of Comte Aucoin's land to the other. Only the chateau had been spared but the ground around it was littered with hundreds of those red-curse crosses that mean death to the recipient. They hoped to make it appear that François' servants had turned against him and planted the crosses as a sign of their loathing. When the fires finally burned out, the Magistrate found Aucoin's wife and five children all dead, murdered along with every servant in the chateau."

Chastel stopped him. "Five children?" he asked.

"Five," Armand confirmed. "Three girls and two boys."

"There were six," Chastel protested. "Four girls and two boys. I know. I spent many nights at this chateau before that tragedy."

There was a moment of silence and then Devin heard the sound of muffled weeping, heartbreaking and desolate. Chastel jumped to his feet and had the keys to the wine cellar in his hand before Marcus could stop him.

The wolves whined and wound uncertainly between Chastel's legs as he fumbled for the padlock. Marcus stood in the kitchen doorway, his pistol braced in both hands, as the bolt on the inside of the door slid back with a screech. The door creaked open and a slender girl launched herself into Chastel's arms with a cry. "Monsieur Chastel?"

Chastel held her a moment, one hand stroking her long brown curls. Gently he pushed her back to look at her face. His hands traced the angle of her jaw and came to rest cradling her cheeks in his palms. "Angelique?" he asked.

"Yes, *monsieur*," she murmured. "I could not believe it when I heard your voice. I had to be certain it was you before I revealed myself."

"God, child," Chastel muttered. "How did you escape?"

"After Papa left for Viénne, Mama was restless, her face pale and worried. She suggested that we children play hide and seek. I ran down to the wine cellar and hid in one of the empty casks. I waited for what seemed like hours but no one ever came to find me," she said. "I fell asleep waiting. Finally, I was very hungry. When I came upstairs ..." Her voice faltered. "... Mama, my brothers, my sisters ... they were all dead."

"That was twelve years ago," Armand pointed out.

"She was four years old," Chastel remarked, his voice

42

hard. "Four years old and alone in the world. How on earth did you manage? How did you live here alone?"

Angelique shook her head. "I was not alone at first. Marie survived, too. She was our nurse. She hid my little sisters in the closet in the upstairs hall but Jocelyn started to cry and the soldiers found them. They knocked Marie unconscious when she tried to protect them. They left Marie lying on the floor, after they had murdered my sisters. Perhaps they thought she was dead, also."

"And where is Marie now?" Chastel asked.

"She caught lung fever and died two winters ago," Angelique answered bleakly. "I have lived here alone since then."

Devin imagined a four-year-old child waking to find a houseful of dead family members and servants, then living in secret for years with only a servant for company. He offered her his chair at the table. "I am so sorry," he said because he could think of nothing more eloquent to say.

She eyed him darkly. "And who are you, *monsieur*?"

"Devin Roché, the Chancellor Elite's youngest son," Devin answered quietly.

"And you have the audacity to break into my house and eat my food?" she hissed. "After what your father did to my family!"

Devin shook his head. "He didn't know," he protested. "My father would never have ordered this."

Angelique glared at him. "Your father, *monsieur*, was the only one other than my family and our staff who knew Papa was going to Viénne. I have the letters to prove it."

"You have letters?" Marcus demanded.

"I do. Papa hid them well. When the soldiers tore this chateau apart looking for his personal correspondence, they found nothing."

43

"Where are they now, Angelique?" Chastel asked. "We must have them. The empire is divided. The government is apparently being controlled by a secret association. Those letters might help us to identify those responsible."

"The Chancellor is responsible," Angelique responded, her pretty face hard as stone. "What kind of leader can he be if he cannot control his own people?"

"He's a good man," Devin whispered, "a father with children of his own. He's trying to change life in the provinces for the better."

"So was my father," Angelique replied. "Look where it got him! And you will have to try very hard to convince me that your father didn't play a part in his death."

"Enough," Chastel said gently. "Will you help us, Angelique? Perhaps we can bring these killers to justice."

Angelique glared at him. "Even if one of them is Llisé's Chancellor Elite?"

Chastel held her eyes with his, as though he was soothing a frightened wolf cub. "Yes, my love, even if the Chancellor, himself, is responsible."

Angelique's hand slammed down upon the table. "Do you think I haven't read those letters a thousand times? I have searched again and again for some clue as to what might have gone wrong, and there is nothing. All I know is that Papa left for a secret meeting with the Chancellor and he was killed on the way."

"Perhaps, between us, we can discern more," Chastel said. "May we see them?"

Devin thought she would refuse. Her expression didn't soften at Chastel's tone or request. Yet, suddenly she wilted, sagging into her chair so abruptly that he thought she might be ill.

"It hardly matters anymore, does it?" she murmured. "Everything I have ever loved has been taken away from me. Do you know it's been two years since I spoke to anyone? Thank heavens Marie taught me to read, because I read aloud every night now, just to hear the sound of my own voice. This is my home and yet every hallway, every room, is marred by the memory of death and blood. When I sleep, I hear their voices crying out to me for help. The walls of this house will be forever haunted by the screams of all those innocent people dying. Oh God, I am so tired of living alone here with my ghosts."

Chastel knelt before her, taking her small hands in his. "You're not alone anymore, Angelique. There are men here who will care for you and protect you. You can't stay here."

She smiled grimly. "This is my home, Monsieur Chastel. I have nowhere else to go."

Chastel was adamant. "You will come with us."

Marcus stiffened but he didn't contradict Chastel's offer. Perhaps even Marcus, Devin thought, balked at leaving a sixteen-year-old girl alone.

"I'm sorry. We've eaten your meal," Chastel apologized. "We thought we were stealing food from a thief, which had a certain poetic justice."

Angelique wiped her sleeve across her eyes abruptly and rose from the table. "Did you have enough? There is more. Marie's sister lives in the village. She leaves bread and cheese on a stump in the forest every Wednesday and Saturday. I still pick them up and leave her some coins." She put a hand to her face. "She doesn't know about me, only that Marie survived. So, I couldn't even tell her when Marie died, because there would have been no more food. Marie said neither of us could show our faces here again, or surely whoever killed the rest of my family would return to kill us."

"So Marie hadn't seen her sister in all this time?" Marcus asked.

"Only once, right after the attack. Her sister said she would give her food but Marie must never come to her house again."

Marcus made a disapproving sound in his throat.

"She was afraid!" Angelique retorted. "These murderers killed the children of a Council member with no compunction at all. The death of a villager would mean nothing to them. You have no idea what it's like to always be afraid for your life."

"We're beginning to understand what it is like," Devin said. "We have people tracking us, at this very minute."

Angelique jumped to her feet, her face pale and frightened. "Someone may have followed you here?"

"There's no way to be sure," Chastel said.

"Then we need to leave this room." She brushed the crumbs from the table with her hand and grabbed handfuls of leaves from the floor to scatter randomly across its surface. She grasped the wine bottle by the neck and the candle in her other hand. "Follow me," she said.

They followed her into the wine cellar while Armand barred the door to the hallway. The wolves whined and scratched at the threshold, angry at being left behind. Chastel spoke a low command and silence ensued. "I've sent them off to hunt. They'll be back by morning," he explained.

The wine cellar's stairs had rotted. They supported the weight of an agile sixteen-year-old girl but a misstep sent Marcus sprawling, while the others scrambled unsuccessfully to break his fall. He clambered up from the stone floor more embarrassed than hurt.

Angelique touched his shoulder tentatively. "I'm sorry, *monsieur*. I cannot repair the steps. I cannot go to the village to buy new wood and the sound of a hammer might call attention to the house."

Marcus brushed at his clothes with a scraped hand. "I do understand."

"I sleep here," she said, "inside the wine cask where I hid as a child. I think some nights that maybe when I awake, this will all have been a dream and my family will all be here to welcome me. Or, perhaps, if I should die in my sleep, I can join them again. Either way, I would be happy. Even death is preferable to this."

"There will be more to life, Angelique," Devin replied. "We will find the men who did this and punish them."

She shook her head. "That will not bring my family back, *monsieur*, and I have no one else."

"You have me," Chastel said. "Your father was one of my dearest friends. I felt as at home here as I do in Lac Dupré. When this is over, my dear, you will come to live with me."

She graced Chastel with a stunning smile and laid her hand in his. "I would like that very much, *monsieur*."

She turned to the others and gestured. "I can only offer you the floor to sleep on. Anyone who searches the house will have to break that door down and we will have time to escape."

"How?" Armand asked.

Again, she smiled, a certain nonchalance creeping into her stance. "Don't you know, *messieurs*? All these old chateaus have secret passages."

CHAPTER 7

New Wine in Old Casks

Devin found himself crawling through an empty wine cask, following Angelique's slippered feet, the candle bobbing in her outstretched hand.

"There's a false bottom," she whispered, setting the candle down to pry at the wood. It rolled back easily and she rested it against the curved side of the barrel. She drew up her knees and dropped lightly into the dark abyss on the other side, the candle flame flickering wildly in a draft of cool, damp air. "Come on!"

Devin dropped more cautiously onto the stone floor and took the candle from Angelique's hand to light the others' way. "Your family could have hidden here," he said. "They would have been safe."

She turned on him, a bright flush splashed across her cheeks. "Don't you think I know that? Don't you think it has haunted me every day of my life, that I was the one who survived while they were brutally murdered? We had no warning, Monsieur Roché! We sent Papa off with hugs and kisses and the next thing I knew, I was alone in a house full of corpses!"

"Now, children," Armand remonstrated. He straightened carefully, his cane supporting him. "We must work together if we are ever to solve this trouble."

"Some troubles can never be solved," Angelique retorted.

Armand chastised her gently. "You are not the only one to have lost someone you loved. None of us has escaped the violence this group perpetrates."

Chastel joined them and Marcus came last, helping Angelique to put the cask bottom back in place. For the first time, Devin paused to look around him. The escape route had been well stocked for an emergency. A table and chairs stood near the center, while trunks, blankets, and crates of wine lined the sides of the tunnel which seemed to go on forever ahead of them.

Angelique riffled through a trunk and brought out several sheaves of letters tied with cord and put them on the table. "These are Papa's letters. The newest ones are in this packet here. He stored them here before he left for Viénne."

Chastel sat down, untying the cord and scattering the letters on the table top. "I'll need some help here. Perhaps we could each read one and give a short summary to the group when we are finished."

Angelique brought a bottle of wine and set it on the table. "There are no glasses," she apologized.

Devin slipped a letter out of its envelope and immediately recognized his father's handwriting. The message was dated just a week before François Aucoin had died.

My dear François,

When you arrive in Viénne, stay at the St. Charles on Beauchamp's Square. I will make arrangements for you to be met and brought to me as quickly as possible.

It is extremely important that no one know of your errand or the book you mentioned in your correspondence. I do realize the risk you are taking by coming to me with this. May God protect you on this errand.

Devin looked up. "Angelique, what is this book my father mentions?"

"He called it 'The Bishop's Book.' It's only referred to once before." She searched through the letters, seized one that seemed more rumpled than the others, and handed it to Devin. Chastel intercepted it while Marcus leaned in to read over his shoulder.

I am more than intrigued by The Bishop's Book. Is it in your possession or does the Priest at St. Gregory's still have it? I can send someone trustworthy to retrieve it, as soon as the weather breaks, if you prefer not to journey to Viénne but I feel it is paramount that I see the contents. I must also caution you not to put yourself or your family at risk over this. I will wait on your decision to formulate my plan of action.

Chastel raised his eyebrows. "Has anyone heard of this book before?"

No one had.

"Why didn't you mention this earlier?" Chastel asked Angelique.

"Because I wasn't certain that I could trust you before," she answered with a solemn face.

Chastel flattened a hand against his chest. "You weren't certain you could trust me? I've known your family since long before you were born."

"I don't know who to trust," she said. "Someone betrayed my father."

"These letters don't sound like my father intended to betray yours, Angelique. They are filled with cautions to protect him and your family," Devin pointed out.

Angeline shrugged. "You cannot blame me for assuming that the man who asked him to deliver the book might be to blame for my father's death. If it wasn't the Chancellor, then it was one of our staff – all of whom are dead."

"Are you certain of that?" Armand asked.

"Very certain," Angelique answered. "Marie and I identified each body."

Devin turned his head. He couldn't even imagine what she had been through.

"The traitor may have been killed too," Marcus suggested. "What about your father's bodyguards?"

Angelique shrugged. "I know he trusted them implicitly. Marie's sister said they were killed too, so who is to know?"

"How many bodyguards were there?" Devin asked.

"Four," Angelique replied.

"Does the Chronicle say how many men were killed?" Devin asked Armand.

"It's not specific," Armand answered.

Devin looked at Marcus. "Does the official report tell how many bodies were found on the road?"

"If it did, I don't remember. You are the archivist. Shouldn't you know such things?"

Devin smiled. "Archivists don't know all the answers, Marcus; they just know where to find them. I'm afraid my resources aren't at hand at the moment."

Chastel tapped the table with an envelope. "It is possible

someone escaped – or was allowed to escape. Angelique, have you ever tried to contact this priest?"

"I have contacted no one," she replied. "I am supposed to be dead and Marie thought it better that I remain that way."

"Where is St. Gregory's?" Devin asked.

"In the village," Angelique said.

Devin probed further. "Is this priest your father mentioned still alive?"

"He was at the time of Marie's death. I almost contacted him then. Just to have him say a few words over her body, but I was afraid," Angelique replied. "I buried her myself in the garden under a full moon by the flowers she used to love."

Knowing she would hate him for asking, Devin blundered on: "And what about your family and the servants? Who buried them?"

"No one," Angelique said bitterly. "The Magistrate and his men burned their bodies because it took too much time to identify and bury them individually."

Chastel covered her hand with his. "Perhaps it's just as well, because someone who knew the family well might have realized you and Marie were missing."

CHAPTER 8

Unnecessary Destruction

Devin lay on the floor, one arm bent beneath his head, staring up toward the vaulted ceiling of the wine cellar which was now shrouded by complete darkness. Marcus had recommended against locking the cellar's door. He'd reasoned that the men looking for them would find the cellar empty and assume no one had been there. The lock would only convince them that someone was hiding. Once they broke the door down, they would tear the place apart looking for a secret passageway. Chastel had positioned two wolves to patrol the downstairs. They would be their first line of defense, apparently having wandered in through a half-open back door.

The plan required that someone stay awake to listen for any sound of intruders, and Devin had chosen the first watch. It wasn't that he didn't feel tired. He did. But he doubted he could sleep. Angelique had told them that the chateau had been thoroughly searched when her family had been murdered. That suggested that Comte Aucoin's murderers had not found The Bishop's Book with him when he traveled toward Viénne. He had gone specifically to deliver it to the Chancellor and yet it must have been missing when he was accosted. There were very few possibilities of what might have happened to it.

Perhaps one of Aucoin's bodyguards had been carrying it and escaped. Or maybe, and this seemed less likely, Aucoin had a chance to hide it before he was killed. It seemed imperative that they search the scene of the murders and also discover for certain whether all the bodyguards had been killed. Determining that was going to be hard to do without arousing suspicion.

Devin stiffened as a wolf padded through the hall upstairs. The click of nails on the floorboards was unmistakable but the sound was still jarring in the silent wine cellar. Angelique had retreated to her wine cask where she felt safest. Marcus lay sprawled on the floor near the bottom of the rickety staircase, Armand and Chastel had lain down next to each other, their faces deceptively alike before Marcus had blown out the candle.

A year ago, Devin couldn't have imagined this night. His planned pilgrimage to the provinces had seemed so thrilling. With Gaspard for company, the trip would have been riotous and merry, not the somber, morbid thing it had become. He wondered if he would know instinctively if Gaspard died. There had been no momentary stab of terror or sudden realization that his friend had left this world brutally, at the hands of his kidnappers. Nor could he ever give up on Jeanette. It was obvious that she had disappeared along with the entire village of Lac Dupré but nothing in his heart made him think that she wasn't still alive somewhere. Perhaps she'd been hidden and protected by Adrian's forethought and he'd died guarding her secret.

Marcus would denounce him as unrealistic and sentimental but he felt that love and friendship exacted an emotional toll, weaving bonds that were more than physical or intellectual. If he were honest, a part of him truly believed that both Gaspard and Jeanette were alive and somehow they would meet again.

***

Devin wakened as Angelique opened the end of her cask. She was so thin, her mother's old dress hung on her like a shroud, her brown hair cascading down her shoulders and back. It was obvious that she had been crying.

Devin sat up. "What is it?" he whispered, trying not to wake the others.

She shook her head. "The same old nightmare."

Devin patted the floor beside him. "I have nightmares, too, Angelique. Come and tell me about it."

She tiptoed across the space between them and dropped down close to Devin.

For a moment, she said nothing, her hands twisting the front of her dress into a mass of wrinkled fabric. "The nightmare is always the same. We are playing hide and seek and I crawl into the wine cask and fall asleep. When I waken, in my dream, I am cold and hungry and crawl out and I go upstairs." She hesitated, tears streaming down her face. "There are bodies in the hall. My father's guards are dead, hacked up like meat in the butcher's shop. There is blood everywhere – on the fine paneling and the tiled floor – and I don't want to go any further. But it is so quiet, even the birds seem to be silent in the face of such brutality and I know that something even more horrible awaits me. I find my father's two old hounds slaughtered at the front door and then I turn toward the stairs and ..." Her voice trailed off for a moment. "My mother ... my dear, sweet mother is dead, too, her new blue dress drenched in blood. And so is my brother. There is so much blood, Devin. I try to wake them up and I get blood all over my hands and I start crying for Marie, running up the stairs toward the nursery, and then I see my sisters in the hall ... and Marie is lying there, too, and I know there is no one left to help me." She bowed her head against his shoulder, sobbing silently.

Devin put his arms around her. "I am so sorry," he murmured. "I can't even imagine what you've been through, Angelique ... how frightened you've been."

Her voice was shaking. "There have been days when I felt that I couldn't bear it any longer and yet, I have." She raised her face to look at him through tear-drenched lashes. "I've hoped that someday I'll find the man responsible."

"Perhaps we can take care of that," Devin said. He glanced at the others sleeping around them. Only Marcus remained awake, standing watch. "I was thinking about your father last night, Angelique. I have a few more questions, if you don't mind answering them."

She wiped her face on her sleeve and shook her head. "I don't mind." She nodded at Chastel and Armand who were still asleep. "Let's go upstairs."

Marcus preceded them, somehow climbing the stairway without demolishing the remaining steps. They found him in the kitchen with two of Chastel's wolves, a half empty wine bottle in his hand.

Angelique extended a cautious hand toward one of the wolves. "I don't understand about the wolf pack. Did Comte Chastel train them?"

Devin cleared his throat. "I believe so. He has a certain affinity for wolves."

Angelique laughed, a sweet melodic sound, which Devin had never heard her make. "Oh, I know all about The Wolf Comte. Even when I was a little girl there were terrifying stories that my brothers tried to frighten us with at night. I never believed any of them. Monsieur Chastel has never been anything but kind to me."

"Or to me, either," Devin agreed.

"Last night I heard Armand tell the story of my father's death. He said that our family was ancient, that 'their roots were nurtured in Arcadian soil,' but I believe the Chastels grew out of the very soil of Ombria. They are a part of its forest and its earth, just as the wolves are. It is no wonder that they understand each other."

"Well said." Chastel spoke behind her.

Angelique graced him with a smile that transformed her face. "Can I pat this one?" she asked, pointing to the small gray wolf at his side.

Chastel murmured something that Devin didn't understand but the wolf's ears pricked up. "Of course," Chastel added to Angelique.

She advanced a finger to be sniffed and, receiving no rejection, stroked it between the ears as gently as though she touched the fragile wings of a butterfly.

"There," Chastel said with satisfaction. "See, she likes you!"

"Do they have names?" she asked.

"Not in the way you mean," Chastel replied. "They designate each other by character traits. It's difficult to explain."

"To a person?" Devin asked.

Chastel smiled. "Yes, to a person. They aren't dogs, even though they may appear that way at times."

There was an awkward silence which Devin rushed to fill. "I was thinking last night about Comte Aucoin's death. Angelique said the chateau was searched. It sounds to me as though The Bishop's Book was never found."

"I thought the same thing," Marcus said, pulling out a chair to sit down. "Either it's been hidden or someone took it from the scene of the murder before it could be discovered. I still keep going back to the number of bodyguards and whether one of them might have escaped."

"I don't suppose you know where your father hid it when he had it here?" Devin asked.

Angelique shook her head. "He put his most important papers in the escape tunnel before he left. If he had left it, it would still be there – but it isn't. I have looked through everything."

"How about the library? What better place to hide a book than among others of its kind?" Devin suggested.

"If he left the book here, Devin, it would have negated his trip to Viénne. What would have been the point?" Marcus asked.

"I don't know, but if the information was so important, is it possible he left a copy of some of the most vital material behind? He knew what he was carrying and that it would make him a target. Perhaps he left something here that will steer us in the right direction."

"I guess anything is possible," Marcus admitted.

"I can take you to the library," Angelique offered. "It was practically destroyed. Come on, I'll show you."

They wound down several hallways to an arched wooden door marked by cruel gouges and slashes. The room inside was a shambles. Every book had been torn from the shelves and piled in the middle of the room. An unsuccessful fire had consumed a few volumes but the heavy leather books must have proven too much for the flames. They lay sprawled and moldy, the bindings cracked and broken. The room stunk of smoke and decay.

"God," Devin murmured kneeling down. For an archivist, it physically hurt to see fine books treated in this manner. In a rural province, where reading wasn't even taught, this room had represented a treasure house of information and learning. The bookshelves reached the ceiling on all sides except for two windows that matched their height on the front wall. The mantel was devoid of decoration; its autumnal painting lay smashed on the hearth. The desk had been vandalized. Its drawers lay upside down, their contents spread at random across the floor. Even the cushions of the chairs had been slashed, the stuffing strewn in piles. Devin's voice caught in his throat. "Is the rest of the house like this, too, Angelique?"

"Yes," she answered in a small voice. "There was hardly anything worth saving except clothing. They were particularly ruthless here in my father's library. I think they assumed, as you did, that perhaps he had left something incriminating here. Maybe they found it. I never saw what they took with them."

"Thieves stop looking when they find what they want. The fact that nothing here is untouched makes me think the book was never found," Chastel interjected.

"I haven't ever tried to do anything with the books," Angelique admitted. "If I had straightened them up, they would have known someone was here."

"I realize that," Devin said, his hands caressing a wounded

first edition of Gautier's *Elegy* with the binding split in half.

"This is hopeless," Marcus said in frustration. "If we stayed here for a month, you couldn't sort through all this. There is nothing you can do here, Devin. Leave it. Obviously, nothing was found before."

"That's what we are assuming," Chastel answered. "But I think we need to speak with the priest at St. Gregory's. If he trusted François with that book then maybe we can assume he is trustworthy also."

"What if he was the one who betrayed Aucoin?" Marcus pointed out.

"Then he would also have implicated himself," Chastel responded. "It's worth the chance."

"And who will speak to him?" Marcus demanded.

"If I'm not mistaken," Chastel answered, "it's Sunday. I believe I'll go to Mass."

CHAPTER 9

Memories

"I'll just stay here," Devin said despondently from the floor. "Maybe there's something I can salvage."

"Suit yourself," Marcus commented roughly. "But it's a fool's errand."

Angelique sank down beside him. "You blame me, don't you?" she asked. "For not caring for these books better."

"What?" Devin asked distractedly, pulling his eyes away from the moldering pile to look at her face. "No, never! It's just difficult to see your father's library like this. Some of these volumes are worth more than the chateau itself."

"You must love books," she said.

Devin laughed. "I do. I'm an archivist. Did we not mention that? I came to the provinces to learn the Chronicles. Armand is Ombria's Master Bard and my first teacher. I felt I would never truly know Llisé without having learned the Chronicles, just as I learned the Archives."

She nodded. "I wondered why you had come. I thought perhaps it was a holiday."

"A strange sort of holiday," he murmured. "My best friend and Armand's daughter were both kidnapped and the entire village of Lac Dupré is missing."

Her face blanched. "The village?"

"The people of the village," he clarified. "There's no one left. Even the cats and dogs are gone. And Armand's apprentice, Adrian, and Shérif Picoté were both murdered. We found their bodies."

"So these assassins are the men that are tracking you?"

"I'm afraid so," he admitted. "I'm not sure what or who we may have led to your door."

"My door is already stained with blood, Monsieur Roché," she answered solemnly. "Perhaps it's time I took a stand instead of hiding away like a child."

"Angelique," he protested, "you've done nothing wrong. What more could you do without anyone to advocate for you?"

Tears shone in her eyes. "I could have left this haunted shrine and traveled far away to make a new life."

"With what?" he asked. "You hardly have the money to start a new life."

"Oh, I have money. My father provided well for us. The tunnel in the cellar is filled with gold. So much gold, I could never have carried it myself."

The trunks, Devin thought. They lined the side of the escape tunnel. Monsieur Le Comte was an amazing man. "I wondered where you had gotten the coins for the bread and cheese. Your father thought of everything to keep his family safe."

"It was not enough," she answered mournfully. "All his planning was for nothing."

Devin resisted the urge to pat her hand. "It kept you safe,

Angelique. You are all that remains of his legacy and we will see that you live to carry it on."

His hands fell on a leather-bound volume with ornate gold trim. The pages had been scorched by flames but the book itself was remarkably intact. Beside it another book appeared completely unscathed. He picked up one in each hand. "Both of these books have value. Do you know which appeals to me more?"

"The undamaged one?" Angelique guessed.

Devin shook his head. "No, this one with its pages singed. It survived impossible odds and still remains serviceable. The other one escaped destruction by chance." His voice softened. "You remind me of the damaged one."

Angelique frowned, her lower lip sticking out like a child's. "Is that supposed to be a compliment?"

"I meant it as one," Devin replied. "Do you know what the odds of your survival were? You beat the monsters that killed your family, Angelique. You have kept yourself safely a secret for twelve years and with our help, you can bring these people to their knees."

"But I don't know anything!" she protested. "I never saw the men who killed my family."

"But Marie did. Surely, the two of you have discussed that day many times. I want you to try to remember anything she might have told you."

Angelique pulled her knees up to her chin, her arms clasped around them. Her eyes evaded Devin's. "I've tried to forget. My own memories of the aftermath haunt me constantly. I don't want to remember anything more."

"Not even if it meant bringing these men to justice?"

"It won't change anything," she snapped. "Can't you understand that? Nothing can bring back the people I love."

"It could prevent others from losing their families," he said gently. "The men behind this are ruthless."

She sighed and looked up with red-rimmed eyes. "What do you want to know?"

Devin stretched his legs out in front of him and leaned on one hand. "What did the man that hit Marie look like?"

"He was tall and had dark hair. She said he had a cruel face with a scar that pulled down the corner of his mouth. He was wearing the uniform of the *militaire*. Marie tried to stop him when he yanked my sisters from the closet. That's when he hit her. She only remembered her head hitting the wall and then nothing more until I found her."

"That's very good information," Devin said. "Did she have any idea how many men there were?"

"Marie said she hid my sisters as soon as heard the front door crash open. She said my father had warned both her and my mother to get to the wine cellar if they felt threatened. But there wasn't enough time."

"Surely, your father left guards to protect you," Devin protested.

"I'm sure they were killed first. I never saw them."

"Could they have been bribed?"

"If they were, they were murdered for their trouble. Marie found their bodies."

"Traitors are often murdered so there is no chance they will repeat the truth to some other person who might try to bribe them," Devin said.

"I hadn't thought of that," Angelique answered.

Devin idly paged through a book of maps on his lap. "Is it possible that your father might have had one of his bodyguards carry the book? Perhaps he gave instructions for it to be hidden or taken somewhere. Was there one man he would have trusted more than any other?"

"Jules," Angelique said without hesitation. "He confided in him, trusted his counsel. I remember when Marie would have us all ready for bed; we would parade down to father's study and stand in a line for kisses. Papa would swoop out of his chair and swing each of us girls into his arms for a hug and a kiss. The boys, he tickled first and then kissed them goodnight, too. Jules was there nearly every evening. I think I said goodnight to him as many times as I did to my father."

"And you never saw any stress between Jules and your father? They didn't argue or disagree?"

Angelique fixed him with a glare. "How often are you privy to your father's interactions with his bodyguards? I was four years old, Monsieur Roché. Most days I only saw Papa at bedtime."

Devin laughed. "I'm sorry. You're right. Believe me, there are months when I don't see my father at all. Now, my mother is another story. If I don't check in at least once a week she sends someone to track me down."

Angelique's face brightened. "Mama was with us constantly. Marie was our nurse but Mama seemed to really enjoy attending our lessons and playing with us," she paused, her voice lowered to a shaky whisper. "Did you know they stabbed her? She bled to death on the stairs with my youngest brother beneath her. She was only trying to protect her son, and they stabbed her to death."

Devin reached out and took her hand. "That was all part of the conspiracy. They couldn't have shot anyone because peasants aren't allowed to own firearms, so they stabbed everyone, to make it appear that your family had been killed by the villagers. I'm sure that's why they scattered the red crosses, too."

"They didn't stab everyone," Angelique said bleakly. "Emile, the stable boy, was beaten to death."

Devin jumped to his feet. "Marcus!" he yelled. "Come in here!"

CHAPTER 10

Conspiracies

Marcus rounded the corner at a run, a pistol in his hand. His glance took in Devin standing and Angelique sitting on the floor surrounded by books. "God!" he blustered. "I thought there was something wrong. It would have been easier on my heart if you'd come to find me yourself, Devin."

"Sorry," Devin apologized. "I've just run across something I think you should know."

"It better be good," Marcus growled.

Devin ignored him. "Angelique says that everyone at the chateau was stabbed except for the stable boy, who was beaten to death."

Marcus raised his bushy eyebrows and gave a low whistle.

Angelique rose gracefully from the floor. "I don't understand. Why is this important?"

"It's important," Marcus said, "because he was probably beaten to obtain information. If your father and his bodyguards discussed anything about their trip in the stable, the stable boy would have overheard it."

"And yet you don't believe they found the book they were looking for," Angelique protested.

"It wasn't for lack of trying," Devin said. "They obviously tore the chateau apart."

"Apparently, the book wasn't with your father when he was killed," Marcus added, "and yet he was taking it to Chancellor Roché."

"Is it possible he sent it with someone?" Devin asked. "What about Jules? You said your father trusted him more than any of his other bodyguards."

Angelique shrugged. "I suppose it's possible, but as far as you know it never arrived in Viénne, did it?"

"I have no knowledge of it, at all," Marcus said.

"So Jules must have been killed or injured ..." Devin speculated.

"Or he went into hiding," Marcus added.

"Do you think he still has the book?" Angelique asked.

"I think it's possible," Marcus replied. "He may have been afraid to take the book to its final destination because he wasn't sure he could trust the Chancellor."

"Or he may have hidden it," Devin suggested, "or returned it to the priest who gave it to him. Trying to find Jules now would be nearly impossible. After twelve years the trail has grown cold. People who might have helped us have died and after all this time, it's possible that Jules, himself, is dead."

"I always imagined that he died at my father's side," Angelique whispered.

"He very well may have," Marcus answered. "If there is a recurrent theme here, it is death."

"I would agree," Chastel said from the doorway.

"God, now what?" Marcus asked.

68

"The priest at St. Gregory's fell from a ladder last week and broke his neck. His replacement has yet to arrive."

"Well, that's convenient," Marcus growled sarcastically.

"You've no idea how convenient," Chastel continued. "The church didn't own a ladder and there was apparently no reason for him to have been on a ladder. The man was in his eighties. The men in the village did any maintenance that the church required."

"So he was murdered?" Devin asked.

"It would seem so," Chastel remarked.

"They may have suspected we might come here," Marcus said, "perhaps because of Chastel's friendship with Aucoin's family."

"It doesn't make sense," Devin protested. "They have ignored the loss of the book for twelve years. Why would they be afraid that we might find it now?"

"I don't know," Marcus answered. "Something else may have changed. Maybe I'm wrong in assuming it has something to do with us. But it makes me uneasy about our safety here."

"My wolves are still patrolling," Chastel reassured him.

"Pardon me for relying on other safety measures as well," Marcus replied.

"Where is Armand?" Devin asked. "I haven't seen him all morning."

"He's been nosing around the chateau," Marcus said. "I think he's upstairs."

An uneven clatter came from the stairway and Armand limped into view. "There's a man approaching from the north!" he gasped.

"Damn!" Marcus snapped. "Devin, you and Angelique go to the wine cellar. Armand, you go, too. Chastel, you're with me."

Even as Devin pushed Angelique in front of him, he had a very odd sensation that time hung suspended for a moment. He was sure that they wouldn't reach the wine cellar in time just as Angelique's family hadn't either. They were still in the hall when a man's shadow darkened the doorway in the kitchen.

Marcus shoved Devin and Angelique against the wall, his cocked pistol in his hand. Devin grabbed his arm. "Don't! It's Gaspard!"

Marcus' pistol didn't waver even when Gaspard stepped through the door. "Where have you been?" Marcus demanded.

Gaspard's face was still in shadow, his shoulders slumped, his hands behind him. "I'm sorry, Dev," he murmured.

Devin dove to the floor, yanking Angelique down with him, as Chastel wheeled to fire at the front door. He saw Gaspard go down as a group of men rushed in behind him. The gunshots were cut off sharply by savage snarls as Chastel's wolves joined the fight. The cries of the dying filled the hallway. He could feel Angelique shaking, her face pressed against the floor, and he put his hands over her ears. Unbelievably, the massacre was over in minutes. The stillness was almost as unnerving as the screams.

Marcus placed a hand on Devin's shoulder. "Are you all right?"

Devin nodded. He sat up and reached for Angelique who shrank from his touch. She shook her head silently and straightened to lean her back against the wall, her face white.

Devin jumped to his feet and ran into the kitchen. One of the wolves backed away from its kill and snarled at Devin. "No!" Chastel snapped. It dropped to the floor, its eyes wary and wild.

The room reeked of blood. Two men lay across the threshold, another sprawled on the kitchen floor, his glassy eyes staring sightlessly at the bottom of the table. Devin stepped over a lifeless body and knelt beside Gaspard.

Gaspard started at Devin's touch. "God," he whispered. "Is it over?"

"Yes," Marcus answered as he joined them. "Are you hurt?"

"No," Gaspard admitted. "I fell down, hoping they'd think I'd been shot. Can you untie me, Dev?"

Devin cut the cord that bound him with a kitchen knife. Gaspard's wrists looked raw and bruised, as though he'd been bound for days. He glanced back to the hall and saw that Chastel had taken charge of Angelique. Somehow, she had allowed him to take her in his arms, her sobs muffled against his shoulder. Around them, the hall lay littered with bodies, wolves winding between them, their noses rooting at the motionless corpses.

Devin glanced around wildly. "Where is Armand?"

He stepped away from Gaspard and made his way to the library. Armand was sitting against the wall, his head bent against his knees.

"What is it?" Devin asked. "Are you hurt?"

Armand drew a shuddering breath and raised his head. His lined face looked ten years older than when Devin had first met him six weeks before. "They're all dead, aren't they?"

"Yes," Devin assured him. "The wolves killed them. We're safe for the moment."

"We'll never know, now," Armand whispered. "There's no one left to tell us what happened to Jeanette and the rest of the people of Lac Dupré."

Devin reached out a hand to help him to his feet. "Come to the kitchen. Gaspard's alive; maybe he can tell us."

Chastel and Angelique were gone when they went into the hall. "Chastel took her to the wine cellar," Marcus explained when they reached the kitchen. "I think it's the only place she feels safe."

Gaspard beamed. "There's still a wine cellar? Why didn't you tell me? Do you know how long it's been since I had a drink?"

"I don't really care," Devin said. "You have a lot of explaining to do!"

Gaspard splayed a hand across his chest. "I do? I'm the victim in this! I was kidnapped by my father's men."

"To what end?" Marcus asked.

Gaspard grimaced. "A bad one. I was the bait to reel Devin in. They planned to kill us both."

Devin raised his eyes. "That's nice to know. Have you been following us all this time?"

Gaspard shook his head. "No, they lost you a couple of times. When they realized you'd come here they waited until you seemed to feel a little less threatened. They thought that this morning seemed the perfect time to assassinate us both."

"Your father ordered this?" Devin asked incredulously.

"Yes! Don't you just love the old man?" Gaspard replied gaily. "I can't believe I had actually decided to go home! He had it all planned. You and I were to serve as an example that the people of the provinces are violent and undisciplined. Imagine the outrage in Coreé when the Chancellor's own son and the son of a Council member were killed by a mob of peasants. It would squelch any talk of access to education or medical care for the next fifty years."

"What about Jeanette?" Armand demanded.

Gaspard frowned. "What about her? Didn't you leave her with Adrian?"

"Adrian and Picoté are both dead, Gaspard," Marcus said quietly. "We found them along the trail after we left Chastel's. They were beaten to death."

Gaspard shook his head. "I honestly didn't know. Why do you think something happened to Jeanette?"

Devin sighed, feeling as though the entire problem had suddenly become more entangled than ever. "Everyone in the entire town of Lac Dupré is missing, Gaspard. There isn't even a cat or dog left."

"I know nothing about this!" Gaspard objected. "I was held for the past two weeks by eight of my father's men. None of them even mentioned Jeanette or Adrian."

"Eight?" Marcus asked. He whirled and went down the hall.

Devin grimaced at Gaspard's puzzled expression. "He's counting bodies."

Armand gave Gaspard a hard look. "So your disappearance and the missing residents of Lac Dupré aren't connected?"

Gaspard shook his head. "I swear I don't know anything about that, Armand. I would tell you if I did."

Armand slumped down in a chair, one hand supporting his head. Devin sat down beside him. "We'll find her," he said softly. "I love her, too, you know."

Armand roused, his face contorted. He pointed a finger at Devin's chest. "You have no business loving her! None of this would have happened if you hadn't come to Ombria."

Devin took a deep breath. "You're probably right. But I came here with the best intentions." He rose from his chair. "If it comforts you to blame me, please continue to do so."

Armand pounded his fist against his chest. "Nothing comforts me! I feel as though my soul has been torn in two! Jeanette was everything to me – everything!"

"Armand, I haven't given up hope of finding her," Devin replied. "And neither should you."

"How can we find her when every step leads us farther from where she disappeared?" Armand demanded.

Marcus returned, ignoring the flaring tempers and accusations. "They're all dead."

"So we're safe, then?" Gaspard asked.

"No, I wouldn't go so far as to say that," Marcus replied. "There seems to be more than one thing going on here and I can't believe they aren't connected in some way. If Picoté and Adrian weren't killed by the men who were holding you, then there is a second group who took the people from Lac Dupré. And the priest's death confuses me further."

"These can't all be isolated incidents. Someone is orchestrating the whole thing, but to what end?" Devin asked.

"We have one motive but surely that's not the only one." Marcus looked at Gaspard. "Did you hear anything else at all while these men were holding you?"

"Nothing that will help you. They constantly taunted me by saying I was worth a great deal more dead than alive to my father. I don't know why I was so stupid as to think that he would welcome me home. Why did he write those letters asking me to come back if he planned to kill me?"

"My letters from my father were all missing from my room," Devin said. "Your letters were gone from your room, too. Everything was gone, all of our belongings. They probably planned to use your Father's letters as evidence of his concern for you. If you had been killed, no one would ever know any differently."

"René Forneaux won't let this rest," Marcus warned. "You two are a liability now. We need to get out of here."

Devin gestured at the bodies scattered on the floor. "Shouldn't we bury these men first?"

"I have a better idea," said Angelique from the hallway. Chastel stood behind her, a shadowy protective form. "If we are truly leaving, there is a cistern at the side of the chateau. If we weigh their bodies down with stones, no one will know what happened to them."

Devin looked away from the resolute look in her eyes. Her voice was chilling. A few moments before, she had been paralyzed with fear and now she was proposing how to deal with the disposal of bodies like a soldier.

Marcus nodded his head. "A viable solution for the bodies but the hall will have to be scrubbed. And when we leave we need to go by way of the secret passage in the wine cellar. This chateau must appear untouched."

Devin and Armand dealt with the clean-up while Marcus and Chastel dragged bodies outside. Both Gaspard and Angelique disappeared into the library and no one seemed inclined to call either of them back to the task at hand.

"I don't understand why the wolves didn't alert us before these men attacked the chateau," Devin said, a scrub brush in his hand.

"Wolves are wolves," Armand commented drily. "I imagine they were lured away with fresh meat. No matter what their allegiance to Chastel, they are still wild animals. A full belly trumps guard duty."

Devin sat back on his heels. "So their protection is tentative at best?"

"They saved our lives today, Monsieur Roché. Don't take their guardianship lightly." Armand gestured at the bucket of murky water. "Could you dump that, please?"

Devin carted the bucket out to the small tangled garden. The blooming plants still damp and fragrant from last night's storm made him realize that he might never forget the smell of blood and death. How much worse must it be for Angelique?

He poured the water on the ground and nearly stumbled into a huge wolf on the way back through the door. Its gaze was steady and unyielding, fiercely intelligent. "Chastel?" he asked softly. It turned tail and preceded him back into the chateau.

"Yes," Chastel answered from the kitchen.

Devin's cheeks burned. He felt naive and foolish to have imagined that he had actually just faced the nobleman in disguise.

"What is it?" Chastel asked, stepping through the door.

Devin glanced at the kitchen behind the Comte. The room was devoid of wolves or people. Only the sounds of Armand scrubbing filled the hallway. "Nothing," Devin stammered.

CHAPTER 11

A Den of Thieves

They hid in the wine cellar for the rest of the day after scattering dust, leaves and twigs on the freshly scrubbed hallway. They packed up enough of Comte Aucoin's emergency supplies to outfit them for the journey ahead. Only with Angelique's permission did they fill their pockets with gold.

Angelique remained noticeably quiet. She spent the afternoon sewing all of her father's letters inside the lining of her cloak. Despite the chateau's grim past, Devin sensed that it was difficult for her to leave. Had it not been for Chastel, he doubted that she would have gone at all. She never let him out of her sight; her eyes followed him relentlessly around the cellar.

They were packed and ready, waiting for dark to continue toward the caves in Arcadia. Devin leaned his head against the wall and closed his eyes. He kept examining the pieces of this complicated puzzle that seemed to hold their lives within its frame. There were so many players that it was hard to keep them straight: Comte Aucoin and his infamous book, Jules, his bodyguard, who might and might not be dead, René Forneaux who had decided that his son's death was invaluable as a political device, and the priest at St. Gregory's who might have been killed simply because he had knowledge of some arcane book.

He sat up suddenly. "We're looking at this all wrong!"

Marcus stopped sharpening his array of knives and looked up. "Looking at what wrong?"

"Chastel, you said that the priest at St. Gregory's died in a fall from a ladder," Devin explained, "even though physically, he had no business being up on one."

Chastel sat down next to Angelique, ready to shield her from some new and terrible revelation. "What's your point, Devin?"

Devin continued, his voice rising with excitement: "Maybe the priest did have a reason to be on the ladder. Maybe he was hiding something."

"The book!" Marcus said.

"Maybe he wasn't murdered. Maybe he fell. He was an old man. Perhaps the responsibility of that book was weighing on him. He may have been afraid that he would die and it would be discovered among his things. He was trying to put it in a safe place while he was still able to do it and, tragically, he fell while accomplishing his task."

"It's a good theory," Armand agreed. "Chastel, did they tell you where he fell?"

"At the foot of the bell tower. The people thought he might have been untangling the ropes. The stairs to the tower crumbled years ago."

Devin jumped to his feet. "That's perfect! If he left the book in the bell tower, it would be safe!"

"This is all conjecture," Marcus grumbled.

"So, do you think that he was murdered?" Devin said. "Surely, it's worth investigating."

"We are leaving tonight," Marcus said firmly.

"Couldn't we at least look in the bell tower before we leave?"

Silence crept in from the edges of the room and gathered at Marcus's feet. After a moment, he sighed. "My only responsibility is to return you to your father in one piece. All the rest of this, as intriguing as it is, is superfluous."

Gaspard snorted. "God, Marcus, that's a hefty word for a bodyguard."

Devin laughed. The release of tension was exquisite. How long had it been since they had laughed together? Angelique giggled and suddenly everyone else joined in. Even dour Marcus had to chuckle, too, at his choice of such a lofty term.

Devin regained his composure first. "Even if it's …" He grinned and paused for effect. "… 'superfluous,' it may hold the answers to part of this puzzle at least."

"We don't have a ladder," Marcus replied obstinately.

"I have a ladder," Angelique said. "It's lying on the rafters in the stable. It's old but it would hold my weight or Devin's."

"I believe she is referring to the incident on the stairs," Chastel remarked cheerfully, waving a hand at the broken, missing step.

Everyone roared again at Marcus's expense but he laughed with them, some of the more recent lines around his eyes easing in the darkened, candlelit room.

This is how it's done, Devin thought. This is how men survive war, and torture, and butchery. They find some small thing to make them laugh and somehow it brightens their spirits enough to make it through another day of hell.

"All right," Marcus agreed. "But I am vetoing the ladder. If we have to run, the ladder will only make others draw the same conclusions we did."

"How about a rope?" Devin suggested. He'd had plenty of experience escaping the Chancellor's residence as a child.

Gaspard grinned. "A rope is perfect! I'll spot you, Dev."

Marcus sighed. "Why do I have the feeling this will end badly?"

Only four of them walked to the churchyard after dark: Marcus, Devin, Chastel, and Gaspard. The wolves shadowed them. Armand stayed with Angelique. In the event the others were captured, he was entrusted with getting her to safety, however he could.

They carried a rope and an unlighted lantern. The squat stone church stood in a small clearing. Haphazard tombstones loomed darkly around it in a macabre semblance of a fairy ring. The tower wasn't terribly tall but the door at its base was cracked and broken.

"We'll have to secure the rope near the top," Marcus whispered. "Perhaps if I aim for the roof, I can hook the base of the cross. I just pray it will hold your weight." He lifted the rope with its attached hook. "Everybody stand back."

Devin watched with admiration as Marcus's first attempt caught briefly and slid off. The noise on the tiled roof made them all cringe but the only building close by was the priest's house and it was dark and deserted. Marcus swung again and the rope held as he pulled it taut.

Marcus turned to look at Devin. "You don't have to do this."

Devin laughed. "I want to do it. Think of how insufferable I can be if I find what we are looking for!"

"That's what I'm afraid of," Marcus said without cracking a smile. "Be quick about it."

Devin tested the rope even though Marcus had done that a moment before and then threaded it through his belt. He leaned back, placing one hand above the other on the rope, and planted his booted foot against the stone. He had expected the climb to be a strain but the weeks of walking had left him much stronger physically than when he had set out from Viénne. The biggest problem was that moss covered most of the tower. It gave way beneath his feet and he had to scrape it off the stones to secure his footholds.

It really wasn't much of a climb. He reached the top in only a few minutes and tied off the rope on the window frame. He could see the bell through the window and slid forward, pausing to sit on the sill. A flutter and then a flurry of wings made him shield his face as a flock of pigeons flew straight at him. He waited out their assault and then opened his eyes.

He'd forgotten the lantern! The tower was in deep shadow. Below him, Devin could just make out the broken stairway. A rope descended into the abyss. A large knot secured a second length of rope so the bell could be rung from the first floor. The remains of the bell tower floor tilted down precariously but there was no way to search the tower without using the floor. He stepped on it gingerly, keeping one foot against the inside wall. The resounding crack did nothing to reassure him. He heard Marcus swear softly below him.

Chastel thought the priest had fallen from this side of the tower. Devin was certain he hadn't braved this floor to secret his book. So, it had to be hidden close by. He ran has hand along the inside of the floor as far as he could reach, succeeding only in smearing his fingers with pigeon droppings. He stood up to wipe his hand against the wall and encountered a niche in the stones. His heart hammered in his chest as his hand closed over a book. He pulled it out and held it, slipping the smooth leather tome beneath the front of his shirt.

An ominous crack split the silence. As the floor gave way beneath him in a cloud of dust and debris, he snatched desperately for something to hang onto. The bell rope miraculously grazed his palm and he held on for dear life. It burned his hands as he slowed his descent, the clear voice of the bell announcing their presence to the entire countryside. He slithered down, landing in a pile of rubble. Marcus dragged him out roughly.

"You stink as a thief," he hissed between his teeth. "Get out of here as fast as you can!" With one mighty yank, he pulled the rope from the tower, leaving the cross wobbling precariously.

They turned and ran. As they neared the chateau, Gaspard fell behind gasping. Devin turned in alarm to see him bent double with laughter.

Devin slapped him. "You scared me to death! I thought there was something the matter with you."

"I scared you!" Gaspard accused him, wheezing wildly. "I wish you could have seen Marcus's face when the floor collapsed! You just about gave us all heart failure and then you landed without a scratch, ringing the bell like a saint on his way to glory. That's about the funniest thing I've seen in a long time!"

"I've had enough of both of you for one night!" Marcus snarled. "Gaspard, the only time Devin acts like an adult is when he isn't with you! If you're not careful I'll send you back to your father."

For some reason Devin and Gaspard both broke into gales of laughter and even Chastel had to keep his mouth tightly pinched to avoid joining them. Marcus stomped away over the withered fields toward Comte Aucoin's chateau.

They gathered in the wine cellar. Both Armand and Angelique looked relieved to see them safe until Marcus broke into a tirade, announcing their failed mission. Devin let him rant, relishing the fact that no one knew their undertaking had actually been a startling success.

He chose his moment carefully. When Marcus finally fell silent after all his fuming and fussing, Devin withdrew the book from his shirt and held it up so they could all see it. "I found it," he announced, "just as the floor gave way."

Marcus glared at him. "You realize that is just a Bible?" he snapped.

Devin turned it around. He hadn't realized that but ultimately it made no difference. A Bible could be used to hide information just as well as any other book. "There is probably a code or some notes," he said, flipping the pages.

Chastel extended a hand. "May I see it?"

Devin shifted it gladly into Chastel's hands. Leave it to Marcus to spoil the moment. He had actually succeeded. Marcus was just too grumpy to admit it.

"There are a lot of notes in it," Chastel said, as Angelique hung over his shoulder. "It will take some study to figure out what the message is here or if there really is one."

"Marcus is a Biblical scholar," Gaspard quipped. "Maybe he should look at it."

Devin snorted as they put the book on the table and gathered around it. There were underlined words but nothing that made any sense.

"It's just a Bible," Marcus repeated.

Devin turned to the inscription on the first page: *To Father John Mark on the day of his consecration as a Bishop.* "No, it's not just a Bible," he said. "It's The Bishop's Book and it's up to us to take it to my father."

CHAPTER 12

After Darkness, Light

They set off by lantern light into Comte Aucoin's escape tunnel. Everyone but Marcus could stand upright. Devin's bodyguard shouldered his way through cobwebs and dangling roots that threatened to entangle them. His hunched shadow holding his lantern aloft projected a macabre dance against the stone and earth that surrounded them.

None of them knew exactly where the tunnel led. They were trusting Comte Aucoin to have chosen a safe place somewhere in his native Arcadia for his family to find refuge. The journey might take hours or days and it was the uncertainty that concerned Devin the most – that and Chastel's wolves which surrounded them. Their breath blew hot against Devin's legs in the enclosed space and their coarse hair brushed against his hands as they competed for position in the narrow tunnel. The musky smell of their fur permeated the air, making him feel on edge and inescapably pursued. Perhaps, it was simply ingrained in man's very nature to fear wolves. But then, Chastel walked like a king among them, speaking in that odd guttural tone that they seemed to respect and understand. The provinces were filled with wondrous things that those in Coreé would never even dream of.

Devin tore his mind away from the wolf pack and considered how much time it must have taken to construct a tunnel of this magnitude. How many servants had been involved in its creation and how many chances did that leave that its existence had been discussed outside of Aucoin's inner circle at the chateau? Was it possible that a group of soldiers were awaiting them at the far end? Or maybe the construction of the tunnel preceded the Comte and he had only adapted it to his own needs. Perhaps the secret had been passed down from father to son for centuries and he had only carried on the tradition. Part of it followed a natural formation, evident in the varying heights of the ceiling and the distance between the walls.

They had been walking about an hour when Gaspard stopped abruptly to pick something up from the earthen floor. Devin ran into him. All of them hushed suddenly without a word from Marcus. There was the faint sound of voices, old men singing, the clink of glasses, and laughter. Gaspard pointed up and pantomimed raising a glass to his lips. The ceiling had become wood, not earth or stone. Gaps between the floorboards revealed glimpses of light and the overwhelming smell of alcohol and unwashed bodies. The tunnel ran directly under the floor of a building. It must be a tavern in the village, which meant they were traveling west, not north toward the mountains.

Gaspard grinned and held up a coin. The lantern light glittered on many more littering the floor at his feet. Gaspard stooped and gathered them in his hands.

Devin stepped forward in the narrow space. "Surely, we are under part of the village now," he whispered.

"Perhaps not," Chastel explained softly. "For several miles on either side of the border between Arcadia and Ombria there are a number of small taverns that cater to travelers."

Marcus, uncharacteristically silent, simply motioned them forward.

They walked carefully, afraid to make any noise lest they be discovered. The sounds from the tavern faded but the tunnel continued, its depths dark and vacant ahead of them.

It seemed they walked for hours. Angelique stumbled more than once. Devin took her arm, suspecting she was asleep on her feet. The monotony of the earth walls became hypnotic. Distance was difficult to judge, time even more so. Surely, it was close to dawn but how could they ever tell in this endless passageway?

Hours later, Marcus finally motioned for them to stop. "We need to rest. Make yourselves as comfortable as possible. I'll leave one lantern burning. Extinguish the rest to save oil."

Devin was only too glad to save lamp oil. The thought of all the lamps burning out simultaneously terrified him. He couldn't imagine being trapped underground in complete darkness. While his childhood held none of the trauma Angelique's had, he had never felt at ease in the dark. He had a vague memory of being shut in a dark closet by one of his five older brothers that he hadn't thought of in years. Oddly enough, it nagged at him now when their only light depended on the supply of oil they had brought with them.

He was glad to sit down and apparently the others were, too. Gaspard collapsed in a heap, gray with exhaustion. Had anyone doubted the truth of the story he told about his captivity, they had only to look at his ashen face and emaciated frame to have proof of his claim.

Angelique cleared a place to sit next to Chastel, staking a spot right in the middle of his wolves for herself. Something of her childlike-self remained in her trust and handling of these wild beasts. She treated them like dogs and in return they nuzzled her hands and accepted her caresses.

Armand sat with his back against the tunnel wall. He looked exhausted as well. He'd been through so much in the last month and each crisis seemed to have carved a new crease in his face. A small gray wolf, misplaced by Angelique, flopped down on the ground beside him. Armand never even noticed; his eyes had already closed in sleep. Only then did some of the deep crevasses in his cheeks relax.

Marcus sat on Chastel's other side. Devin could hear them speaking softly but if he hoped to overhear their conversation, his body had other priorities. His eyes closed quickly, finding sleep easily in this bizarre spot.

Devin wakened some time later. The others were still sleeping but he heard voices behind them in the tunnel. The words were indistinguishable but the conversation rose and fell with at least three and maybe four voices participating. Were they being followed? He sat in silence trying to differentiate the words but heard nothing specific. Afraid to speak himself, he crawled across to Marcus and shook his arm. Marcus woke with a start, his hand reaching for his pistol before his eyes focused on Devin's face.

"What is it?" he growled.

"Voices," Devin whispered. "There are three or four men behind us in the tunnel."

Marcus waved his hand for silence and listened for voices in the depths of the earth. He shook his head at Devin. "I hear nothing," he said, his voice low. "Perhaps you heard water flowing or the shifting of rock."

"It was voices," Devin insisted. "I couldn't hear specific words but it was definitely men talking."

Understanding dawned in Marcus's eyes. "Could it have been one of your dreams, perhaps?"

"It wasn't like that," Devin assured him, regretting once again his penchant for waking dreams. "What if we are being followed?"

Marcus stood up. The others were stirring around him, blinking with sleep.

"God, Devin," Gaspard protested. "Did you have to do this now? I can't walk another step. I'm exhausted."

"We're all exhausted," Marcus murmured. "But if there is any chance we have been followed, we need to get out of here."

They silently gathered their things, listening uneasily for voices in the tunnel behind them. Chastel straightened suddenly. "I hear something, too."

Suddenly the wolves scattered from under their feet, dashing up the darkened tunnel ahead of them.

"Move!!" Marcus shouted.

Behind them something cracked, rocks shifted and small stones rained down from the ceiling. The tunnel collapsed in a crash of rock and rubble, a cloud of dust spewing out to surround them as they scrambled for safety. Marcus led them forward, away from the cave-in and possible death and destruction, his bobbing lantern barely visible through the dust.

At last they stopped, far beyond any risk of another collapse. Marcus gave each of them a cursory glance. "Everyone all right?"

They all nodded, still choking and coughing from the dust. Their faces and clothes were as black as coal miners.

A wolf sneezed sharply as Marcus stood back and pointed a finger at Devin. "If I ever question your dreams again, Devin, remind me of this day. You saved our lives."

"I lost my lantern," Devin said, embarrassed to be singled out.

Marcus laughed unsteadily. "Better a lantern than your life. What else did we leave behind?"

"Some of the water," Chastel said.

"And part of the food," added Gaspard.

"But we have some of everything," Marcus said, as each of them checked their remaining supplies.

"At least now, no one is following us," Gaspard said with relief.

Marcus looked grim. "Someone may have collapsed that tunnel to kill us. It would have been an effective means of execution, or the tunnel may just have given way. One thing is certain; we would all be dead if it weren't for Devin. Now we have nowhere to go but forward. I pray there have been no other cave-ins along this route. Let's move on. This dark is getting to me."

The tunnel seemed darker and more sinister now. Devin's mind kept going back to the conversation he had heard when he wakened. Years before, a doctor who specialized in sleep disorders told him that waking dreams always held some element of truth. If you dreamed of being attacked by a tiger, perhaps the family house cat had just landed on your chest. If your nightmare involved mistrusting a friend, then maybe unconsciously you did. Whatever had wakened him, whether it was assassins or divine intervention, they were lucky to be alive. He ran his fingers through the rosary in his pocket and wished they weren't so vulnerable. He tried not to think what would happen if this tunnel ended in another cave-in. There would be no way out. They would simply starve to death slowly or run out of air to breathe.

Gaspard bumped Devin's shoulder as he leaned in to whisper, "Can you imagine if we'd been caught in that rock fall? No one would ever know what happened to us. We would have just disappeared."

"But we didn't," Devin said.

"But we might have," Gaspard continued. "Only the goons that set those rocks to cave in and my father would ever know the truth." He stopped. "What if they believe they were successful? What if they assume we are dead?"

"You can walk faster if you don't waste breath talking, Gaspard," Marcus growled, as though he were addressing a subordinate officer.

"Think about it," Gaspard whispered to Devin. He silently moved on, matching his steps to Marcus's with a comical swagger and a silly salute.

Devin barely avoided laughing but he heard a faint giggle from Angelique. It was amazing, after all she'd been through, that she could still see the humor in this situation. She still walked with a spring in her step. But then, they were following the route Comte Aucoin had laid out for her. She had complete confidence in her father and his directives even though the realm had changed a great deal in the twelve years since he'd been murdered. She was certain that he would bring her to safety.

They stopped several hours later to rinse their mouths and swallow a bit of their precious water. As they sprawled on the ground, Angelique passed bread and cheese around. Gaspard produced a bottle of wine he'd filched from the Comte's wine cellar, to share. It was then that Marcus's lantern began to sputter.

"Who has the other lantern?" Marcus demanded.

Gaspard produced it from his scattered supplies. Marcus hefted it in one hand, jiggling it gently. "There's only a bit of oil left here."

Gaspard gulped. "It must have spilled when we were running from the cave-in. God, I'm sorry. How many hours do we have left?"

"Not many," Marcus replied. "Perhaps we'd best cut short our break and move on."

How far could it be? Devin thought. Aucoin had left this escape route for his wife and six small children. He'd left three lanterns filled with oil. Devin had lost one and Gaspard had spilled the oil from another. They could be a mere third of the way with a little more than a third of the oil for the lanterns. Those weren't very good odds.

He wished he knew how far they had come; better yet, how far they had to go. No one spoke but their thoughts must all have been running along parallel lines. It was not his imagination that Marcus picked up the pace as they continued. Only Armand had trouble keeping up but Angelique linked her arm with his. She was a daughter who had lost a father and he was a father who had lost a daughter. They had a lot more in common than Devin might first have thought.

In just a few hours the lantern flame dwindled again. Ahead the wolves had stopped and were sniffing and scratching in the darkness. The group covered the last few yards quickly, anxious to see what the fading lantern would reveal or to at least stand in the warmth of its light for one last time.

Marcus held the lantern aloft so everyone could see. A carved stone door blocked the end of the tunnel. The stone arch around it was embellished with vines carved deep in the surface. It was padlocked.

"What now, Angelique?" Chastel whispered.

Angelique looked tired beyond words; circles dark as soot marked the skin below her eyes. She pulled a large key from her pocket. "Papa called this the key to our salvation. He left it hanging on the wall inside the tunnel so we could take it with us."

"You know nothing more than that?" Marcus asked quietly.

Angelique shrugged wearily.

Devin couldn't avoid smiling; the gesture was endearing. Angelique combined the formality of the ruling class with country manners seamlessly. His mother would have been shocked to see a young woman shrug but somehow, Angelique carried it off with grace. No doubt it came from being raised by a servant even though she was Comte Aucoin's daughter.

Marcus's brow was furrowed in thought. "If there are soldiers waiting, we are lost."

"We have the wolves," Chastel reminded him.

"Wolves can be slaughtered, too," Marcus said coldly. "We're taking a big chance by opening this door."

"And we will die if we don't," Armand pointed out. "There is no future in this tunnel without food, water, and light." As though to emphasize his words, the lantern flickered ominously. "Do you trust Aucoin or not?"

Marcus withdrew a knife and stuck it into his belt. "It's been twelve years since the Comte was murdered. Things may have changed."

"This was built a long time before that," Chastel assured him. "Did you notice there were no branches off this tunnel?

There was no way that his wife and children could take a wrong turn. Some provision would have been made for changing times. Comte Aucoin led us here, to this door, and provided a key. I, for one, have no fear of capture here."

"I hope you are right," Marcus said. "Devin, I want you and Angelique in the back. Chastel, can you keep the wolves up here with me? I want whoever is waiting for us to be faced with a strong front."

They held their breath as Marcus inserted the key in the lock. It ground against metal as it turned but the door swung open easily. They stepped out into an opulently appointed sitting room. Ornate draperies hung at the shuttered windows. A fire burned low on the hearth. The floor was covered in richly colored carpets and before the fire, an old woman was seated, a cup of tea in her hand.

The wolves rushed into the room, sniffing the floor, the draperies, and the fireplace, and the old woman who sat quietly by the fire. She extended her hand and they lay down at her feet as though they had been commanded to do so.

The woman placed her cup carefully on a side table and smiled, her soft rosy cheeks wrinkled with age. "I have prayed that this moment would come for years," she said softly. "Which of you are Comte Aucoin's children?"

CHAPTER 13

Revelations

Devin looked at Angelique but there was no sign of recognition in her eyes. They all stood a moment in awkward silence, unsure what to do next.

Angelique took a step forward. "I am Comte Aucoin's youngest daughter, Angelique. Do I know you, *madame*?"

"No, dear," the old woman said. "But your father knew me. François was my son."

Angelique's voice was barely a whisper. "You are my grandmother?"

The old woman nodded. "I knew some of your brothers and sisters a long time ago, before fear kept us apart."

"Why didn't you live with us?" Angelique asked.

"At one time I did," she replied. "Several years before he was killed, your father thought it best that I move here. This was an isolated hunting lodge that the Aucoins have owned for centuries. The escape tunnel has always led here but I think François thought it would be good to have someone here to welcome you if the situation became dangerous. I've never lost hope that one of you escaped the massacre at the chateau. My dear Angelique, are you the only one left?"

Angelique nodded, tears running down her cheeks. She crossed the room and collapsed in a pitiful heap at her grandmother's feet, her head resting on the old lady's knee.

Her grandmother stroked Angelique's hair with a gentle hand. "You must be exhausted," she said, taking them all in with her glance. "Please sit down. I'll send for something for you to eat."

The wolves lifted their heads briefly to look up as a bell jangled in her hand; then subsided immediately when a servant arrived. "Breakfast for seven," she requested quietly.

Chastel bowed. "Madame, I am Jean Chastel from Lac Dupré."

She acknowledged his introduction with a nod and a gentle smile that crinkled the lines around her eyes into small sunbursts. "I'm Madame Aucoin. Jean, you were my son's dearest friend. I always worried about how you weathered the news of his death."

Chastel grimaced. "Not well, *madame*. I miss him very much. However, I am very relieved to find Angelique alive. Any service I can provide for her will be a service to François, as well."

Despite his weariness, Armand swept forward with theatrical grace and bowed, his cloak swirling around his legs. "Armand Vielle, Master Bard of Ombria."

Madame Aucoin beamed at him. "I have heard such wonderful reports of your storytelling. Would you honor me with a performance when you have rested?"

Armand smiled, the first glimmer of pleasure that he had shown since Jeanette's disappearance. "Of course, *madame*. The honor would be mine."

"I'm Devin Roché," Devin announced, stepping forward as well. "This is my friend Gaspard Forneaux and my bodyguard, Marcus Berringer."

"You are Chancellor Roché's son?" Madame Aucoin gasped.

Devin nodded. "Yes, *madame*."

"My dear boy," she said. "You and your friend Gaspard have been reported as missing and presumed dead."

Devin turned to look at Marcus. "That's disturbing news. Is there any safe way to send a message to my father assuring him of our safety?"

"Not at the moment," Marcus replied grimly. "*Madame*, how did you come by this information?"

Madame Aucoin picked up the newspaper from her side table. "I have the newspaper from Coreé sent once a week. The news is always a week old but at least I am able to keep track of what is happening in the capital. This was on the front page of the one that arrived yesterday."

Marcus snatched it up before anyone else could and read it out loud. "The news of unrest in the provinces has escalated this week with reports that Chancellor Roché's youngest son, Devin, has been reported missing and presumed dead. Gaspard Forneaux, Councilman René Forneaux's oldest son and heir ..."

"Heir?" Gaspard snorted.

"... oldest son and heir," Marcus repeated, "had accompanied Devin Roché on a trip to memorize some of the provinces' oral Chronicles. The men had only visited the province of Ombria and both disappeared from the Chateau of Jean Chastel the night before their departure. Comte Chastel is also missing and may be implicated in the deaths of these young men. Chastel is currently under investigation by Council and troops have been dispatched to Ombria for his arrest. Our sympathies are with both the family of Chancellor Roché and Councilman Forneaux during this difficult time. Memorial arrangements have been postponed until more definitive information has been received."

"Well, that's a relief!" Gaspard barked. "I'd hate to return home and have to visit my own grave!"

Devin took the newspaper from Marcus's hand. "My apologies for having brought you into this, Chastel."

Chastel laughed unexpectedly. "I haven't had this much fun in years! I don't believe I've ever been a wanted man before. Sitting alone in a moldering chateau day after day is not nearly as entertaining."

"It's hardly moldering," Gaspard remarked. "You've got a lovely stable and a very well stocked wine cellar!"

Devin wondered about Castel's personal physician. "What about Dr. Mareschal? Is he safe?"

"I sent him away," Chastel replied. "Perhaps it's best if no one knows where."

Devin studied the paper. "If this newspaper was printed more than a week ago, how could they be so sure that the kidnapping attempt would succeed?"

"They weren't certain," Marcus answered. "But if it failed, they assumed you would go into hiding rather than head back to Coreé. Apparently, we played right into their hands."

"What can I do to help?" Madame Aucoin asked.

"Hide us for a month and ensure we will avoid pursuit when we leave," Marcus said gloomily.

Madame Aucoin beamed. "I can do that. But let's eat first."

Devin looked down at his filthy clothes. "We can't eat in these clothes, *madame*. Your dining room will be ruined."

"All things wash, Master Roché," Madame Aucoin said

calmly. "This is a hunting lodge. The chairs are upholstered in leather and easy to clean. Come and eat, please."

They sat down in a cozy dining room that looked out on the mountainside. The shutters had been thrown back revealing spectacular tree-lined slopes. A small river cascaded over rocks, the white spray rising in a lingering mist. Madame Aucoin even encouraged the wolves to lie under the table after they had visited the kitchen for a well-earned breakfast themselves. There was very little space for anyone's legs and feet as the wolves sprawled, satiated and drowsy.

Assorted breads, fruit, eggs, and sausages lined the small table. Devin thought the freshly brewed coffee smelled exquisite.

"Oh my God – sausages!" Gaspard exclaimed, raising his hands in supplication.

Devin shifted away from him. "I'm not sure I want to sit by you. You're practically drooling!"

"Do you know how long it's been since I had hot food?" Gaspard complained. "Life as a hostage isn't all fun and games, you know!"

Marcus eyed him critically. "You're lucky to be alive, Gaspard. If all you've lost is a few pounds, consider yourself fortunate."

"Oh, I do!" Gaspard answered. "But it doesn't stop me from being grateful for sausages." He piled them onto his plate in delight.

Chastel turned from staring out the windows. "This place is remarkable, *madame*. Even with all the hunting we did together, François never mentioned it."

"This was his safe house," Madame Aucoin said. "The family secret, passed down from father to son. It wasn't only his generation that had to make use of it."

"Nicholas Aucoin!" Armand gasped. "I didn't make the connection until now!"

"He was my husband's grandfather. You are familiar with his story then?" Madame Aucoin asked.

"Oh yes, *madame*," Armand answered.

"Thank God for that," Madame Aucoin answered. "I fear the Chronicles are in danger of extinction, along with our bards."

Armand laid his fork down on his plate.

"*Comte Nicholas Aucoin came to the defense of a young woman who was accused of theft by the local shérif. The girl, whose name was Margaux, was employed by the Comte himself. After a party at the chateau one spring evening, several of his wife's pieces of jewelry went missing. The shérif was called to investigate. Several days later, he claimed all evidence led to Margaux, the servant girl, who Comte Aucoin had recently promoted to a lady's maid. Margaux was imprisoned in the local jail and sentenced to be whipped the next day.*

"*The young woman entreated the Comte to visit her before the sentence could be carried out. He came immediately. Margaux fell down on her knees and claimed she had taken nothing from the chateau and that her loyalty to the Comte and to his lady wife was without question. Nicholas believed her. That night, Margaux disappeared mysteriously from her jail cell.*"

Armand turned to Madame Aucoin. "I am assuming that the Comte broke her out of her cell and after returning her to the chateau, made use of the tunnel to get her to safety?"

Madame Aucoin nodded, "He did, but you may not add that fact to the recitation of this tale."

"I understand completely," Armand said before he continued.

"Nicholas asked one of his personal guards to begin a discreet investigation into the crime while the shérif combed the village and mountains in vain for Margaux. The guard discovered that Margaux had angered the shérif several times in the last few months when she had refused his advances toward her. Further investigation revealed that the jewelry had been sold in a neighboring town by the shérif himself. Comte Aucoin had the shérif arrested for theft and falsifying evidence. He was stripped of his title and imprisoned for ten years. Margaux was never heard from again."

"Margaux served in this house as a servant for many years. She married and raised a son. Nicholas felt it was best for her to remain here in case the former *shérif* planned any kind of retribution against her," Madame Aucoin finished for him.

Devin smiled. "That is a very nice ending to the story, *madame*. So few of the Chronicles end happily. Perhaps I should mention that the tunnel will probably never be used again. One section collapsed moments after we were resting there. It is completely blocked back toward the chateau."

"I have no use for it now that my granddaughter is home safely," said Madame Aucoin. "We will lock the door and throw away the key."

"There is a small possibility that the tunnel was collapsed intentionally," Marcus interjected. "Devin thought he heard voices behind us just before the cave-in."

Madame Aucoin rose from the table. "I will lock the door this minute, although no one from the other side will be able to make it through either. I doubt you have anything to worry about."

They had plenty to worry about, Devin thought. If only she knew.

But she was ushering them off upstairs. "Please don't allow me to keep you at the table. You must all be exhausted. Go upstairs and rest. Rooms have already been prepared for you and hot water will be waiting. Sleep as long as you need to. There will be a hot meal waiting when you waken."

They all thanked her profusely, feeling relaxed and safe for the first time in days. Angelique could barely keep her eyes open and Devin was unbearably sleepy himself. He and Gaspard followed a servant upstairs where a copper tub brimming with hot water had been brought to their room. Devin would have liked to have fallen into his bed face-first but he peeled off his filthy clothes and bathed.

Nightclothes were laid out on the two gigantic beds and an assortment of clothing had been added to the armoire in their room, everything from shirts and trousers to jackets and boots. There were more than enough for several days' use.

"God, I've forgotten how good hot water feels," Gaspard commented from the tub. "Sometimes, I wonder why I let you talk me into this crazy adventure."

"I didn't talk you into it," Devin reminded him. "I kidnapped you."

Gaspard laughed. "Oh, right! Of course, how could I have forgotten that?"

CHAPTER 14

Safety

Devin wakened shortly after noon to find clean clothes laid out for him. He dressed and left Gaspard snoring peacefully. He walked down the long central staircase, which faced a magnificent floor-to-ceiling window with an incredible view of the waterfall. Whoever had designed this house had skillfully incorporated the scenery into the plan. The entire building and its surroundings exuded calm and serenity.

He found Madame Aucoin alone in her chair beside the fireplace untangling her knitting from the paws of a huge orange cat. He knocked gently on the open door. "Am I disturbing you, *madame*?" he asked.

She smiled as though there was no one she would rather spend time with. "Of course not, Devin! Join me, please. You have no idea how lovely it is to have visitors."

He chose the armchair across from her. "You're very gracious, considering we came barging into your sitting room in the wee hours of the morning."

She threw up her hands and abandoned her knitting to the mercies of the delighted cat. "I cannot count how many days I have sat here waiting to hear a key turn in the lock of that door. You have brought me more joy than I can ever express by bringing my granddaughter safely to me."

Devin turned to look for the door where it lay deftly hidden in a wall of carved stone. The flowing curves and arches reminded him of the sanctuary of a church. He was struck again by how beautiful this house was and perfectly designed for its purpose.

He cleared his throat. "I should probably allow Angelique to tell you this herself, but she has faced some terrible things in her life. She and the other children were playing hide and seek when the chateau was attacked. Angelique hid in a wine cask. Only she and Marie, a servant, survived. She spent years hiding in the chateau with nothing but a kind servant to talk to. Then two years ago, Marie died and Angelique has been alone ever since. Luckily, Marie taught her to read and write. She had her books but she has been alone most of her lifetime."

"My son taught all his servants to read and write," Madame Aucoin said. "I imagine he never dreamed that one would in turn teach his youngest daughter." She paused a moment, one hand to her cheek. "Please tell me that Angelique didn't see her family after the chateau was attacked."

Devin avoided her eyes. "She did," he answered softly. "The memory continues to haunt her. She has terrible dreams where her mother and siblings cry out to her to save them."

"Oh, the poor child," she murmured, tears sparkling on her lashes.

Devin stood up, his back to the fireplace, his eyes on the staircase. "I thought you should know what she's been through. She's easily frightened and yet a part of her is very cold. We were attacked by some of René Forneaux's men at the chateau yesterday. Between Marcus and Chastel and his wolves, all eight men were killed. It was Angelique who suggested weighting their bodies with stones and dropping them in the cistern. It scared me to hear her say that. She is fragile and vulnerable and then ruthless, all in the space of a few minutes. She needs care and someone dependable to love her. We intended to take her with us. Chastel has already offered her a permanent home. She seems to feel safe with him but now, according to the newspaper, he is considered a criminal until we can straighten this mess out. I don't know if any of us will ever make it back to Coreé alive."

Madame Aucoin tilted her head. "My dear boy, what are you trying to say? Of course, Angelique will stay here with me. I never considered anything else."

"Thank God," Devin murmured, slumping back into his chair. "I'm just worried about her. The last thing she needs is to be roaming the countryside with men who may be murdered at any moment."

Madame Aucoin leaned forward, a little smile playing over her lips. "I would never allow my granddaughter to accompany five men anywhere, so please put your mind at rest."

Devin laughed. "When you put it that way, it seems quite inappropriate!"

"As it would be under normal circumstances," Madame Aucoin agreed with a smile. "But I thank you from the bottom of my heart for bringing her home to me."

Devin relaxed against the chair back and stretched his legs out in front of him. "Your son had meticulously planned an escape for his family. I've often wondered why Angelique never followed that tunnel herself."

"Fear of the unknown, perhaps?" Madame Aucoin suggested. "As much as the chateau repelled her, she couldn't bring herself to leave it because it was her home. Sometimes the familiar is appealing even though its memories haunt us. I will take care of her now and she will be as safe here as I can possibly make her."

Devin grinned. "Do you have your own personal army?"

Her laugh was light and musical, like a young girl's. "You might be surprised at the forces I have at my disposal, Devin. We will talk to your man, Marcus, later to see how best I can help you."

"Is he still sleeping?" Devin asked in surprise.

"As far as I know."

He laughed. "It is a compliment to you, *madame*, that he feels safe enough here to relax his vigilance and get a good sleep."

"We had a short talk about vigilance before he went up to bed. I think he is more than satisfied with the safety precautions we have taken here." Madame Aucoin rang the bell at her elbow. "You must be hungry, Devin. I believe my cook made some excellent cinnamon buns while you were sleeping."

"Thank heavens I woke up first. If Gaspard finds out he'll eat them all!"

"Too late," Gaspard said from the doorway, a half-eaten cinnamon bun in his hand. "I've already been to the kitchen!" He was dressed in clean clothes but his hair was uncombed and tousled. He sauntered into the sitting room and gracefully dropped into a chair. "You'll have to learn to get up more quietly if you don't want people following you downstairs."

"I hope you left a bun for me," Devin said.

Gaspard took a large bite and made appreciative noises. "There might be one left and they are brewing the most heavenly coffee, too."

Devin laughed. Only a few days ago he wondered if he would ever see his best friend again. He'd have given up every cinnamon bun in the world just for the assurance that Gaspard was still alive and unharmed. "It's good to have you back!" he said. "I've missed you!"

CHAPTER 15

Old Acquaintances

It was almost time for dinner before Angelique finally came downstairs. Devin heard her light footsteps on the stairway and left the other men in the sitting room and went out into the hallway to greet her. Apparently, her grandmother had outfitted her well, with a soft-blue dress that flowed like water down the stairs behind her as she descended. Her eyes had lost some of that haunted look. She graced Devin with a smile but her glance went over his head as the front door opened. Devin turned. A broad-shouldered, bearded man stood frozen in the doorway, his eyes fixed unwaveringly on Angelique, as hers were on him.

"Jules?" Angelique whispered.

"Angelique?" the man gasped. "My little Angelique?"

Devin stepped out of the way as they rushed to each other.

Jules grabbed Angelique and lifted her off her feet, as he must have so many times when she was a child. "Thank God," he said reverently. "Thank God you are safe, my little one!" He set her down gently as though she were a porcelain doll. Angelique couldn't stop smiling.

"I can't believe that you are alive, Jules!" Angelique cried, clinging to his hand. "How did you get here? I assumed you died with my father."

Jules put an arm around her shoulders. "Believe me, little one, it was my duty to die at your father's side but he entrusted me with something that he felt was more important than his life. He asked me to return it safely and then to come here, to your grandmother."

"Why didn't *Grandmère* tell you I was here?" Angelique asked.

"I haven't spoken to Madame Aucoin yet. I only returned just now, myself," Jules explained. "I have been away for two days."

Madame Aucoin appeared in the doorway of the sitting room, her face wreathed in smiles. "My visitors arrived early this morning, Jules. Angelique has been living alone in the wine cellar of my son's chateau. Her friends persuaded her to follow the tunnel to safety."

Jules put a hand to his chest. "*Mon Dieu*, I have failed in my duty to your father, Angelique. I should have come for you. I should have made certain that any survivors were rescued, no matter what the risk."

"You might have endangered her life," Madame Aucoin said softly. "The chateau has been watched for years in hopes of retrieving The Bishop's Book."

Devin started. "I have it with me. It's upstairs in my room."

"You have The Bishop's Book?" Jules asked incredulously. "How did you get it? I returned it to the priest at St. Gregory's."

"The priest was killed in a fall from a ladder," Devin said. "We thought perhaps he had fallen while he was hiding the book in the bell tower. I found it hidden in the stone-work."

"Thank God it is safe, too!" Jules said. "François died for that book and its contents."

"We have yet to discover what is significant about the contents," Devin said. "Was there some sort of code or key to decipher it?"

Jules shook his head. "Not that I know of. François took only the book with him when we left for Viénne. He gave it to me and told me to leave at the first sign of trouble and return it to St. Gregory's."

"Obviously, it will take some more study then," Devin said. "Perhaps you can help us interpret it."

"Of course," Jules replied with a little bow. "Who do I have the pleasure of addressing?"

Devin extended his hand. "Devin Roché."

Jules' face darkened. He made no move to shake hands. "The Chancellor's son?" he asked.

"Yes," Devin answered.

"And you have The Bishop's Book?"

Devin saw the suspicion in Jules' eyes that the book had fallen into the wrong hands. He nodded. "Yes, I do."

"What made your father send you for it now?" Jules demanded. "It's been twelve years since its disappearance."

"My father didn't send me for the book," Devin replied defensively. "I didn't even know it existed until Angelique showed me her father's letters."

"Then what in God's name made you visit the provinces at a time like this?" Jules demanded.

"A time like what?" Marcus asked, flanking Devin in a protective stance.

Jules's voice echoed in the elegant hallway of glass and

110

stone. "Villagers are disappearing all over Ombria and Arcadia! Many are blaming the government. Some people are withholding any exports to Viénne until they can be assured that they are safe from retribution. We are on the verge of revolution!" Jules gestured at Devin. "And you, *monsieur*, seem to have been the catalyst for all of this!"

"My visit has always been a peaceful one," Devin replied, forcing himself to answer quietly. "I am an archivist, Jules. I came to the provinces to memorize the Chronicles. I began in Ombria under the tutelage of Armand Vielle. Since then, I have been targeted by assassins, hunted by wolves, and seen the whole town of Lac Dupré disappear without so much as a whisper. I have lost several people that I care deeply about. I am as much the victim in this as those villagers."

Madame Aucoin moved between them, her voice exuding calm. "Would you all join me in the sitting room for a glass of wine before dinner? It seems we have a great deal to discuss, but I believe we are all on the same side here. Perhaps we can arrive at a solution to this problem if we all work together."

They followed her into the sitting room, Jules determinedly aligning with Angelique and her grandmother. His defensive stance escalated Marcus's vigilance and they faced each other across the room, two men so alike in both build and determination that they should have been brothers in arms rather than adversaries. When Madame Aucoin offered them wine, both of them refused it.

Madame Aucoin broke the silence first. "The newspaper didn't include the information about the villagers' disappearance."

Jules snorted, his eyes never leaving Marcus's face. "Coreé

prints only the news it wants its citizens to read about. Conditions in the provinces have always been a well-kept secret. Few Councilmen know or are interested in the truth."

"And yet, François Aucoin was a Councilman," Devin pointed out.

"And because he disagreed with the current thought in Coreé, he was assassinated for his views. No doubt the intent was to wipe his entire family from the face the earth!"

"My father didn't order his assassination, Jules," Devin replied. "There are more factions at work here than you know about."

Jules leaned back in his chair with his arms folded over his chest. "Then perhaps you will enlighten me, Monsieur Roché."

Devin shook his head. "I wish I could. There are forces that we haven't completely identified. We do know that René Forneaux planned to kill both his son and me here in the provinces to further alienate the residents of Viénne from the provincial people."

"I see he was unsuccessful," Jules replied drily.

"And we pray that he will continue to be," Madame Aucoin inserted quietly. "Perhaps our time might be better served discussing the problem at hand instead of rehashing old hurts, Jules."

"The problem at hand is so big that none of us will be able to solve it," Jules replied. "The situation has escalated beyond resolution. The Empire of Llisé has reached a tinder point – one spark and we will all go up in flames."

"There has to be some way to defuse the situation," Chastel said. "All of us know that Gaspard's father ordered his assassination and Devin's, too. If we can make that known, it might undermine Forneaux's authority."

"I have no secure way of sending a message to the

Chancellor," Marcus replied. "I was given contacts and troops at my disposal when we left Coreé but I have no idea to whom they owe alliance now."

"Could we just go home, Marcus?" Devin asked.

"Oh God, please! I don't want to go home!" Gaspard protested dramatically.

"It's impossible now," Marcus replied.

"My prayers have been answered," Gaspard said, throwing his hands in the air in triumph and heading for the wine bottle. "Can I get anyone else a refill?"

Devin watched his friend fill one glass and down it and then refill it again before he went back to his seat. "This is deadly serious, Gaspard," he said in exasperation.

Gaspard raised his eyebrows. "Don't you think I realize that? I was held hostage for two weeks and I was never certain from one moment to the next whether I would be killed or not! They mocked me with dozens of different means that they could use to kill or torture me."

"Gaspard!" Armand said sharply.

Angelique had gone quite pale and Jules was scowling at Gaspard as though he might kill him himself.

"We're sorry for what you endured but this is not the time to discuss it," Armand continued.

"Did you hear other names mentioned besides your father's?" Devin asked hopefully.

Gaspard shook his head. "My guards didn't speak about anything important in front of me. In fact, other than taunting me, they hardly spoke at all."

"Devin," Chastel said. "I'm sure both you and Marcus can come up with a list of men who might side with Forneaux if this all came down to some kind of vote. It shouldn't be hard to know who is taking sides."

Devin shrugged. "It is and it isn't. Many of these men agree publicly to one thing and say quite another in private. And believe me, no one was any more surprised than I was that René Forneaux would actually think of sacrificing his oldest son to make the provincial people look barbaric and dangerous."

Gaspard balanced his glass on the arm of his chair. "Not everyone has a father who loves him, Dev. I've told you before that you have no idea of the way the world actually works."

"Well, it's up to us to prove René wrong," Chastel remarked. "We have to show him that the provincial people can be very different from the way he portrays them."

"How do we do that?" Gaspard asked. "The papers will be reporting boycotts and riots. If we can't control the news, then we can't influence the leaders of the Empire."

A servant appeared at the door. "Dinner is served, Madame Aucoin."

"We'll simply have to be more creative than our enemies," Devin said as he stood up. "I'm certainly not giving up."

"Nor am I," Chastel affirmed.

CHAPTER 16

Confidences

Dinner was more relaxed, although Jules sat right next to Angelique and Marcus sat next to Devin. Madame Aucoin was seated at the head of the table, gentle and discreet as ever. Devin wondered if she ever raised her voice. She emanated calm and graciousness, carefully steering the conversation away from controversial topics.

"So, your assignment was to memorize all fifteen Chronicles?" she asked Devin.

"It is really only fourteen Chronicles, *madame*. Viénne's history is well preserved in the Archives. And it wasn't an assignment," Devin clarified. "It concerned me that one of the Chronicles had already been lost after the death of the Master Bard of Perouse. I thought that if I could memorize them, then Gaspard could write down the songs and ballads and they would be preserved for another generation, at least."

"I'm surprised your father allowed you to come," Madame Aucoin said.

"My father was against this trip from the beginning. It

was something I wanted to do personally. The heritage of Llisé lies in the history of its people."

Madame Aucoin shook her head. "Our own Master Bard was assassinated recently. His apprentice has disappeared. No one knows whether he is alive and in hiding or dead at the hands of the same men."

"I have memorized Arcadia's Chronicle," Armand reminded them. "Perhaps I can find an apprentice brave enough to learn it from me."

"I doubt you'll find a willing participant now," Jules said. "In order to attract someone, you would have to reveal your own location, which would breach our security and your own."

"I want to learn it if you have time to teach me," Devin offered.

Jules stabbed a finger at Devin from across the table. "You can never apprentice to be Master Bard of Arcadia, Monsieur Roché. You are a resident of Viénne!"

"That was not my intention ..." Devin began but Armand rose to his defense.

"Arcadia has no Master Bard at the moment, Jules," he retorted. "You have me and a frightened or dead apprentice. Unless you intend for Arcadia's Chronicle to be buried along with its Master Bard, the rules will have to be bent as to how the Chronicles are passed down."

"If we bend the rules," Jules replied, "then the integrity of the Chronicles will be lost!"

"Only if you let it," Chastel said. "The fact remains that Master Bards are in short supply. The more people who can tell the stories of your province, the better. It is your history that unites you."

Madame Aucoin looked up at a servant and smiled sweetly. "I believe we are ready for dessert now."

Devin, Chastel, Armand, and Marcus walked outside after dinner to watch a spectacular sunset over the mountains. The clouds were edged in pink and gold, as the sun's final shafts of light threw rainbows through the mist of the waterfall. The air smelled damp and woodsy, redolent with rotting leaves and spruce and fir. The evergreens stood silhouetted against the sun, like sentinels guarding the chateau from danger. All the turmoil in Llisé seemed very far away.

"Do you know what the chateau is called?" Devin asked.

"La Paix," Marcus said.

"Peace," Devin repeated, "how appropriate."

Chastel's wolves snuffled in the ferns and fallen branches beneath the trees. Sending a rabbit out of hiding, they bounded into the forest, their noses to the ground. They were gone in seconds, lost to the shadows and mist of the forest, but their chilling howls still rang across the ravine.

Devin looked at Chastel, who was observing them intently. "What's it like," Devin asked, "to run with your wolves?"

Chastel lifted his chin and took a deep breath before answering. "Do you enjoy riding, Monsieur Roché?" he asked.

Devin nodded. "I do, very much."

"Do you know that moment, when you and the horse become one being, moving in tandem but united?"

"Yes," Devin agreed.

"That is a small taste of what it is like to run with wolves." Chastel turned to look at Devin. "A very small taste, because it is so much more than that. When I take the form of a wolf, I can still think as a man but I have the senses, the instincts, and the aptitudes of a wolf. It's strange, but I have changed on this trip. I am not certain why. Perhaps it's the tension of being on alert all the time. I am

117

never simply a man, or simply a wolf, but always one waits behind the other, suppressed but ready, if the need arises for the other self to appear."

Devin swallowed. "I appreciate your candor. I hope I haven't offended you by asking."

Chastel gave a wry smile. "It was bound to come up, if not from you, then from my brother." He glanced at Armand. "Are you repelled or fascinated?"

"Fascinated," Armand said. "I can't help but wonder if it is possible that the same instinct lies within me. Since Jeanette's disappearance I have savored the thought of bringing vengeance on those who took her. I am haunted by dreams of brutalizing those men."

"Wolves kill to eat or survive, Armand – they don't plan vindictive attacks on those who have injured them," Chastel said gently. "I think your feelings are very human ones. We are, without a doubt, the more violent of the two species."

"And yet, as a wolf, with a man's intellect, I might have a better chance of killing them," Armand replied. "Will you teach me?"

Chastel shook his head. "Not if that is your motivation for learning to shape-change."

Armand's eyes were cold. "Suit yourself then! Perhaps I don't need a teacher. You apparently taught yourself how to shape-change and so can I." He turned and left them standing in the rapidly darkening night.

Devin sighed, watching Armand limp toward the front door of the chateau. "He's grieving, Chastel. He doesn't mean half of what he says these days."

"Don't you think I know that?" Chastel replied. "We are all grieving. I hurt for him and for you and for myself. I love Jeanette, too. She is my only heir. I had hoped that at some point, I might be permitted to treat her as my niece and welcome her into my home. Through your intervention, I believed there might actually be a chance of that. Without Jeanette, the Chastel line will die out."

"You could still marry and father children," Marcus suggested from the shadows.

Chastel scoffed. "I have been without a spouse for many years because no family would allow their daughters to marry the Wolf Comte. I think my abilities preclude my establishing any kind of marital relationship."

"Are there no other families that can shape-change?" Marcus asked.

"I don't honestly know. Both the Chastels and the Aucoins trace their families to the first settlers of Llisé. My father believed that early tie to the earth and forests set us apart. As close as we were, François and I never discussed it, although after Angelique's experience in finding her family slaughtered, I would have thought any tendency might manifest itself in her then."

"What do you mean?" Devin asked, perching on the stone wall that bordered the edge of the falls. Behind him the water tumbled and rushed, masking their voices from anyone beyond their immediate circle.

"The emblem of the Aucoins is a falcon," Chastel said. "I've often wondered if the falcon is to their family what the wolf is to mine. When Angelique's family was murdered, she might very well have shape-changed into a falcon and flown away."

"She was only four years old," Devin reminded him. "Surely shape-changing requires years of practice."

Chastel placed one booted foot on the wall and gazed down at the water. "You'd be surprised. My father never spoke of our family curse until some of the village boys taunted me one day and called me 'wolf child.' I came home crying and he sat me down in his study in that same chair where I explained the whole sordid tale to you. He told me the story of my Uncle Charles and his death. When he was finished, I asked him if he had ever been able to shape-change. He swore to me that he had never taken the form of a wolf and wouldn't have the faintest idea how to do it. I believed him."

"Then how did you ..." Devin began.

Chastel held up a hand. "I'm getting to that. As a child, I rode for hours around the chateau. My father made no demands except that I return well before dark when the threat from wolves was most credible. On my twelfth birthday, my father gave me a new horse. I was so anxious to ride it that I was gone most of the day, roaming the countryside around the estate. On my way home, a flock of ducks took flight, which startled my horse, and it threw me. I wasn't hurt but I was miles from home and my faithless birthday gift went galloping off toward the stables hoping for a full measure of grain. It started to get dark and I was scared. I heard the howls of wolves and I ran.

"The howls grew nearer and I knew they were behind me. I remember racing over the ground and then suddenly I had this euphoric feeling that I could almost fly. I wondered why I had never been able to run this fast before, and then I looked down at my feet, and they were paws. I was so astounded that I stumbled and fell – an ungainly ball of fur and claws, rolling over and over in the dirt.

"I was terrified and to make matters worse, the real wolves darted out of the shadows of the trees along the road. They circled me, sniffed me, pawed at me playfully, and all the while I could do nothing but sob little puppy squeals of terror. One female broke the circle and licked my face. And then quickly, they turned and left me, as though they recognized me as one of their own. I lay on the ground, and as my breathing finally returned to normal, I changed back into a dirty, tear-stained little boy. A few minutes later, one of my father's men arrived with my runaway horse and took me home."

"Did you tell your father?" Devin asked.

Chastel shook his head. "Never. I was sure I had done something shameful. I couldn't even imagine telling him what had happened. I felt like a freak, some horrible aberration. I was convinced that he would have to shoot me, just as Grandfather had shot Uncle Charles years before. After a while, I was able to convince myself that it had never happened. It wasn't until after my father died that I read my grandfather's journal. Perhaps it was a result of boredom or youthful experimentation, but I decided to try again.

"I was convinced that by concentrating hard enough, I could shape-change. I tried time after time and nothing happened, at all. It was like one of those experiments we all try at *Université*, like trying to bend a spoon with your mind. I continued to try as hard as I could but nothing changed. I remained a man. Again, I began to think that I had imagined the whole incident from my childhood. The idea that wolves would spare a child simply because he was frightened was so foreign to what I knew to be true and yet, at the time, I had chosen to believe it." Chastel shook his head. "There was a certain relief in agreeing to accept that my experience was only a figment of my imagination."

"What made you try again?" Devin asked.

"I was coming home late one winter afternoon. My horse lost a shoe and I was walking him. The skies were heavy with snow and it was almost dark. I heard the wolves before I saw them; they came up behind us. They slowed down and started loping parallel to my horse. I was frantically trying to pull out my pistol, but I never fired a shot. It was pointless. There was a whole pack of wolves. They could easily have brought my horse and me both down but they didn't. They slowed down and kept pace with us. When we reached the chateau, they veered off into the forest. It was the strangest thing. It was almost as though they were providing us with an escort home.

"That night, after arriving at the chateau, shaken and awed by the wolves' behavior, I discovered the passageway out of the study. I'm not even sure how it came about. I'd had a couple of drinks and was standing at the mantle, a glass of wine in my hand, and somehow I bumped the latch. There it was!"

"Your father never showed it to you?" Devin asked in disbelief.

"No, he never mentioned it."

"Perhaps it was originally an escape tunnel," Marcus said, "like the one in Aucoin's chateau."

"If it was, then why wouldn't my father have mentioned it?" Chastel replied. "Either he didn't know about it or he intended to keep it a secret from me."

"Maybe he hoped that the tendency to take wolf form had died with Charles. He might have thought that the passageway would only serve as a temptation to anyone who inherited the master's study," Devin said.

Chastel laughed. "You are too gentle in your judgement, Devin. On the wall in the passageway, there is a list of names and dates. My father's name was the last on the list before I added mine and the day of my twelfth birthday." He moved his foot to the ground and took a deep breath, giving Devin a direct look. "My father was able to shape-change, too. He just didn't want to admit it. You see, not only are the Chastels shape-changers but they are excellent liars, too."

Devin raised his eyebrows. "I'm not sure what to say."

"You don't need to say anything. There you have it – the Chastels' dirty little secret. We have all lied about it."

Devin laughed suddenly. "I must admit, you do lie well! You insisted that Charles was never some strange hybrid who could change from man to wolf at will."

Chastel laughed, good-humoredly. "Well, the transformation is much more complicated than that, Devin. I couldn't have you going back to Coreé and reporting that the Chastels were werewolves, because we aren't."

"That's true," Devin replied, suppressing a chuckle. "And I, for one, am happy that you have that particular talent because without you along, we might all be dead by now." He glanced at the chateau. "Will you ever teach Armand to shape-change?"

Chastel shrugged. "I'm not sure it can be taught. I've often wondered if it doesn't happen by chance. That's why I wondered about Angelique and the falcons. That situation would have been the perfect one to reveal her latent tendencies."

"And yet she, herself, wasn't at risk. She slept through the massacre and when she did find her family dead, her nurse was there to take care of her."

"True," Chastel answered.

"So much is passed down from father to son in these old

provincial families. It makes me wonder why your father didn't share this with you," Devin said.

"Because this shape-changing business is a burden," Marcus replied unexpectedly. "Why give your sons knowledge that will only complicate their lives?"

"I researched all the names and dates in the passageway," Chastel said. "They skip several generations, so being a Chastel doesn't necessarily mean you can shape-change. The other interesting part is that most of the dates, which I assume represent the first manifestation, range between the tenth and fourteenth birthdays of my ancestors who are listed."

"So if it does happen, it is before a boy becomes a man," Marcus said.

Devin looked out at the forest over Chastel's shoulder. Fireflies danced in the dark, lending a magical quality to the night. "Maybe Armand couldn't learn even if he wanted to."

"I don't know," Chastel replied. "But I have bared my soul to you tonight. I want your word that this information will go no further. It is my family's personal business – our curse, if you care to see it that way. It cannot go beyond the three of us. I will tell Armand the whole story sometime, when and if I choose."

"Of course," Devin said, extending his hand. "You have my word."

"Mine, as well," Marcus added, shaking Chastel's hand.

"There are only two other people I have shared even part of this with. One is Dr. Mareschal; he has been my friend and my physician for a long time. His services became necessary a number of times when I hurt myself in wolf form and limped home for his ministrations. I had to offer him some justification for my recurring injuries."

"I wondered if he knew," Devin replied. "It seemed likely when he lives at the chateau."

"He lives with me as compensation for keeping my secrets and caring for my wounds. I have had no greater friend."

"You said you told two people your secret," Marcus said. "Who was the other?"

Chastel's face darkened. "René Forneaux, and I regret that more than I can say."

CHAPTER 17

Storytelling

The front door opened, sending a shaft of light across the quiet woodland garden. Ferns and bell-shaped white flowers swayed gently in the light breeze as mist crept stealthily across the ground, giving it an otherworldly appearance. Jules stood silhouetted in the doorway, hostility emanating from the rigid stance of his massive shoulders.

"Madame Aucoin requests that you join her in the sitting room," he boomed across the yard, a lantern in his hand.

"We will be there in a few minutes," Devin called back, feeling reluctant to leave both the camaraderie and the magic of the woodland night.

Jules didn't wait. The door slammed.

Chastel inclined his head and smiled. "We have been summoned."

"Apparently," Devin agreed.

Marcus didn't find the situation amusing. Devin could feel his irritation radiating like a cloud around him as they headed up the stone path toward the house. A lone wolf howled just as they reached the doorstep and Chastel turned, a look of undisguised yearning on his face.

"Perhaps you'd prefer to stay behind," Devin suggested quietly.

Chastel dismissed the suggestion with a wave of his hand. "However would you explain that to Madame Aucoin?" he asked with a wry smile.

The candlelit house felt too bright in comparison to the serenity of the shadowy garden. Jules stood waiting in the hall, as though anticipating that they might dare to disobey a direct order that he had delivered personally. Devin walked past him with no more than a cursory glance and entered the sitting room. Armand was ensconced in the customary Master Bard's spot, next to the fire. Angelique sat at Madame Aucoin's feet, her head resting against her grandmother's knee. She looked happy and relaxed for the first time since Devin had met her. Gaspard sprawled indolently on the carpet, his back against a chair and a half-filled wine glass between his knees.

"I thought you'd all gone to the local tavern without me," Gaspard protested, his words slurred.

"The nearest tavern is miles away," Jules informed him coldly. "Should you choose to avail yourself of its wares, be careful. We wouldn't want you to fall into a chasm or be eaten by wolves."

Gaspard raised his glass high in an inebriated salute. "Thank you for your concern, Jules! We hardly even know each other and already you are looking out for my welfare. That's very nice."

Devin smothered a smile and sat down, carefully shifting Armand's old harp where it lay resting against the chair.

"I've asked Armand to entertain us with a few stories

127

from Arcadia's Chronicle," Madame Aucoin remarked brightly. "He suggested that you might play a few ballads for us, too, Devin."

Devin bowed his head. "I will acquiesce to my teacher's expertise. I prefer that you enjoy the best first and I will follow."

"Whatever you wish," Armand replied, his mood only marginally improved. "For my first story I have chosen 'The Two Brothers'."

Madame Aucoin's brow furrowed slightly before she turned her attention fully to Armand.

"About two hundred years ago," Armand began, *"a prosperous farmer had two sons. The oldest, Pierre, excelled at woodworking. He kept his father's barns and fences in good repair and took great pride in his work. The younger son, Remy, spent his days in the surrounding woodlands gathering herbs, roots, and mushrooms. He knew every edible wild food on sight and the family ate well because of his ability, even when harvests were meager. Pierre admired Remy's talent and offered to teach Remy woodworking if Remy would in turn teach him to identify the edible plants in the area. Remy refused, even though Pierre persisted. Remy claimed he had no interest in learning woodworking. He said that spending time with Pierre would lessen his own time in the woods collecting food for the family, so matters continued as they were for some time.*

"Autumn came and Pierre was often gone all day, checking the fences and gathering firewood before winter. Remy disappeared into the forest and returned every night before dinner with a variety of wild foods to supplement the stews and cassoulets that his mother prepared. The brothers saw little

of each other; they went to bed early and got up before dawn to finish their appointed tasks. One particular afternoon, Pierre had been working hard all day with only a break to eat the bread and cheese his mother had packed for him. He stopped about mid-afternoon. Tired and hungry, he sat down in the grass. As he sat on the hillside, his eyes took in the black berries growing on small plants near the hedges along the field. They looked very much like the ones that Remy often brought home as a treat for dinner. He gathered a handful and popped them into his mouth, pleased with their sweet taste."

Madame Aucoin gave a little gasp of distress but Armand continued.

"Pierre did not return by nightfall and Remy and his father went out with a lantern to look for him, repeatedly calling his name in the area where he had been working. It was not until morning that they found Pierre's body, his hand stained purple from the berries he had consumed. Remy was immediately seized by remorse that he had not taken the time to teach his brother about which plants were safe to eat and which were poisonous. But it was too late and Pierre was dead. Remy had to live the rest of his life with his guilt."

Armand glanced at his audience in the calculated way he had of judging the effect his words had on his listeners. Madame Aucoin had her hands to her face. "He ate *Morelle Noire*!" she said in horror. "Surely, even children are warned about Black Nightshade? That is such a sad story, Monsieur Vielle. I wonder why I have never heard it before."

Chastel chuckled in amusement. "My dear lady, contain your sorrow. Armand made that story up!"

"What do you mean, Chastel?" Devin objected. "Armand

is very precise about retelling the Chronicles; he would never substitute a fabricated story and pass it off as part of Arcadia's Chronicle."

Armand stood up and bowed, looking pleased with himself. "Thank you for your loyalty, Monsieur Roché, but Chastel is absolutely correct. I did make this one up."

"Why?" Devin stammered.

"To get back at me for our earlier discussion," Chastel explained calmly.

"God, your naiveté continues to amaze me, Dev," Gaspard snorted. "Why do you always expect everyone to be as honest as you are?"

Devin spared him an annoyed look. "Gaspard, you don't even know what he is talking about, so don't pretend that you do!"

Gaspard splayed a hand across his chest unsteadily. "Excuse me for commenting. Does anyone want another drink?"

"No!" Devin snapped. "And neither do you!" The resulting silence made him wince. Angelique was staring at him as though he had suddenly grown horns on his head and Jules seemed apt to throttle him at any moment. "I'm sorry," he apologized. "This just took me completely by surprise."

"I was trying to make a point," Armand explained agreeably. "I beg your pardon, Monsieur Roché and Madame Aucoin, if I have lost credibility in your eyes."

"It was an excellent story," Madame Aucoin remarked diplomatically. "But could I request something lighter? Perhaps 'The Black Fox of Rowan'?"

Devin decided that silence would serve him better than entering into any further discussion. He slid back in his chair, his arms crossed in front of his chest. When Gaspard tentatively waved the remaining contents of his glass at him as a peace offering, he took it and finished the wine.

He realized, as Armand settled into his recitation, that he had forgotten to pay close enough attention to memorize the story, which was totally out of character. He was still stunned by Armand's attempt to bend Chastel to his wishes. He remembered the first time he had heard Armand tell "The Beast of Gevandan" at Chastel's chateau, only to realize later that the Master Bard had added an extra part to the story that wasn't actually included in Ombria's Chronicle. Did Armand bend the rules only where Chastel was concerned, or did he make a habit of it? Appreciative clapping broke his train of thought.

Armand bowed smugly to his audience and then held out a hand to Devin. "Please Monsieur Roché, entertain us with a ballad of your choosing."

Devin chose Lisette's Lament only because he was rattled and unprepared to start. Fortunately, his fingers flowed effortlessly over the strings of the harp, evoking a far better backdrop for his voice than he could have hoped for under the circumstances. Angelique and her grandmother were both in tears when he finished, earning him another glare from Jules.

Angelique clasped her hands in front of her. "It was beautiful, Devin! Her love for him was beautiful! Sing another love song, please!"

He hesitated only a moment, avoiding Armand's eyes. "Since the precedent has already been set to include selections that are not part of the Chronicles, this is a song I wrote in honor of Jeanette. It's a work in progress," he added. "But I'll share what I have completed."

He played the opening bars of a familiar ballad and then began to sing the words he had written to it.

> *Great roots lie tangled, vines entwine,*
> *Like lovers' arms the ivy binds,*
> *And only death can separate,*
> *Leave one alone to mourn and wait.*
>
> *My days seem dark, my heart bereft,*
> *My life lies barren since she left.*
> *But in my dreams I feel her close,*
> *And hold the one that I love most.*
>
> *If I could pledge to her my heart,*
> *I swear this life would never part*
> *Me from her side, or her from mine,*
> *Our love as tight as ivy binds.*
>
> *If God ordains that she return,*
> *I'll pledge my heart to her in turn.*
> *Till then, I know that I must wait*
> *To hold her hand or touch her face.*

Devin stilled the harp strings with his hand just as Armand left abruptly, muttering about something in his eye. No one else said anything for a moment and then Angelique looked at him hopefully. "Tell us Jeanette's story, please. I want to know more about her."

Devin shook his head. "It's not part of the Chronicles, Angelique. She is Armand's daughter. She disappeared the same night the rest of the residents from Lac Dupré went missing. I have no idea where she is or whether she is alive or dead. I cared a great deal for her but I wasn't man enough to stand up to Armand and make certain he knew that. I have regretted it ever since."

"I believe Armand threatened you to stay away from her," Chastel said quietly. "I wouldn't be too hard on yourself."

Madame Aucoin smile gently. "Jeanette may still be alive," she whispered. "The provinces are filled with amazing stories of people who have survived unbelievable odds. If you are supposed to be together then God will see that you are."

"Do you truly believe that, *Grandmère*?" Angelique asked. "Do you believe Jeanette is alive?"

Madame Aucoin smiled. "I believe we have a gracious and loving God who wants us to be happy in spite of the terrible things that may happen in our lives." She pulled Angelique close to her in a hug. "He brought you to me, after all these years, my dear. So, yes, I think that means that anything is possible."

CHAPTER 18

Thieves in the Night

Devin came down to breakfast, leaving Gaspard to sleep off a terrible headache. He stopped by the kitchen and asked the cook to reserve some sausages in case Gaspard's appetite revived later along with his good spirits. The entryway off the kitchen reeked of wet dog or more precisely, wet wolves. Chastel's pack lay grooming their dripping pelts, making a formidable barrier for anyone who needed to go in or out the door.

The dining room held none of yesterday's warmth and light. There was no sunlit waterfall to greet them this morning through the windows. Leaden clouds engulfed the tops of the evergreens and rain dripped steadily off the roof. The ravine below the waterfall was adrift with fog as tendrils of mist snaked eerily across the garden, obscuring the stone walls and ferns. The mountains echoed with distant thunder.

Madame Aucoin and Angelique were already seated next to each other. Angelique's hand lay on her grandmother's lap, their heads tilted together as though they were young girls chatting about what their plans for the day were. Jules had his eye on the garden and so did Marcus but neither talked to the other one. Chastel and Armand sat at opposite sides of the table, still at odds over last night's discussion.

Devin slid into a chair next to Armand and exchanged the expected pleasantries with everyone before the meal began. Coffee arrived, hot and fragrant, along with an assortment of fresh breads, cheese, fruit, and sausages. It was a huge improvement over Devin's daily ration of berries as they trekked through the mountains. With Viénne's newspapers reporting his disappearance and probable death, only his parents' apprehension over his wellbeing marred the cozy serenity of La Paix this morning.

"I wish there was some way to get a message to my father to assure him that I am all right," he said, when they had all been served.

Madame Aucoin gave him an encouraging smile. "I believe that can be accomplished, dear. Please don't worry about it."

Marcus laid his fork carefully on his plate. "How, *madame*?" he asked. "I hesitate to use my own routes as they may have already been compromised."

Madame Aucoin added cream and sugar to her coffee before speaking. "I can send the message verbally by a trusted messenger."

"If what the newspaper is reporting is true," Marcus replied, "security may be tight in Coreé. Anyone without vital business within the capital may be denied access."

"I can invent vital business," Madame Aucoin assured him. "Landowners in both Arcadia and Ombria have reason to be concerned for their holdings. I believe I can demand that Jules receive an audience with the Chancellor."

"Jules?" Marcus asked. "Surely his life is in danger, too, from what I'm told."

135

"It's been twelve years since my son was murdered, Monsieur Berringer," Madame Aucoin replied. "Jules has aged; his appearance has changed, as have the appearances of those who murdered my son. I think the chance of casual recognition from either of them is slim."

"Still it's a risk," Devin said, glancing at Jules. "I would prefer he not undertake it simply for the sake of a message."

"I'm willing to do whatever Madame Aucoin requires of me," Jules answered. "I owe my life to her family."

When Jules declined to elaborate further, Madame Aucoin spoke up. "Do you remember the story of Margaux?" she asked. "Jules is her grandson. He was actually raised in this house and went into service here. Of course, this was just the family retreat at the time but a complete staff of servants was always on site. When my husband died and François became Comte, he needed a bodyguard. Jules was assigned to the other chateau to serve in that capacity."

"Did you know about the escape tunnel when you lived here?" Devin asked.

Jules shook his massive head. "No, *monsieur*. I was in Monsieur François Aucoin's employ for a number of years before he divulged that secret. When the family traveled from the chateau to La Paix the route was circuitous and took four full days. It was only when Monsieur Aucoin became more outspoken about his views on education in Council, that he felt the need to assemble supplies in the escape tunnel to protect his family."

"He trusted you," Angelique said, bestowing him with a brilliant smile. "There was no one else on his staff that he trusted more."

Jules looked down at his plate. "Your father treated each

of his servants well. He was just and fair. Any one of his bodyguards would have died for him."

"Some of them did," Marcus remarked lightly.

Jules looked up, angry and defiant. "And I would have, also! I would have preferred to die at his side but I followed his orders to deliver that infernal book to St. Gregory's! I wish it had never been given to him because then perhaps, he would still be alive today."

"Do you know what prompted the priest to give it to him?" Devin asked, attempting to stifle the smoldering confrontation between Marcus and Jules.

"He didn't tell me," Jules replied. "He simply said that the Chancellor needed to see it. I know Monsieur Aucoin spent a great deal of time studying it, but he did it alone. I have no idea what it contained and he preferred it that way. He felt that if any of us were captured, we wouldn't be able to reveal its secrets."

"We haven't been able to decipher its secrets either," Devin said. "It appears only to be a Bible with a lot of underlined passages. That's why I asked you if there was some kind of code or key to the information it contained."

"As far as I know, there never was," Jules said, "but it is also possible that Monsieur Aucoin held the key. If I can help you translate its contents, I will."

"And you have no idea, at all, what the information pertained to?" Devin persisted.

"No, *monsieur*."

"Was there anything in particular that was going on politically at the time?" Devin asked.

"Monsieur Aucoin planned to introduce legislation regarding education in the provinces. He knew his stance would be unpopular and create enemies but he also felt that something needed to be begun in his lifetime. He hoped the relatively newly appointed Chancellor might be more receptive to his views."

"It's unfortunate that his life was cut short by his eagerness for reform," Chastel commented. "I wonder if he would have been so quick to act if he had realized that it would cost him his life and the lives of his wife and children."

The dining room fell silent. "He did what he felt was right," Madame Aucoin said quietly. "He became a hero to the people of Arcadia even though they were wrongly blamed for his death. And there are still landowners who agree with his stance, even though they may be afraid to admit it. That is why it is important that the news of your safety should reach your father, Devin."

"It's more than just a message," Jules added. "Your father's policies and priorities might be influenced if he has more accurate information. I am willing to undertake that risk to inform him that you are safe."

"Thank you," Devin said in surprise. What had suddenly softened Jules' attitude toward him and his father?

"The trip could take a week both ways. It may be a fortnight before I could return. How long do you plan to remain here?" Jules asked.

Marcus nodded to Madame Aucoin. "If it wouldn't inconvenience you, *madame*, it would suit our purposes very well to spend several weeks in hiding."

Madame Aucoin smiled graciously. "I am delighted to have your company, Monsieur Berringer. Please consider this your home for as long as you have need of it. Decide what your message to your father should contain, Devin, and let Jules know. He can leave tomorrow if necessary."

Angelique clapped her hands in delight. "This is wonderful!

It will be so nice to be with all of you for a while. It has been so long since I have lived in a house full of people." Her lips extended in a slight pout. "But I will miss you, Jules. We have only just become reacquainted and already you will be away for two weeks."

"I will be back, little one," Jules replied, his expression softening as he glanced her way, "just as quickly as I can."

The change in Angelique was astonishing. She had gone from a terrified child to a beautiful, passionate, young woman in a little over a day. Her transformation seemed almost too good to be true. Surely, she couldn't leave what she had seen and what she had been through so easily behind her, Devin thought. Her immediate attachment to her grandmother was understandable, but this complete personality change was slightly disturbing.

While the food and accommodations exceeded anything they had experienced before on their trip except at Chastel's chateau, the prospect of several weeks of inactivity didn't appeal to Devin. After breakfast, he cornered Chastel and Armand in the hall. "Could you spend a few minutes with me this morning to look at The Bishop's Book?"

"Of course," Chastel answered immediately.

"I thought that you and I could begin Arcadia's Chronicle," Armand replied.

"We can," Devin reassured him. "But if Comte Aucoin believed the book was vitally important, I think we owe it to him to try to discover its secrets."

"I will try to help you," Armand said grudgingly. "There is a study just across the hall. I had asked Madame Aucoin if we could use it to work on the Chronicle. If you wish to discuss the book first, bring it down."

"Thank you," Devin called, taking the steps two at a

time. He opened his bedroom door softly, so as not to waken Gaspard, and crossed to the table in front of the window where he had left the book. It wasn't there.

"What …?" Devin muttered. He searched beneath the table, ran his hand across the windowsills behind the drapes and combed the tops of the armoire and chest of drawers. Finally, he dropped on his knees to feel under his bed.

"What in God's name are you doing?" Gaspard growled, his face partially obscured by his pillow.

"The book's gone!" Devin told him. "I left it on the table by the window. It's not there."

Gaspard struggled to a sitting position, one hand to his forehead. "What book?" he asked.

"The Bishop's Book!" Devin snapped. "What other book do I have with me?"

Gaspard swung his feet onto the floor. "Open the drapes, so you can see. It has to be here somewhere."

Devin pulled the drapes back and tied them, earning a moan from Gaspard as the subdued morning light filtered in. "I'm sorry," he apologized. "I was trying not to waken you."

"It's all right," Gaspard said. "I'm proving to be a very bad house guest, drinking too much of my hostess's wine and sleeping until all hours of the morning. Let me help you."

They went over the room again, even searching the huge armoire that stood in the corner. It wasn't as though they had brought much of anything with them to clutter up the room. The book simply wasn't there.

Devin sank down in a chair. "Now what? We assumed we were safe here and already the only truly valuable item we have has been stolen."

"Or misplaced," Gaspard suggested.

"I didn't misplace it!" Devin insisted. "I looked at it last night before I went to bed. Then, I got up and left it on the table by the window."

Gaspard nodded at the rumpled covers of Devin's bed. "You're sure you didn't fall asleep looking at it?"

"I did fall asleep looking at it," Devin admitted. "But I was sitting at the table when I fell asleep. When I got up to go to bed, the book was still lying on the table."

They pulled the covers from his bed, shaking and then folding them over the ornate footboard. There was no book.

Behind them the door creaked open. "Is everything all right?" Chastel asked, looking in.

"No," Devin said. "The Bishop's Book is missing and I suspect that someone in this house intentionally took it."

Chastel closed the door behind him. "That's quite an accusation, Devin. There are few prospects. We three and Angelique knew that you had it. You told Jules and Madame Aucoin that it was upstairs yesterday. The thief has to be either one of us or one of them."

"I'd bet my money on Jules," Gaspard said. "He wasn't happy that Dev had the book in the first place."

"And yet this morning at breakfast, he volunteered to take a message to my father in Coreé," Devin said. "Do you think he plans to take the book with him?"

Chastel shook his head. "He is taking the message as a service to Madame Aucoin. He doesn't trust you or your father. I can't imagine him turning it over to the Chancellor."

"Jules is Madame Aucoin's most trusted servant," Devin pointed out. "He eats at her table just as Marcus does with me. After her incredible hospitality, I can't accuse him of stealing my belongings."

"Perhaps you need to just ask him directly," Chastel suggested diplomatically.

Gaspard flopped back on the bed. "At least take Marcus with you when you go, Dev. Jules could squash you like a fly!" he remarked gaily.

"There will be no squashing," Chastel said grimly. "This will require finesse. Perhaps we could ask for Jules' help in locating it. We might avoid any appearance that we think he took it."

"Even though you do," Gaspard replied bluntly.

"It seems the only possibility," Chastel said thoughtfully. "I can't even imagine that Madame Aucoin would have any use for it. She didn't even seem to know of its existence until you mentioned it yesterday."

Devin sighed. "It has to be Jules. Can he have hidden it somewhere for safekeeping out of some strange sense of duty to François?"

"Perhaps, or maybe he just feels that you shouldn't be the one in charge of it. He thought it was well hidden according to his master's orders, and then the son of the very man that he holds responsible for François' murder happens to discover its hiding place. I think I can understand his distress," Chastel said.

"Could we leave it until morning and hope that the book is returned?" Devin asked.

"That's not a good idea with Jules slated to leave tomorrow," Chastel advised. "This needs to be dealt with now."

Gaspard stood up and rummaged for a short time in the chaos they had made of their room. "Let me get dressed. I'll come with you," he said. "There is strength in numbers."

"Why is nothing ever easy?" Devin protested.

CHAPTER 19

Dresses and Dancing

When they went downstairs, Angelique and her grandmother were looking at fabric in the sitting room. "*Grandmère* is having new dresses made for me," Angelique informed them happily, twirling around the floor with a length of pink satin draped over her shoulders. "Isn't this beautiful?"

She looked so pleased with the beautifully colored fabrics scattered all around her that Devin couldn't help but smile. No doubt she'd been wearing her mother's dresses for the past few years, each one at least a dozen years old, sagging on her slight frame, and filled with bittersweet memories. "It is very beautiful," he agreed and pointed to another one. "I also like this blue one right here. I think you would look stunning in it."

Angelique discarded the pink and pulled the other fabric from the stack – a periwinkle blue with tiny embroidered white flowers. "This one?" she asked, wrapping it around her like a cape.

"Yes," Devin confirmed. "It looks lovely with your complexion." The words had tumbled from his mouth with no prompting, as though he were Angelique's older brother and he simply enjoyed building up her confidence. She blushed a beautiful rosy pink and he was so glad that he'd taken the time to comment.

Madame Aucoin laughed. "Well, we will definitely put that one aside for the dressmaker. I can't have my grand-daughter looking less than stunning!"

Gaspard, who always seemed to know just the right thing to do where ladies were concerned, bowed deeply and took Angelique's hand in his own. "May I have this dance, my dear?" he asked with exaggerated politeness.

She grinned and nodded mutely, his question intensifying the blush in her cheeks.

Gaspard lifted the bolt of blue cloth aloft with his free hand and spun her merrily around in a circle while he sang off key. They cavorted around the room, becoming more and more impossibly tangled in a voluminous swath of blue until they collapsed breathless and laughing onto a small upholstered settee.

Angelique continued to giggle – a spontaneous, youthful sound – and for a moment Devin believed that Madame Aucoin was right: maybe anything was possible. Here was a girl who had spent the last twelve years sleeping in a wine cask, who had been given this chance at a wonderful new life. "I am so happy that you and your grandmother have found each other," Devin said softly. "Perhaps fairytales do come true."

Madame Aucoin blinked and reached for Devin's hand. "I have you to thank for that," she said, giving his hand a squeeze. "What can I help you with? You men surely didn't come downstairs to offer fashion advice and dancing lessons."

"We didn't," Devin admitted. "But I wouldn't have missed this for the world."

Chastel stepped forward. "We were actually looking for Jules. Devin wanted to speak with him about the message he wants to send to his father."

"Oh, I'm so sorry," Madame Aucoin said. "Jules just left on some errands for me. I thought if he was going to be gone for two weeks, I'd better have him take care of a few things before he leaves. He probably won't be back until late afternoon."

"That's all right," Devin said, vaguely relieved. "I'll speak to him later."

"I'll send him to find you when he returns," Madame Aucoin promised, turning her full attention back to untangling Angelique and Gaspard from the bolt of fabric.

Gaspard ducked out from under its folds looking rather pleased with himself. "Thank you, *mademoiselle*," he said with a courtly bow. "Perhaps we can practice again another day."

Angelique clapped her hands. "I'd love that! Maybe Devin would even accompany us on his harp."

"Oh, there's no need to bother him," Gaspard replied conspiratorially. "We did very well on our own."

Devin laid a hand on his shoulder. "She was trying to be polite, Gaspard. She wasn't impressed by your singing and neither were the rest of us."

Angelique was quick to deny it. "I didn't mean that! I just thought …"

"That my harp music would be preferable," Devin said with a grin. "Believe me, we all understand."

She laughed then. Devin realized she must be unused to teasing after living alone for so long. She was probably too little when her family died to remember the silly banter of siblings. They excused themselves and went out into the hall, leaving her to the happy task of planning a new wardrobe with her grandmother.

With the rain pounding on the roof and sluicing down the windows, they all retreated to the study. It was amazing how a house so filled with light only a day before, descended into darkness as the storm intensified outside. Armand was already annoyed that they had kept him waiting. His fingers drummed on the table. "Where is the book?" he demanded of Devin. "I thought that's why you went upstairs."

Devin shut the door quietly behind him. "It's missing. Someone took it out of our room, either last night or this morning."

"Jules?" Armand suggested. "I can't think of anyone else who would have anything to gain by stealing it."

"That is the general consensus," Chastel agreed. "And of course, he has just left La Paix to do errands for Madame Aucoin and won't be back for hours."

Armand leaned back in his chair. "Well, I hardly think she is involved."

"Nor do we," Devin replied. "But Jules is conveniently out of reach at the moment and we are without the only clue we may have had to exposing François Aucoin's killers."

"You'll have to ask Jules when he comes back then," Armand retorted. "Are you ready to work or would you rather ransack every corner of the chateau and humiliate our hostess?"

Devin sat down opposite him, puzzled by his irritability. "I think you know me better than that. There is no reason to embarrass Madame Aucoin; in fact, I would like to avoid involving her, at all."

"I'll be interested to see if that's possible," Armand responded. "Diplomacy only goes so far." He tapped the polished oak table with his fingers. "Since you've nothing else productive to do, Monsieur Roché, we need to get busy if you truly want to learn Arcadia's Chronicle."

"I'll leave you to it then," Chastel said.

"And I'm off to the kitchen in search of stray sausages," Gaspard announced.

"I asked the cook to save you some," Devin told him.

Gaspard laughed from the doorway and patted his stomach. "I'm internally grateful!"

Devin groaned at his pun and turned his attention to Armand.

Marcus didn't leave but instead perused the bookcases that lined the walls. He clasped his hands behind his back and scanned each shelf from top to bottom. After several minutes, he selected an aging volume of maps and settled into an armchair by the fireplace.

Armand paid no attention to him; instead he removed his harp from his lap and set it gently on the floor. Devin noticed how thin the bard's hands had become. Armand's body had turned gaunt and angular on their journey, his limp more pronounced, his shoulders slender and stooped. It was ironic that sorrow could actually sculpt a man's bones, winnow him like a strong wind through harvested grain, wiping away the extraneous and leaving only the strongest substance behind.

Armand ignored Devin's scrutiny and began. "You will be relieved to know, Monsieur Roché, that it is not necessary for you to learn the lives of a completely different set of saints. The saints are canonized as such by the church as a whole. Ombria's saints are Llisé's saints. You have already learned all of their stories in Ombria's Chronicle. Occasionally, there will be a local legend associated with a particular saint in an individual province, but there are none for Arcadia."

"That will make things easier, then," Devin said.

"Not necessarily," Armand replied. "Arcadia has more ballads than Ombria does. We'll begin those tomorrow but I want to teach you 'Bellamy's Garden' today. You can perform it tonight after dinner; I believe it may ease Madame Aucoin's grief over her son's death."

Devin met his gaze. "That's very thoughtful of you."

"Those who mourn recognize the strain of grief in each other, Monsieur Roché," Armand replied. "If we can do nothing else in this cruel world, we can attempt to comfort each other."

CHAPTER 20

Accusations

Late afternoon found the table in the study littered with the remains of lunch and multiple cups of coffee, when someone knocked on the door. Jules cautiously opened it and stood awkwardly in the doorway. "Madame Aucoin said you wanted to see me."

Devin wished Chastel were there to ease the conversation around to the topic that concerned them most. "Thank you," he said standing up. "Come in and close the door. There's something I wanted to discuss with you."

"You can just give your message for the Chancellor to me verbally," Jules said. "It will be much safer and I swear, I will remember it."

"I will do that," Devin agreed. "I actually have another problem that I hope you can help me with. The Bishop's Book seems to have disappeared from my room."

"What?" Jules demanded. "Where did you leave it?"

"On the table by the windows," Devin told him. "I was looking at it before I went to bed last night. When

I was finished, I left it on the table before I went to sleep. It was gone this morning."

"And you have searched the room?" Jules asked.

"Several times! It isn't there. I don't want to worry Madame Aucoin. I thought maybe you could help us."

"Maybe one of the maids shelved it in the bookcases down here," Jules suggested, walking to the rows of books along the walls.

"I have already checked," Marcus said. "It isn't here."

"I cannot believe you have lost it!" Jules thundered. "Good men died to assure the safety of that book!"

"I haven't lost it," Devin clarified. "It was taken from my room, which is a very different problem. Can you think of anyone who might have had an interest in it?"

"Oh, I see where this is going!" Jules' face burned an angry red. "You think I took it and this is your poor attempt to disguise your suspicions!"

For a split second, Devin hesitated. "Actually, it is," he replied calmly. "I have to admit that your name was the first that came to mind when the book went missing. However, judging from your performance just now, I honestly believe that you had nothing to do with it. Will you help me find out who did?"

Jules swayed unsteadily for a moment, as though he'd lost his footing on a slippery river bank and just regained his balance. He recovered enough to continue as the suffuse color began to drain from his face. "I can't imagine," he muttered. "All of Madame Aucoin's servants are intensely loyal. There is no one who has been recently hired; everyone has held positions of long standing here."

"There has to be someone," Devin said.

"Perhaps one of your companions took it," Jules suggested

harshly. "Have they earned your complete trust? Can you depend on them?"

"I can," Devin replied. "They have earned my trust and I have earned theirs."

Jules folded his arms over his chest. "Then we are at an impasse."

Devin frowned. "I would regret having to involve Madame Aucoin in this."

"Please don't," Jules said quickly. "Allow me to make some discreet inquiries first. If that fails then we will consult her."

"You are leaving tomorrow morning," Devin pointed out. "This needs to be resolved."

"It will be," Jules replied. "I will speak to you after dinner."

Devin inclined his head. "Let me know, then."

Jules closed the door and was gone.

"Nicely done," Armand commented. "That might have gone wrong in so many ways."

"I'm convinced that Jules didn't take it," Devin said.

Marcus nodded in agreement. "I agree. He couldn't have feigned his reaction. He has no idea where the book is."

"I think I may have an idea where it is," Devin replied. "There is only one other person that might have reason to want it, however innocent that reason may be."

Angelique was in high spirits at dinner. She wore a dress of apricot satin, possibly her grandmother's, but tailored and tucked to fit her perfectly. Her dress lent a creamy glow to her skin but her flushed cheeks were the result of a conversation she was having with Gaspard. His soft voice and Angelique's appreciative giggles provided a backdrop to the other conversations in the room.

Jules arrived late and slid into his chair just as they began serving.

"Are you ready to leave tomorrow?" Madame Aucoin asked.

Jules shook his head. "I'd hoped to get off very early but there are some things that need to be resolved before I go. Hopefully, I won't be delayed more than a day."

Devin took a deep breath and glanced at Marcus. Apparently, Jules hadn't been able to acquire any further information on the book. He took a spoonful of the excellent cream soup they had been served but his mind was elsewhere. "Madame Aucoin, how does La Paix maintain its security? It appears no one knows it exists but you have to receive your supplies from somewhere."

Madame Aucoin smiled graciously. "Of course, I can't divulge all our secrets but I do maintain another home. The ordering of supplies is made through it and they are delivered there before being transferred here. It is one of things that Jules handles so seamlessly."

"So you have another life?" Devin asked with a smile.

"I do indeed," she replied. "It has been so long since La Paix has been used as a hunting lodge that any of the men who stayed here are long since dead and buried. To the Aucoins, its usefulness as a safe place in times of danger far outweighs its value as a hunting retreat."

"How did it happen that you were here the night we arrived?" Devin asked. "Was it just coincidence?"

"Not at all, Devin," Madame Aucoin answered. "I spend the summers at La Paix. I tell my friends that I am off to visit cousins in the mountains and I will return in the fall. I have done it for years. No one questions my whereabouts. There is always a full staff here, in case they are needed. It was a dream come true for me, that I was lucky enough to be here on the night that my granddaughter returned."

Angelique turned from Gaspard and beamed at her grandmother. "It was for me, too. If I had known that our very long, long tunnel would lead me to you, *Grandmère*, I would have made the trip many years before."

"You had neither your father nor your mother to guide you, child. I am just sorry that you spent so many years alone."

Angelique straightened her shoulders. "But it is over and now thanks to you, I can begin again." She looked at the men sitting around the table. "And thanks to all of you, too."

"What will happen when the summer ends?" Chastel asked. "Will you return to your home?"

Madame Aucoin nodded. "I will, but I will be taking my 'cousin's daughter,' Angelique, with me for companionship. She will live with me in town over the winter and return here for the summer, just as I do!"

"Deftly plotted, *madame*," Chastel said with a laugh. "You are an excellent strategist!"

After dinner, Jules excused himself, while the rest of them gathered in the sitting room. Devin took the bard's seat at the hearth-side. He had promised to tell "Bellamy's Gardens", the story that Armand had taught him earlier that afternoon.

He took a moment to compose his thoughts while the others settled down on brocade chairs, sated with exquisite food from La Paix's kitchen. The nights of raw venison seemed very far removed from this scene.

"Madame Aucoin," Devin said, as conversation lagged, "Armand chose a story for you and asked me to tell it."

Madame Aucoin touched her chest and blushed. "For me?" she asked. "How lovely!"

Devin bowed. "I hope you enjoy it."

"*There once was a prosperous farmer named Bellamy, who was famous for his fragrant lavender and medicinal herbs. He had a real talent for growing plants and his business rapidly became a success. As he grew wealthier, he acquired more and more land, planting flowering shrubs and trees and flowers of every color and kind. People came from miles away just to see Bellamy's gardens in full bloom. Young lovers lay beneath the trees in his orchards and old lovers held hands on the benches Bellamy placed along the paths between the trees. Children flew kites and floated tiny paper boats on the ponds. Bellamy's gardens grew more extensive and more beautiful each year.*

"*As he grew older, the large number of gardens became harder for Bellamy to tend. But even though his knees and back were creaky and sore, every day he would go out to pull weeds that might choke his tender new plants. Every day, he planted seeds and bulbs in anticipation of the next growing season.*

"*Bellamy's two sons were much more interested in the financial part of their father's business than actually growing things. Every day they tallied the profits of the business and began to discuss how it might be even more lucrative if their father would plant all of the land in herbs that could be sold for profit rather than providing gardens for strangers to wander aimlessly through.*

"*They proposed the change to the old man but Bellamy would have none of it. He loved seeing the pleasure that his gardens brought to people and he was determined to continue cultivating them. Bellamy grew very old but his gardens remained his first priority. One day, when Bellamy didn't return for lunch, his youngest son found him lying*

under an apple tree, his hat on his chest, his hoe laid care-
fully beside him. Bellamy had died caring for what he loved
most. His sons buried him under the apple tree and half of
the province turned out to mourn the loss of their beloved
Bellamy and praise his beautiful gardens.

"*Bellamy's sons accepted the condolences and gifts that*
people brought them but they also immediately made plans
to cut down the orchards, uproot the flowers and shrubs,
and plant only herbs to sell. Because there was so much
land, some of it simply wasn't needed for their enterprises,
at all. It became overgrown with brambles and weeds. The
Bellamy brothers continued the business their father began,
simply growing and selling for profit, but the customers
were not as numerous or as faithful as before.

"*Before long, Bellamy's grandson, Florian, entered the*
business. He remembered playing in his grandfather's
gardens as a child. One June morning, he walked out to
survey the extent of the land. He discovered old apple trees
unpruned and sprawling, and rose bushes growing wild over
broken benches and walkways toward the back of the prop-
erty. Florian went to speak to his father and asked what
had happened to the beautiful gardens that had once graced
the area around their business. When his father answered
that they had been sacrificed to grow herbs for profit, he
asked for permission to try to renovate the gardens.
Surprisingly, both his uncle and his father agreed. After all,
the gardens had drawn more customers, even if they required
more work, and now business was slow and not as profit-
able.

"*So, Florian cultivated his grandfather's gardens, putting in*
long, hard hours tending the soil, pruning, and planting. It
took five years before he had restored what the years of neglect

had buried. It wasn't long before news of the restoration of Bellamy's Gardens reached the neighboring villages and people began to visit again. The gardens were so popular that the visitors increased revenue for all of the businesses in town. Restaurants served more meals, taverns served more drinks, bakeries sold many loaves of bread and dozens of pastries, and the Bellamy brothers sold many more herbs than they ever had before. The village became famous throughout the province and much more prosperous because of Bellamy's beautiful gardens. The townspeople decided to rename the town for the person responsible for its fame. From then on it became known as the town of Florian, named for the grandson who carried on his grandfather's dream long after his death.*"

Madame Aucoin, Angelique and Chastel clapped. And Devin bowed, feeling that Armand deserved the credit. "I chose 'Bellamy's Gardens', *madame*, because it reminded me in some ways of your son, François," Armand explained. "He spent many years putting his views into practice and trying to influence others to his way of thinking, only to die before the reforms he espoused could be put into practice. Perhaps in your granddaughter's lifetime, his ideas will come to fruition."

"Perhaps," Madame Aucoin said quietly. "The story reminded me of François, too. It is difficult when the work of a lifetime is discarded as if it were nothing. His chateau lies deserted; that great old house was built by his ancestors and treasured by his family. Life can be cruel and ugly and unkind but there are always flickers of hope: like a Chancellor's son who risks his life to uncover the truth and men who are willing to help a girl they don't even know and bring her to safety." She smiled at all of them. "You have restored my faith, gentlemen."

They all hastened to assure her that Angelique had helped them also and that no matter what, they would have cared for her. Chastel had offered her his home and even Marcus hadn't objected to allowing her to travel with them.

"Gentlemen," Madame Aucoin said, "you are only validating my sentiments. You are an unusual group of men and I am grateful that I have been given the opportunity to get to know you better."

Angelique was strangely silent, watching her grandmother's face with a mixture of affection and sadness. Gaspard took her hand in both of his own and kissed it. "We are simply happy to have you safe, with a place of your own to live in and someone who loves you to care for you, Angelique. Don't be sad, love. This is one of those few stories that has a happy ending."

Angelique pulled her hand from his, tears running down her face. "I don't deserve your concern," she said. "I let my family die and I never made a move to help them!" She turned and ran from the room, her footsteps clattering up the stairs.

"I'll go talk to her," Madame Aucoin said, rising from her chair. "She has been very emotional in the last few days. Somehow, she blames herself for her family's deaths. It isn't rational; just some peculiar manifestation of her living alone for all those years. She was four years old when it happened. It breaks my heart that she feels she had some responsibility where that tragedy was concerned."

"Perhaps she did," Jules said grimly from the doorway.

CHAPTER 21

Innocence

"Whatever do you mean, Jules?" Madame Aucoin demanded.

"*Madame*, this took me by surprise just as it will you," Jules replied. He held up The Bishop's Book and a small leather-bound journal.

"Thank God, you found it," Devin murmured.

Jules continued. "Monsieur Roché questioned me earlier today about The Bishop's Book. It was missing from his room this morning. I thought that maybe one of the maids might have put it in the study but it wasn't there. I knew no one on the staff would have taken it but I did wonder if maybe Angelique might have. I found it under her bed a few minutes ago, along with this."

"That book cost her father his life and the extinction of her entire family," Madame Aucoin answered. "Maybe she wanted to know what it contained that was so important."

"We would all like to ascertain that," Jules said. "But it is the journal that interests me more."

"Is it Angelique's?" Madame Aucoin asked. "If so, you have no right to read her personal thoughts, Jules."

"Perhaps not, *madame*, and I beg your forgiveness for having done so. But your granddaughter hasn't been entirely honest with us. We have always questioned how Comte Aucoin's trip became known to his enemies. May I read a small portion of the journal aloud?"

"Absolutely not, Jules!" Madame Aucoin said. "What she wrote wasn't meant to be shared with anyone else."

"*Madame*," Jules entreated, "I beg your forbearance. This is extremely important."

Madame Aucoin sighed, the color high in her cheeks. "Shut the door," she said. "This goes no further than this room."

Devin stood up. "Would you like us to leave, *madame*?"

Jules eased the door closed behind him. "This actually concerns you, too, Monsieur Roché. With Madame Aucoin's permission, I ask that all of you stay."

Devin sat back down, feeling ill at ease in the middle of this discussion of family business. Jules handed Devin the Bishop's Book and then opened the journal on the palm of his left hand.

"This was written yesterday," he said:

My grandmère is wonderful. She is beautiful and loving and kind. Every time she smiles at me, I feel overwhelmed with the guilt of what I have done. And Jules, finding him alive after all these years is like a miracle and yet I am constantly haunted by what I did to set the tragedy in motion that caused the deaths of all those I loved most.

Madame Aucoin was shaking. "What could she possibly have done?"

Jules closed the book. "She doesn't say."

159

"She was hardly more than a baby," Madame Aucoin insisted. "How could she think she would have been any match for professional assassins? She couldn't have prevented what happened!"

Jules shook his head. "She says she set it in motion, *madame*, not that she should have tried to stop it."

Madame Aucoin's face was white. "I can't even imagine …"

"I think we need an explanation," Jules said. "May I go and bring her down?"

"To face an inquisition?" Madame Aucoin demanded. "I don't think so! Yes, we need to know what happened but not here and not now. I won't subject her to that humiliation. She is my granddaughter and whatever she did, she was four years old at the time. Surely, this is something that has grown out of proportion in her mind. She's had nothing else to think about for the past twelve years. I'm sure that her memory of what happened has been altered by dwelling on it so much."

The door creaked open just enough for Angelique to see into the room. "It hasn't, *Grandmère*," she said softly from the doorway.

Chastel rose and gently took one of her hands to draw her inside.

Her eyes were red and puffy, her cheeks tear-stained. "When I went upstairs, I saw that my journal and The Bishop's Book were gone. I assumed Jules took them. He was the only one who didn't stay for Devin's story. And now you all know what a fraud I am."

"You're not a fraud," Devin answered quickly.

She gave him a sad smile. "Oh yes, I am. I have played the innocent, the sole survivor of a massacre that wiped out my whole family, when I am actually the cause of that tragedy. No one would have died if I hadn't told my Papa's secret."

There was a stunned silence. No one spoke and then Madame Aucoin cleared her throat. "Tell us what you mean, Angelique."

She stood before them trembling. "When I was little, I used to hide under Papa's desk. There was just enough space for me to sit behind the drawers on the right side if I crawled through the kneehole. I could smell the polished leather of his boots and his pipe tobacco. To me those were the best smells in the world. They made me feel safe. I loved just listening to Papa when he talked to Jules, that deep resonance in his voice. I thought that between the two of them they could protect me from anything.

"I was there the day he made plans to go to Coreé. I heard him talking about The Bishop's Book and how important it was, how he needed to deliver it to Chancellor Roché. You would have thought even a four year old would have realized that the information was secret. But I didn't. I only thought about how important my Papa was and that he had business with the Chancellor of Llisé and Jules was going with him.

"After Papa and Jules left, I scrambled out from under the desk. Minette, who was six, was having a riding lesson at the stables on her new pony. I ran down to share my very important news that Papa and Jules were going to visit the Chancellor in Coreé and they were taking this very special book with them. There were two men at the stables that I didn't know. One of the men squatted down to talk me. He said his name was René and he wanted to hear all about my Papa's trip."

"God," Gaspard groaned. "That was my father."

"He went to Aucoin's to buy a horse the week before François was killed," Chastel said. "I had forgotten that. They made the arrangements over dinner at my chateau."

"He seemed like such a nice man," Angelique continued. "He told me he had two little boys at home and he knew how much all children loved their Papas."

"That makes me want to throw up!" Gaspard muttered.

Angelique went on. "So, I told him everything I knew – what day Papa was leaving and which port they were leaving from and that it was a very important trip because my Papa was a very important man. I remember, the man put his hand on my head and thanked me and then he said, maybe it would best if I didn't tell Papa I had mentioned his trip to anyone because he might not like it. So, I never told Papa. If I had, he could have changed his plans. He wouldn't have been murdered along the roadside with his bodyguards, and he and my mother and my brothers and sisters would be alive today!" She stood there with clasped hands as though she were awaiting a death sentence.

Jules turned and left the room, slamming the door behind him. An anguished sob escaped Angelique's lips and she fell to her knees on the rug. "I would give anything … anything … to take it all back. They were killed because of me … because I told Papa's secrets to a man I didn't even know."

Gaspard ran a hand over his face. "You told your father's secrets to a man who apparently would do anything to gain control of Llisé's government, Angelique. You are not at fault, he is. I am ashamed to call the man my father."

"René Forneaux wasn't interested in buying a horse that day," Chastel added. "That was just an excuse to mask his search for information. He was determined to bring your father down because of his sentiments. If you hadn't given him the means, he would have found it another way. You are no guiltier than I am, Angelique, for introducing your father to him. Men like René Forneaux will stop at nothing to achieve their own ends. He was cowardly enough to leave Arcadia the day after he spoke with you. He left the dirty work to his men and was safely back in Coreé before the murders occurred so he could display his shock publicly in Council that such a terrible thing could have happened in the primitive province he had just visited."

Devin held his breath and looked at Madame Aucoin. He had been so impressed by the lady's graciousness and kindness; surely she wouldn't turn away from Angelique as Jules had done.

Madame Aucoin rose from her seat and threw her arms around Angelique, kneeling down beside her granddaughter on the rug in a swirl of cream satin. "My precious child," she said. "I cannot believe you have lived with this burden for so long. Forget it, darling. You were a child and we all do foolish things when we are little because we can't understand the implications of our actions."

"But don't you see?" Angelique sobbed into her hands, her voice muffled and barely audible. "I was the only one who wasn't killed. It wasn't fair that I survived when I'm the one who caused it all."

Devin closed his eyes. No wonder the poor girl had nightmares. It might have driven a lesser person mad.

Madame Aucoin took Angelique's cheeks in her hands. "It would break your father's heart that you have carried this weight for all these years. He would never have blamed you."

"How could he not?" Angelique demanded. "It is the

worst thing I have ever done in my life. I hoped, when the soldiers arrived at the chateau with Gaspard, that I would be killed then. It would have been better than dragging this chain of guilt around for the rest of my life!"

"If you have a chain of guilt, my dear," Madame Aucoin said quietly, "it is of your own making. You have forged those links and you can break them just as easily. There is no one here that holds you responsible for what happened."

"Jules does," Angelique said, looking at the door. "He couldn't even bear to stay in the same room with me."

Madame Aucoin frowned. "Jules is understandably upset. Your story brought back a very tragic time for him. He has trouble dealing with that day, just as you do, because he also survived when so many others died. Give him some time."

"Jules is the only part of my childhood I have left," Angelique said. "I cannot tell you how happy it made me to see him here in this house. It was almost as though part of my father had come back, too. They were inseparable, you know. They were always together, Jules and Papa, like a team of faithful horses that were able to carry us anywhere safely. When both The Bishop's Book and my journal were gone from my room, I knew nothing would ever be the same again. Jules had found out what I did and he would hate me for it forever."

Devin gestured to the book in his hand. "Angelique, do you know how to decipher The Bishop's Book? Is that why you took it from my room?"

"No," she said. "I took it because I thought that maybe if I studied it, I could figure out what message it contained."

"And could you?" he asked.

Angelique shook her head. "No, and I apologize. I should have asked before I took the book. I just thought that

164

whatever it contained was important enough that my father had died for it. I hoped that I could be the one to solve it and maybe make up for some of the trouble I've caused. What could it possibly be? Papa must have known."

Devin shrugged. "Some secrets are passed along verbally because they are too important to write down. But someone was smart enough to leave a message in that book; we just have to find it. It may take time but we will."

"Can I help?" Angelique asked.

"I don't know why not," Devin said. "The book belonged to your father. You have more right to it than anyone does."

"All this time I have assumed that the Chancellor's correspondence was compromised and that's why your father was killed," Marcus said to Angelique. "After your confession, I realize that may not be true. I wonder if it's possible that your father might have revealed the key to the book in a letter to the Chancellor."

"Do you think we should send the book with Jules to Coreé?" Devin asked. "It's simply a Bible. No one would question a man for carrying one."

"How quickly you forget, Monsieur Roché," Armand said patiently. "Jules is a man of the provinces. He shouldn't be able to read or write. If he carries a Bible with him to Coreé and he is searched, he will put himself at risk and François who taught him to read, were he still alive."

"Of course," Devin said, shaking his head. "How stupid can I be?"

"Whatever that book contains, it is up to us to decipher it," Marcus said. "Everyone in this room knows of its importance. We need a number of different ideas to figure this out and everyone's opinion is welcome. We would be delighted to have your help, Angelique."

Devin smiled at this completely unexpected kindness from Marcus.

"The Chancellor has waited twelve years for this information," Chastel said. "It's not imperative that he have it immediately. We can only send it to Coreé when it is safe to do so and when it won't fall into the wrong hands."

"Preferably, when we can return his youngest son to him, as well," Marcus added.

CHAPTER 22

More Confessions

Jules didn't return, leaving both Angelique and Madame Aucoin worried. Devin thought it might be best to let them have some time to themselves and shepherded Gaspard upstairs. The other men followed them, pausing to say goodnight in the hall.

Devin regretted the entire incident about the journal that evening. The information had done little to supplement what they already knew and Angelique had been put on display, humiliated in front of everyone. Jules' motives in reading the journal seemed unclear. Considering their relationship before, he might have expected her father's bodyguard to keep the information to himself in an effort to protect Angelique. To hold a child responsible for the deaths of her family was unreasonable and unfair. Sleep seemed impossible, so Devin pulled a chair over to the table and opened The Bishop's Book. Behind him Gaspard paced the bedroom floor, a bottle of wine swinging back and forth in his hand.

Devin turned to look at him. "What's bothering you?"

"What do you think?" Gaspard retorted. "My father is

167

a liar and a murderer. It's not an easy thing to know that I am descended from that bloodline."

"You certainly have made every effort to distance yourself from him," Devin replied. "Don't burden yourself with your father's transgressions."

"That's easy for you to say. So far your father has kept his hands clean. The same can't be said for René Forneaux."

"You aren't like him, Gaspard," Devin said sympathetically.

Gaspard closed his eyes and tipped the bottle to his lips. "That's where you are wrong, *mon ami*. You've been a better friend to me than I have been to you."

Devin said nothing, knowing that an alcohol-induced confession would follow.

Gaspard stood and stared at him, the bottle hanging limply from one arm. "I went willingly with my father's men that night at Chastel's chateau. They told me it was best to leave without saying goodbye because you would try to convince me to stay. I had already made the decision to go back to Coreé; it didn't seem odd, at first, that my father had sent an escort to take me home. It didn't seem odd at all, really, until they tied me up and put me on a horse. I thought they were going to kill me, Dev, but they only wanted me to get to you. They planned to kill us both and make it appear that we were attacked and killed by peasants. Thinking back, I imagine that was my father's plan from the beginning. He knew how I would react to his lecture at Antoine's the night before we sailed. He expected me to go out of spite and I would have, but you knew me so well that you took me with you, even though I was three sheets to the wind when Marcus dumped me in my bunk."

"But your father wrote to you, Gaspard, threatening to disinherit you if you didn't come home," Devin pointed out.

Gaspard took another drink. "That is how he works. He thinks of all the details before he plans the finale. If anyone found his letters, it would appear that he had done everything in his power to lure me home."

Devin frowned. "This doesn't make sense, Gaspard. Later he came out in favor of our trip when he spoke to Council."

"Because I refused to come home!" Gaspard said. "He had already planted the seed of suspicion that our trip might be ill advised; his support showed he hoped for the best. He allowed his son and heir to go into dangerous territory for the good of Llisé."

"I don't know, Gaspard. This seems very convoluted to me."

"It's how his mind works and it isn't convoluted – it's devious."

"So, in what way have you not been a good friend?" Devin asked. "All you've told me is what a dangerous man your father is."

"I lied about the red cross," Gaspard said before he took another swig of wine.

Devin knew which one he was talking about before he asked. "The one at Chastel's?"

Gaspard nodded, wiping his mouth on his sleeve. "I wanted to go home then. Those crazy wolves terrified me. I thought they would terrify you, too, but they didn't. You had just about had your arm ripped off but you wanted to keep going on your journey. I hoped that if you thought someone was trying to kill us, you might reconsider. I told you Marcus had found a red cross in the driveway. I didn't think you would ask him about it, but you did, and Marcus asked me. I told him that you must have misunderstood me, that you were feverish or maybe you dreamed it."

"He never mentioned it to me," Devin replied. "And if you remember, I told you I wanted you to go home. I didn't want you to be hurt because of me."

"I couldn't just leave you alone!" Gaspard protested.

"I wasn't alone," Devin said. "I had Marcus."

"He's not much fun on a trip," Gaspard said in a slurred whisper.

Devin stood up and snagged the wine bottle. "Give me that," he said, retrieving the cork from the bed and driving it home in the bottleneck. "Do you think that any of this matters to me? Do you think I would put all those years of friendship behind us and hold this one thing against you?"

Gaspard collapsed wearily on his back on his bed. "You'd be justified in doing so."

"I have no doubt you'll do much worse things to me in the future and I'll do worse to you," Devin said. "Let's just forget this and move on."

Gaspard grinned. "It's all right with me if you're sure it's all right with you. It's your big chance to yell at me in justified rage for all my shortcomings."

Devin grinned. "I don't have several hours to spend yelling at you, Gaspard. If I started chastising you, I would want to do it right, so you are safe for now." He turned the pages of The Bishop's Book methodically. "Did you ever take any classes on codes?"

"Never," Gaspard said. "Why?"

"I keep thinking that all these underlined passages are important. Maybe one word from each of them forms a series of sentences."

Gaspard propped himself on an elbow. "They don't look

as though they were all underlined at the same time. The ink is very faded on some passages."

"I know. It's confusing. I don't know if that is important either. I haven't been through this Bible page by page but there is nothing here that points to any kind of message."

"Is it possible that's it's the wrong book?" Gaspard asked.

Devin nodded. "Yes, I think that is entirely possible, but the fact that the priest at St. Gregory's died trying to hide it seems significant to me."

"You don't even know that for sure," Gaspard pointed out. "It's an assumption that we made. He may have had some entirely different reason for climbing that tower."

Devin sighed. "Then that throws everything into question, doesn't it? Is it crazy to spend hours poring over an old Bible that may be nothing more than it appears to be?"

"Do you have anything better to do?" Gaspard asked. "We are going to be here for several weeks."

"I need to learn Arcadia's Chronicle from Armand."

"Well, do that first. If you have any free time, spend it on the Bible. It isn't as though you have to do this yourself. Marcus asked everyone to help and I think that they will. Don't spend any more time on it tonight, Dev," Gaspard begged. "We're both done in."

"Go to sleep," Devin told him. "I'll devote a few more minutes to this." He heard Gaspard's discarded boots hit the floor and the rustle of sheets and then everything was quiet.

He closed the Bible and opened it again at the beginning. The first two pages were blank, the third held the dedication to Bishop John Mark. The first page of Genesis had the first underlined passage. He took a sheet of paper and wrote "Genesis" and then listed the chapter and verse under it.

171

Some pages had notes written beside certain passages and he recorded these, too, on a separate piece of paper. Several books of the Bible weren't marked in any way and others had multiple passages underlined. He continued compiling the list of underlined passages. Some of the notes were difficult to read but he reproduced them as well as he could, underlining questionable words to look at again. After several hours the lines began to blur but he kept at it, striving to finish just one more chapter, then one more book. He finally put his head down on his folded arms on the table and closed his eyes.

Devin woke suddenly. The candle was spitting and gutting on the candlestick, its wick almost gone. Darkness engulfed the room, except for a shadow, thrown by the fitful candle-light, which gyrated in a macabre dance on the draperies. Gaspard was snoring softly, an unidentifiable shape under the rumpled covers of his bed. Devin stacked the papers on the table. He was just about to close the Bible when a floorboard creaked behind him. He whirled around, convinced that there was someone in the room but there was no one there. A draft ruffled the pages of the Bible, skimming through them as though they were being turned by an invisible hand.

"The answer is here, Monsieur Roché," a voice said. "You need to look beyond the pages." The candle went out, plunging the room into darkness.

CHAPTER 23

The Power of Water

The next morning dawned bright and beautiful. Nothing remained of the dark clouds and rain that had trapped them inside yesterday. The only worrisome thing was that Jules did not come to breakfast. Devin didn't ask where he was and Madame Aucoin didn't volunteer the information. Angelique's mood was no lighter this morning. She sat silently picking at her food, her fork scraping the plate in irritating little squeaks. Even her grandmother couldn't seem to reach her. She responded with only one-word answers to Madame Aucoin's questions. Angelique never even made eye contact with anyone else but kept her eyes fixed firmly on the table, while the others talked around her.

As they left the dining room, Devin drew her into the hall. "Have you seen the waterfall yet?" he asked. "It's truly spectacular!"

She shook her head without speaking.

"Would you like to walk outside with me?" he asked, offering his arm. "It's a beautiful morning."

She took a step backward. "No, thank you," she said softly. "My grandmother needs me."

"Nonsense," said Madame Aucoin as she smiled at Devin. "Please, go outside, dear. The fresh air will do you good."

Angelique's shoulders slumped. She reluctantly accepted the arm Devin offered her and walked down the hallway to the front door. Marcus trailed a discreet distance behind.

The trees, bushes, and ferns were still spangled with last night's raindrops, which sparkled in the early rays of the sun. Birdsong filled the forest. The sky was blue and cloudless, pierced by the pointed tops of the evergreens that towered above them as they walked. Devin kept to the stone path where Angelique wouldn't spoil her thin leather shoes.

"How often did you have the chance to go outside when you lived at the chateau?" Devin asked.

"Do you mean before my family was killed or afterwards?" she retorted. She glanced up at him, obviously contrite. "I'm sorry, that wasn't nice. When I was a child I spent every moment outside that I could. I loved the way the air smelled and the feeling of the wind blowing through my hair. Papa called me 'his little wild thing.' I hated to come in for meals. All I wanted was to run through the fields and pet the horses and build little fairy houses out of twigs and stones."

Devin laughed. "Fairy houses?"

She couldn't suppress a smile. "Yes, Mama told me that if I built little houses the fairies would come to live in them. We always chose the best places for them – under a shady tree or beside a little stream. I used twigs for the walls and made a stone path outside. The roofs were made of moss."

"How very clever!" Devin said. "And did the fairies ever come to live there?"

Angelique nodded her head, laughter teasing at the corner of her lips. "I truly liked to think that they did. Sometimes we would leave tiny cakes or berry juice for them. It was always gone in the morning."

"Ah," he answered, enjoying the way the memory had lit up her face. "It sounds lovely." His own mother had avoided everything to do with child-raising, only parading her offspring out when their childish charm might sway one of his father's opponent's hearts. He and his brothers were primarily left to professional nursemaids who enforced strict schedules and had little sense of humor.

"What did you do when you were a child?" she asked, gazing up at him.

Devin stooped to pick up a glittering piece of quartz from the path. "Nothing as entertaining as that, I assure you. I seem to have been blessed with a gift for memorization that developed early. Before I could read, I memorized the books my father read to me. Soon I invaded his library and read everything I could get my hands on. I'm afraid I've spent a good deal of my time there by choice. I'm assuming your father's library wasn't enough to entice you to stay indoors?"

"Afterwards ..." Angelique began raggedly. "After everyone was killed, Marie and I hid for weeks. She was so afraid that someone would come back to check that everyone was really dead. I would have been terrified to linger in the library, although of all the rooms in the chateau, it was always my favorite. The wine cellar was the only truly safe place we had. We ate there and slept there and when Marie left to go and get her sister's bread, she would make me promise to stay there until she returned. I would cry because I was afraid she wouldn't come back. Those men who killed my family ruined being outdoors for me, too. Suddenly, anything beyond the walls of the chateau was dangerous and frightening and I didn't want to go there anymore. It was worse after Marie died."

Devin stopped walking. "I am so sorry, Angelique."

She shrugged her thin shoulders. "All those days long ago when I played outside feel as though they happened to someone else – not to me. That Angelique was a little girl who had a magical childhood, who was safe and loved and had nothing more important to think about than fairy feasts and her fat little pony."

"You still have those memories," Devin pointed out. "You did have a magical childhood for a short time and parents who apparently worshipped the ground you walked on. That's something no one can take away from you and it is something that you can pass on to your own children someday."

"I hope my children have a kinder world to grow up in," she said forlornly.

"I do, too," Devin agreed. "But even if they don't, you have shown me what childhood should be like and I am sure you will find a way to give that gift to them and perhaps other children, as well." He took her hand and walked toward the falls. "I brought you out here to cheer you up. I'm not doing a very good job of it. Tell me one good thing that has happened since your parents' death."

"I learned to garden," she said, without hesitation. "Marie taught me how. We had to be careful not to make our patch look too neat because it would indicate that someone was living in the chateau. But after Marie died I was so afraid that I might be seen that I even tended my little vegetable garden when it was dark."

Devin laughed. "I imagine that was hard on the plants. How many vegetables did you pull out by accident?"

Angelique spun to face him, her face completely serious. "None, *monsieur*!"

"I'm joking, Angelique!" he responded. "I just imagine gardening in the dark might be difficult."

"Everything about my life for the past twelve years has been difficult. And now, I have come to live with my *Grandmère*. She has promised to give me anything I have ever wanted except for having my family back. I ruined everything last night. I can't imagine what she must think of me now. I wish I hadn't told everyone about how my father's assailants knew where to find him on the day he was murdered!"

"Angelique," Devin said softly, "has anyone treated you any differently since you told us that?"

"Jules hasn't spoken to me!" she replied. "He left last night and *Grandmère* doesn't even know where he has gone."

Devin put a hand on her arm. "It doesn't mean he left because he was angry with you."

She looked up at him with tears in her eyes. "Why else would he have left?"

"Perhaps he was just angry," Devin suggested. "Some people prefer to be alone when they are upset. I would imagine Jules is one of them."

"He hates me," Angelique stated flatly.

"I think you are wrong," Devin said. "I believe he cares for you very much."

"Oh, how I wish that were true," she murmured. "Finding him here was almost like finding Papa alive. The two of them were my heroes – my strength and my security. I cannot bear it if he wants nothing more to do with me."

They had reached winding steps carved into the face of

the rocky cliff. Devin took Angelique's hand and led her down to a stone platform that overlooked the falls.

"Look at this!" he exclaimed, awed again by the incredible scenery. "These mountains are beautiful. Just think, Angelique: You are safe here; you are loved. You do not have to worry about anything right now. Just take a moment to look around you and be thankful that you are living here – not in some old wine barrel."

She turned to face him, her face tear-streaked. "I am grateful, Devin! I truly am. It's just that I feel as though I am carrying this horrible burden around with me and it colors everything I do. I feel like I am the reason that everyone in my family died and I cannot drive that thought out of my head."

"Do you think that's what your father would want?" he demanded. "Do you imagine for one moment that he would require you to live a life devoted to punishing yourself? Your 'mistake' was in trusting a man you didn't know when you were hardly more than a baby. You have confessed it. You have apologized for it. Now, if you must, atone for it in whatever manner you see fit. But do it in such a way that you will bring some good to the world, not drag it down with more sadness and grief."

He didn't wait for her to answer but stepped back and seated her on the steps, out of the mist and spray from the glistening water. "Can I tell you a story?" he asked.

Her laugh sounded more like a sob. "That is exactly what Gaspard warned me about. He said that all you think about is your stories!"

Devin sat down beside her. "That's because life is a story, Angelique. Each one of us is in the process of creating our own story every minute of our days, whether we only tell that story to our friends or it is immortalized in the Chronicles or in books. History is simply the stories of men's lives. If we don't heed what has happened before us, how can we possibly expect our lives to be any better or different? We cannot choose the right path until we know for certain where the wrong path leads."

"It is easy for you to say," Angelique protested. "No one has died because of you!"

"That's where you are wrong," Devin replied solemnly. "Gaspard and I came to Ombria so I could learn the Chronicle from Armand. In fact, I wanted to learn all the Chronicles! I was very arrogant; I honestly believed I could memorize all fourteen of them. On the way to Lac Dupré, we encountered a wolf pack in the forest attacking a deer. They turned and attacked us. If Chastel hadn't arrived when he did, we would all have been killed. I was the only one who was bitten. The wolf nearly tore my jacket sleeve right off. Chastel was kind enough to send it to his seamstress, who mended it, but it still looked pretty ragged. He gave me another jacket and I assumed the torn one had been discarded. We traveled on to The Bardic Hall in Lac Dupré where I began studying in earnest with Armand. Several days later on a beautiful Sunday morning, Chastel told us after Mass that two of his men were shot walking home from the chateau after work. Do you know why they were killed?"

Angelique looked at him, wide-eyed, and shook her head.

"They were killed because one of the men was wearing my old jacket and had the misfortune to have light-brown hair like me," Devin continued. "And he was traveling with a taller man whose hair was dark brown like Gaspard's. Those men were killed because someone thought they were assassinating Gaspard and me. It was my fault."

"But it wasn't your fault," Angelique protested. "How could you know that Chastel's seamstress would give your old jacket to someone else instead of throwing it out?"

"How could you know that the man at your father's stables was anything other than a kind person who enjoyed talking to small children, Angelique?" Devin countered.

Angelique frowned, her lower lip coming out in a childish pout. "It's not the same thing!"

"It is the same thing," Devin assured her. "Neither of us was responsible for the deaths that occurred and yet both of us continue to bear the guilt of them. You have heard us talking about the disappearance of the villagers?"

She nodded.

"Those people disappeared because I came to Lac Dupré. We know for certain that two of them are dead: Shérif Picoté and Adrian, Armand's apprentice. Jeanette and several hundred other people are missing. They may be dead, too. I believe that Armand assumes they are but I continue to hope that there may be some other explanation. All those people's lives rest very heavily on my shoulders, also."

She took his hand. "I'm sorry, I had no idea."

"The point is that whether we intend to or not, everything we do sets something else in motion. It can be good or bad but each of us is constantly the impetus for change. It may be the catalyst that builds a scaffold or saves another man's life, but we cannot walk through this world without changing the future."

She wrapped her arms around herself. "If that is true, Devin, it makes me afraid to do anything."

Devin sighed in frustration. "It should free you! We do the best we can with the light we have, Angelique. No one can ask more of us."

She looked up at him, the youthfulness of her face so in contrast with her expression. "Do you honestly believe that?" she asked.

"I do," he affirmed. "I believe it with all my heart. Angelique, we can only try to do our best in whatever situation we are in. No one can ask more than that."

Her shoulders relaxed a little and her eyes dropped to the ground around them. She shifted, choosing a pink pebble and throwing it into the shimmering water of the falls. As Devin watched her, an idea formed in his mind.

"Angelique," he proposed quietly, "how would you like to go back to being four again?"

Her hand fluttered at her breast. "I would love it! But it is impossible."

He held out his hand. "Give me your shoes."

"What do you mean?" she asked, tucking her feet underneath her protectively.

"Take off your shoes," he repeated, tugging his own boots off. "We are going to play in the waterfall."

"No," she protested. "I will ruin my dress."

"I'll buy you another one," he offered. "Please, give me your shoes."

She extended one foot toward him and giggled as he placed it on his knee and gently slipped her shoe from her foot.

Devin reached out his hand. "Now, the other."

Angelique obediently gave him her other foot.

He hesitated a moment, frowning. "Can you do something about your stockings?"

"Yes, *monsieur*," she said demurely and turned away from him to roll down her stockings into little balls. She tucked them neatly into her shoes.

181

She turned to face him, her bare feet tapping excitedly as though she heard distant music.

He held out his hand and drew her to the edge of the stony platform. Beneath them foaming white offshoots of water bounced and splashed off stony outcroppings while the massive main course of the waterfall plunged down the center of the ravine.

"Devin!" Marcus was beside them before Devin even heard him coming. "This isn't safe."

Devin remained resolute. "I think it is," he said, pointing. "We're going to climb down to that flat rock below us so we can stand in that little stream of water."

"What on earth for?" Marcus asked incredulously.

"Because we want to," Devin replied. "You could help if you like."

"Why would I want to incriminate myself by participating?" Marcus growled.

Angelique's expression darkened. She dropped Devin's hand and stepped back. "Maybe we shouldn't do this."

"You need to do this," Devin insisted. He turned to look at Marcus. "I need to do it, too, and I will, with or without your help, Marcus."

Devin leaned down and put one hand on the rock and jumped down onto the wet projection of rock below him. He held up his hand to Angelique. "Sit on the rock and slide down. I'll catch you!"

She started to do as she was told but Marcus grabbed her arm. Devin opened his mouth to object but Marcus took both her hands and steadied her descent into Devin's arms. She shrieked a little as the cold water swirled around her feet, and then threw back her head and laughed as Devin stepped backward into the spray. He shuddered as the sudden violent rush of icy water completely doused his hair and his clothes. Without hesitation, Angelique threw herself under the water, too, uttering squeals of sheer delight as the icy mountain stream soaked and chilled her.

They danced in and out of the spray, holding their breath at the force and the temperature of the water. Angelique played like a child, diverting water with her hands to splash Devin in the face. The droplets sparkled like magic, glittering a moment in the morning sunlight and then plunging down the ravine to join the rest of the raging cascade. For one precious moment, the glittering water washed the darkness from both their souls and made them laugh and play as though neither of them had a care in the world.

Angelique was shivering when Devin finally pulled her out of the streaming water. "Enough," he said, suppressing a shudder himself. "You're freezing and I'm freezing."

She leaned into him, the warmth of her body trying valiantly to fight her cold, drenched clothes. "Please, I don't want to stop. I don't ever want to stop. I feel new again. I feel clean." She bowed her head against his chest. "Thank you," she murmured. "Thank you from the bottom of my heart."

Devin gently pushed her back and smiled. Leave it to Gaspard to capture her heart; his interest lay more with the state of her soul and his own. Today's frolic had been therapeutic for both of them. "Can you wring your dress out a bit so you don't soak Marcus when he helps you up?" he asked.

Shivering, she did as he asked, leaving the elegant fabric crumpled and still dripping, but nothing destroyed the vibrant look of pleasure on her face. Devin put his hands on her waist and lifted her up into Marcus's waiting arms.

Devin scrambled up the rocky face of the cliff, his bare toes protesting, and stood with relief on the sun-warmed stone.

Marcus stood looking skeptically at both of them. "How do you plan to explain this to Madame Aucoin?" he demanded.

"We were playing," Devin responded, taking Angelique's hand. "And we had a very good time!"

They ran up the stone steps and across the damp earth of the garden barefoot, leaving Marcus to collect shoes, boots, and stockings and follow after them with a suppressed smile on his face.

CHAPTER 24

Family Secrets

They ran in the front door, laughing. Devin's eyes, dazzled by the bright sunlight outside, suddenly focused on Jules' massive form dominating the middle of the front hallway. Devin and Angelique stopped dead, their laughter dying on their lips. They stood hand in hand like guilty children, their clothes dripping steadily on the polished floor.

Jules tore Angelique's hand out of Devin's and pulled her to him. "What in God's name have you done to her?" he thundered.

"We were exploring ..." Devin began cautiously.

"We were playing in the waterfall, Jules," she explained hastily. "We had a very nice time."

"You're soaked and shivering, little one," Jules barked, stating the obvious. "Call your maid and go upstairs and change. And you," he added, pointing at Devin. "You come with me!"

If Angelique had any doubts that Jules still cared for her, they vanished instantly. The smile on her face was like the sun coming out. She obediently headed for the stairway but not without a backward glance to grin at Devin. Her bare feet slapped merrily on the stairs just as Marcus entered like a cobbler with a load of shoes and boots.

Devin relaxed with Marcus at his back. "No one's been harmed, Jules," Devin said, keeping his voice low. "Angelique enjoyed herself this morning. Do you know how long it's been since she was able to forget her family's deaths and do something pleasurable? Your stunt with her journal last night was cruel and unnecessary. Do you know she was convinced that you hated her?"

Jules' hand flew to his chest. "She thought I hated her? My God, why?"

"She thought you blamed her for her father's death, for all her family's deaths. When you left, she felt certain you never wanted to see her again," Devin continued.

Jules' neck reddened. "I never meant for her to feel that way. I didn't think. After she told us her story, I would have killed René Forneaux with my bare hands if he had been in that room. Don't you see? I had to get out of there. I couldn't contain my anger for another moment against a man that would use a little girl to bring about her family's ruin." He flung his arms wide, his fists clenched. "What kind of man does something like that?"

Gaspard had come out of the study and stood leaning against the wall, his hands in his pockets, his shoulders slumped. "Unfortunately, men like my father use any means at hand to fulfill their ambitions. I can't explain it or excuse it, Jules. He has always been that way – never satisfied with any kind of compromise – never content with second best. There is so much that I have only just found out about him that it makes me wonder how I ever survived my childhood. I was never the kind of son he wanted – an heir capable of

186

taking over the shadow empire he had built behind the guise of the legitimate government."

A chill ran down Devin's spine. "Gaspard," he demanded, "how much do you know about all of this?"

His friend shrugged, joining them but still standing a space apart as though his ancestry forbade him from inclusion in the group. "Nothing definitive, Dev, but from the time I was a child, he held secret meetings with some of the top government officials at our house."

"My father wasn't there?" Devin asked in disbelief.

Gaspard shook his head. "Your father was never included, *mon ami*, and neither were any of your brothers, even after they held ranks that might have made them useful."

Relieved, Devin exhaled slowly. He wanted so much to be assured that his father had no part in this, that he was as honest and dedicated as Devin believed him to be. And yet how could he also be completely oblivious to this group that seemed to hold as much power as the Chancellor himself?

Gaspard continued, "They met downstairs in a kind of conference room. I only glimpsed them come in from my perch on the stairs while I waited for my mother to come and kiss me goodnight. My brother used to refer to my father as the King of Llisé. I think sometimes that Father sees himself that way, too."

"We have to stop him," Marcus said.

"How?" Devin asked. "How do you stop someone like that?"

"You kill him," Jules remarked matter-of-factly. "You kill him like the animal he is. He is a detriment to this country and its people and he has to be stopped."

Gaspard put a fist to his mouth and closed his eyes. Devin

put a hand on his shoulder but Gaspard shook it off. "Don't try to comfort me, Dev. Marcus is right. My father is a dangerous man and we are all at risk."

"Perhaps he could be locked up," Devin suggested. "He's surely guilty of treason."

"Men like René Forneaux don't stay locked up, Devin," Marcus said. "Their ideas spread like disease. Wherever they are they recruit new followers. If you threw him into prison he would contaminate his guards with his propaganda. He'd be free in a month and this whole thing would start all over again. We need to eliminate Forneaux and the other top men in his shadow government before he brings down the legitimate government of Llisé."

"Surely, he doesn't have the forces at his disposal to do that!" Devin said.

Marcus sighed in frustration. "We have no idea how many men he has or what his intentions are. It appears he has allowed your father to remain in power for years, perhaps because he was able to influence him. But something has changed – maybe something as simple as this trip of yours, Devin. Forneaux may be afraid of what you will uncover. As strange as it seems, we may be the only ones in a position to prevent an overthrow of the government from happening. Because, at this very moment, we have more information than anyone else has, including your father."

"I didn't come to the provinces to stop a revolution," Devin said. "I don't have the skills for this, Marcus. Archivists record history – they aren't noted for making it."

"You can either help shape the future, Devin, or become a casualty of it," Marcus warned him. "It is not your skills that are so important but where you stand."

"You know where I stand," Devin replied. "I will do

anything my father needs me to do, but we need to join forces – no more petty disagreements. There are very few of us and we need to come up with a plan."

"A plan to kill my father," Gaspard said, rubbing his hands over his face. "God, I never thought I would commit to anything like this."

"You don't have to be involved, Gaspard," Devin said quickly. "No one will blame you if you don't want to participate."

"I would blame myself, Dev, if I help you identify those responsible and then bow out of orchestrating a plan to counteract them. My father has made his feelings toward me very clear. I owe him nothing and I can expect nothing from him in return except a death advantageous to his cause."

"I'm sorry that it's come to this," Devin said. He couldn't imagine any scenario where he would consider plotting his own father's death. As dire as the circumstances were, this seemed too much to ask of Gaspard's friendship.

"We need to pool our information," Marcus said. "I want Chastel and Armand involved. Perhaps you should put off your trip to Coreé, Jules. The longer Forneaux is unsure of whether Gaspard and Devin are alive, the better."

Jules shrugged. "I'll bow to your expertise in the matter, Marcus, but I ask that you include Madame Aucoin, as well. She has a group of loyal friends who may be able to help us also."

"We need to be certain that we have enough proof to implicate Forneaux," Devin said. He glanced at Gaspard. "Would you be willing to testify against your father?"

Gaspard nodded grimly. "I'll pull the trigger myself, Dev. I'll do whatever it takes to stop him."

Devin shuddered. "Please don't say that, Gaspard. He's your father – no one would ask you to do such a thing."

Marcus disagreed. "This may require tough choices," he said. "None of us knows what may be required of him. It's good to know what each of you is capable of."

Rattled, Devin took a step back. He felt sick at his stomach, knowing what they hoped to do. "I'll do whatever I can to help, but please don't ask me to kill anyone."

Marcus's face lost some of its hardness. "I doubt your lack of skill at hand-to-hand combat would be an asset, Devin. Keep in mind we aren't going to storm the capital next week. Something like this requires a great deal of planning. A failed attempt would be worse than no attempt at all because then we will be guilty of treason. I doubt your father's influence would be enough to stop our executions."

"Isn't there some other way?" Devin asked. "Surely we don't have to kill Council members to achieve our purposes." He looked up as Armand's cane tapped on the floor by the study door.

"In an ideal world that might be possible," Armand said. "But there has been dissention festering in Llisé for a long time. It started long before René Forneaux was in charge. It has prevented those in the provinces from ever achieving the level of education and wealth that those in Coreé enjoy. You've seen the archival records, Monsieur Roché. The discrepancies didn't just happen during your father's rule."

"You're right," Devin agreed. "They go back hundreds of years."

"So this conspiracy is very old, as well," Armand pointed out. "And those working in your precious Archives may be involved as well."

Devin's head came up. "The archivists are meticulous,

Armand, just as you are with your Chronicles. The information they document comes to them in the form of reports. They only record what is given to them. Some of those men never even see the light of day. They spend their lives copying and authenticating documents and caring for the archival contents."

Armand raised his eyebrows skeptically. "And this is what you want to spend the rest of your life doing, Monsieur Roché? It's not much to offer a wife, is it? What kind of life would you lead alone among your dusty documents and scrolls?"

"It's hardly any concern of yours, Armand," Devin replied bitterly, "but my father has very carefully chosen the perfect wife for me. She will spend her free time at social functions, planning her extensive wardrobe, and doing charity work. As long as I fulfill my role of providing her with children, I doubt my absence will be noticed." He shook his head. "I'm not certain why this conversation has become so personal, but allow me to say that is one of the reasons I fell in love with your daughter, Armand. When I met Jeanette, it was the first time that I questioned what I had chosen to do with my life. I thought perhaps with her by my side, there might be something more that I could accomplish." He walked around the gathering of men, trying unsuccessfully to keep the irritation out of his voice. "I think I'm finished here for the moment. I'm going upstairs to change."

CHAPTER 25

Acceptance

As soon as Devin left, he wished he hadn't. He had reacted childishly. Here they were, talking about killing Gaspard's father, and he had snapped at a slight from Armand about his work in the Archives! He almost went back and then opted for heading to his room to strip off his wet clothes instead. He craved a little solitude.

Madame Aucoin had provided each of them with several changes of clothes. Each item fit impeccably and Devin wondered how she had managed it. He pulled on black trousers and a white shirt with voluminous sleeves. It reminded him of the shirt he'd borrowed from Chastel to wear the night he'd appeared in Armand's Bardic Hall before a group of angry townspeople. Apparently, he had lost some of his natural tact on this journey. Then he had charmed a village into submission with a few cleverly chosen stories and now he couldn't even refrain from stooping to snipe at his friends.

His toe connected painfully with the massive wooden leg of his bed. "Damn!" he exploded, realizing he'd left his only pair of boots downstairs.

Someone knocked on the door and he grimaced. He was in no mood to continue their discussion of assassination and rebellion. "I'm changing," he called out, knowing that wouldn't deter either Gaspard or Marcus but it might avoid further conversation with Armand.

"I'll just leave these boots by the door, dear," said Madame Aucoin's sweet voice.

He limped across the room, wrenching the door open, to reveal a pair of polished black boots. They were not the same ones that Marcus was holding for him downstairs. Madame Aucoin walked leisurely down the hallway away from him, the faint fragrance of lavender drifting in her wake.

"*Madame?*" he asked of Madame Aucoin's retreating back. As she turned, he retrieved the boots and waggled them in one hand. "How did you know I needed boots?"

She smiled. "My granddaughter needed shoes, Devin. I assumed you needed footwear as well." She glanced down at his toes. "It's difficult to retain one's dignity in bare feet."

He laughed, some of the tension leaving his body with the sound. "Thank you," he said. "I fear my dignity is already in tatters. Hadn't you noticed?"

"I'm not sure anyone has ever talked of treason in this front hall before," she said, nodding toward the stairs. "I imagine boots are a prerequisite for war but perhaps not dignity, as well. I've had no experience there."

He ran a hand across his face "Dear God, *madame*, I hope we aren't talking of war. I'm a scholar, not a soldier. I've no wish to wield the sword of vengeance."

"I'm sure all talents are needed, my dear," she answered. She gestured toward his room. "May I speak to you for a moment?"

Devin's stomach clenched. They had literally been "talking treason" in this gracious woman's home with no consideration for her feelings in the matter. He held the door open and ushered her into his bedroom.

She seated herself at one of the two brocade armchairs beside the table. "*Madame*, I apologize," he began as he reluctantly took the chair facing her.

Madame Aucoin's smile was like Angelique's; it could light up a room. It touched and warmed him, making him feel at ease in her presence. "For what, dear boy? I couldn't help hearing you men talking. Obviously something must be done. For my own sake, I have complete confidence in Marcus and Jules to come up with a plan. They are military men and their judgement is sound. Your offensive will be in good hands. I'm not as certain of Armand or Chastel but perhaps I don't know them well enough yet."

Devin frowned. "You doubt their loyalty to my father?"

Madame Aucoin shook her head. "I doubt their capacity to forward your cause," she said quietly. "Like yourself, neither of them seems aggressive."

Devin was stunned. Then, Madame Aucoin hadn't guessed Chastel's secret. Even with her perceptive mind, she apparently failed to recognize the wolf beneath the man or chose not to speak of it. It certainly wasn't up to him to tell her. He kept his voice causal and ticked off three of his fingers. "A gambler, a bard, and a scholar … Now, if we just had a priest to include in this sorry band, there would surely be a story in this."

Madame Aucoin patted his hand. "I didn't come to discuss mounting a rebellion, Devin. I wanted to talk about Angelique."

Devin's shoulders slumped. Why did he always find

himself apologizing? "I'm really terribly sorry about her dress, *madame*. I will gladly buy her another one."

Madame Aucoin shook her head laughing. "I couldn't care less about the dress. It was an old one of mine that I had altered for her. This is what I care about – when I went down to her room a few minutes ago to take her another pair of shoes, she was singing!"

"She was what?" Devin gasped.

"She was singing," Madame Aucoin repeated. "She was dancing around the room like a little girl, spinning so that her skirt floated out, and singing this darling song she must have learned from her mother. She told me you two played in the waterfall as though that was the most glorious thing that had ever happened to her! Is that what brought about this remarkable change?"

Devin shook his head. "Not entirely. It's been a combination of things. First, she needed to leave her father's chateau. Coming here to this place, and to you, has changed her even more. I only threw in a few stories that have the ability to touch the depths of our souls," he said with a wink. "And a small excursion back to her childhood involving your magnificent waterfall, which I enjoyed as much as she did."

He exhaled and looked up. "I believe that all of us start life completely unburdened. We are faultless babies and somehow, as soon as we begin to walk we start to tally up counts against us: tantrums, broken objects, and angry words. The older we get the more grievous the crimes we commit, until those of us who truly care feel completely weighed down with the baggage of just being ourselves. It's hard to feel good when our memories keep a constant tally of our faults."

He shifted, studying her ageless face. "I wanted to make

Angelique remember a time when she was as carefree and blameless as a young child. For a moment, this morning, she was. I don't dare imagine it will last very long but it gave her a few minutes' respite and a chance to feel innocent again. It only takes one candle to light the darkness. We just have to keep it burning, *madame*. Maybe between the two of us, we can."

"You don't sound at all like an anarchist to me," Madame Aucoin said gently.

Devin smiled and leaned forward, his elbows balanced on his knees. "I am not, *madame*. Our conversation downstairs is so far removed from anything I've ever been asked to participate in before. Who was it that said, 'The word is more powerful than the sword'? I can only hope that there is some way to avoid bloodshed and achieve the same ends."

"Things aren't always so neatly done, Devin. Some people can't hear the voice of reason above the clamor of weapons in their heads," she whispered.

"I'm sure you are right," he agreed.

"Be content that you did some good today, dear. I can never thank you enough for your kindness to Angelique."

Devin shrugged. "I pray to God that this morning soothed her soul."

"And did it soothe yours, too, my dear?" Madame Aucoin asked gently.

Devin rested his head against his folded hands. "For a moment, *madame*."

She stood up and bent to kiss the top of his bowed head. "God bless you," she murmured.

CHAPTER 26

Family Ties

By the time the second person knocked on his door, Devin had squeezed his painful toe into his boot and combed his hair. He was sitting with The Bishop's Book spread out in front of him on the table, continuing to catalog the underlined verses and the comments from the margins. Something told him that this process wasn't going to profit him in any way but he didn't know where else to start. He felt sure he was missing a vital part of this puzzle but he had no idea what it was. Performing a useless exercise seemed better than doing nothing and maybe he might just run across some hint of why this book was so important to Comte Aucoin.

"Come in," Devin said reluctantly. He had decided from now on to limit his involvement with this budding insurrection. He would listen to the plans they were making and keep his comments to himself. He knew absolutely nothing about espionage, sabotage, or murder, nor did he have any desire to know about it. His reactions so far had been purely emotional and that was not helpful. He needed to separate the sensitive side of himself from these discussions. He still couldn't help but feel wretched seeing Gaspard put in the position of planning his own father's assassination. Surely, there was nothing more wrenching emotionally than a conflict that pitted father against son.

The door opened and he was relieved to see Armand. The bard's leg seemed stronger after several days of rest. He crossed the room and sat down in a chair across from Devin. "Are you avoiding me, Monsieur Roché?" he demanded.

"Not at all," Devin said in surprise. "Why do you ask?"

Armand stabbed an accusing finger at Devin. "You're supposed to be learning Arcadia's Chronicle but when you have any free time, I find you with your nose in that damn book!"

Devin marked his place with a folded sheet of paper and closed the Bible gently. "I have to admit, Armand, that it could take me years to discover if there is a message hidden here. I don't have a clue what I'm looking for, only that Comte Aucoin thought it was important for my father to see it and men have lost their lives protecting it."

Armand stretched his legs out in front of him. "To be entirely accurate, you don't even know that you have the right book," he pointed out.

"That's true, too," Devin agreed. "But Jules confirmed that it looked like the right one."

"Have you considered that it may have been the one he was given to take to St. Gregory's but not the one Comte Aucoin was taking to your father?"

Devin shrugged. He hadn't. "Well, if that's true, the original book would have been recovered when Aucoin was killed and any valuable information would have been passed on long before now."

"Probably," Armand answered gruffly. He sat in silence studying the multicolored carpet.

Devin had a momentary pang of concern. "Is something wrong?" he asked.

"I feel we have lost sight of our original plan," Armand muttered. "You've shifted your focus from memorizing Llisé's Chronicles before it's too late to save them, to hiding here and planning a revolution."

Devin didn't disagree. "You're right that we are hiding but the focus on revolution hasn't been mine."

"Arcadia's bard is already dead, Devin. I am the only one left who can pass that Chronicle on to you. It is very important."

"I'm sorry I haven't devoted more time to it, Armand. I really am. But this whole thing with the book just dropped in our laps. I can't help but feel it's important, too. You can have my complete attention for the rest of the day."

Armand sighed. "I wish you had said that yesterday. I'm afraid that won't be possible. I'm going to be gone for a few days."

"Where can you go?" Devin asked. "Your life is in danger too, Armand."

Armand hesitated before answering. "Chastel and I are going to do some exploring."

"Ah," Devin leaned back in his chair. "Just the two of you and the wolves?"

Armand nodded.

"Do you think that's wise?" Devin asked.

"Does it matter?" Armand replied. "I've lost my only child. As a bard, I am a marked man. I think it's time that I cultivated my family's ability to shape-change. Perhaps

Chastel can teach me skills that will help me escape my fate for a little while longer."

Devin held up a finger playfully. "But can fate be avoided? *It seems I remember a story about a Comte who saw the figure of Death waiting in the middle of the road as he drove his family to Mass one Sunday morning. Terrified, he had his coachman turn the coach around and race for home where he felt sure they would be safe and protected. The frightened coachman, trying to avoid death and his master's condemnation, didn't slow the horses down as they passed a cliff where the road curved down to the Comte's chateau. The coach's right front wheel went over the edge and the coach and everyone in it fell to their deaths. The coachman fell to the side of the road only to watch his master's coach tumble over and over in the ravine below. When he sat up, he saw Death leaning over the ravine and laughing. The poor man's heart failed him and he died as well.*"

"You made that up," Armand snorted.

"I did not!" Devin said. "It's one of the few stories my mother told me as a child."

"That's pretty terrifying stuff for a bedtime story," Armand replied. "What dreadful thing had you done before you went to bed?"

Devin shook his head. "I don't remember. I just recall being awed by the effect a story could have on the listener. I never forgot the chill the ending gave me."

"But don't you see?" Armand explained patiently. "If the coachman died too, there would have been no one left alive to tell the story."

"Don't spoil it!" Devin countered. "It still gives me chills just as it is."

"It's a good story," Armand admitted. "So it was your

mother who endowed you with your love of storytelling, then?"

Devin smiled. "Perhaps she did. I never have thought of it that way before, but she may very well have planted the seed. I do remember her telling that story vividly. I think she had a real talent for storytelling but she never used it very often. For the most part, she was very distant and uninvolved in my childhood."

"And yet she left an indelible mark on you," Armand said. "I'd like to meet her someday." He shifted uneasily in his chair. "Chastel and I are leaving in a few minutes. I don't know how long we'll be gone."

"You won't risk your life," Devin stated, realizing how much he depended on Armand to guide him through this provincial maze of customs and curses.

"Life itself is a risk," Armand responded. "Besides, I have no idea whether I will have the knack for shape-changing. Chastel may give up on me in disgust and we will be back in time for breakfast tomorrow."

"As much as you have spent a long time denying it, Chastel blood runs in your veins, too, Armand. I think you can do anything you put your mind to."

Chastel shrugged. "There are some things I may be too old to learn but I intend to try."

Devin stood up and held out his hand. "Good luck, my friend. Be safe."

CHAPTER 27

Mementos

Devin followed Armand downstairs and found Chastel dressed in rough traveling clothes, his wolves gathered around him. He would miss both Armand and Chastel but he felt that Chastel's calm and rational approach was needed in this current fervor advocating war.

Chastel took Devin's arm and led him off to a corner. "I'm leaving four wolves with you for protection," he said pointing out four who stood clustered around his feet.

Devin stepped back from them involuntarily. "They won't listen to me!"

"They will protect you and everyone in this house," Chastel assured him. "I've made sure of that. You can let them out at dusk and they will patrol the perimeter of the chateau. Let them in at sunrise and feed them. Game will be scarce near the building and they will be hungry."

"All right," Devin said uneasily. "How long do you expect to be gone?"

Chastel shrugged elegantly. "I have no idea. A day? A week? We won't be far away should you need us."

"That's reassuring but how would I get in touch with you?" Devin asked.

Chastel laid a hand on the smallest wolf, a silver-ruffed beauty with a lot of gray fur in her coat. "Send her out alone. She will find me and I will come."

"You've trained her that well?"

"Or she has trained me," Chastel replied wryly. "Sometimes I think our minds merge together and we think as one entity. Especially, this one here." He gave the wolf a rough pat and looked back at Devin. "Armand asked for this time together as a favor. No matter what our past history has been, I would like to cultivate a relationship with him now. He is the only family I have. I don't know whether he will be able to shape-change but if trying pleases him, I am happy to oblige." Lines marked his forehead for a moment. "Armand will retain his age even as a wolf. That may present complications in the pack if an older wolf consistently falls behind. I'm not sure how this will work. I'm willing to help him but I question his motives."

Devin glanced at Armand's face as he stood talking to Marcus. Jeanette's disappearance had changed and hardened him. He wasn't certain what Armand might be capable of now. "I believe he wants to kill Forneaux," he said, confiding his worst fear.

"I know he does," Chastel said. "And I resent being used as an accomplice in that murder. The fact that he plans to kill him in wolf form indicates that wants to terrorize him first and then kill him in some horrible, savage way."

"I thought the same thing," Devin said, "but I didn't want to say it. Perhaps he won't be able to shape-change, Chastel. You said it can't be taught."

"It can't. I can only tell him how it came about for me.

I don't want to force him into a dangerous position just to make it happen. If he changes, he'll still be an old wolf with a lame leg and that will make him easy prey."

"For other wolves?" Devin asked.

"Wolves are in danger from a great many things. Physical prowess is paramount in terrain where leaping a gorge or navigating a rocky slope quickly means the difference between life and death. I'll try to keep him out of trouble." Chastel gave Devin a smile. "This is just an experiment. One I trust we will both survive. I'll see you in a few days."

Devin glanced at the gray wolf sitting at his feet. "Does this wolf have a name? Something I can call her?"

Chastel shook his head. "Not that either she or you would understand verbally. My communication with her is purely mental. Believe me when I say, she understands completely what she is to do. She'll protect your life before her own."

"I feel as though I should reward her in some way for such devotion," Devin replied.

Chastel laughed. "Just feed her. The kitchen knows what the wolves like to eat."

"I will," Devin said. "And please take care."

Shaking hands all around, they were off – Chastel, Armand, and a pack of wolves traipsing out into the wooded garden through shafts of sunlight. Devin thought Armand looked happier than he had in weeks. The spring in his step was new and if for no other reason than that, Devin was content to see them go.

The wolf at Devin's feet whined as the door closed and Devin dropped to one knee. "You don't want him to leave, do you?" he said, in the same tone of voice he might have used for one of his mother's lap dogs. The wolf regarded him silently for a moment and then lay down on the floor, its head on his paws. The other three joined her, their noses pointed toward the door.

Devin stood up. "Well, obviously we are second choice!" he said to Marcus.

Marcus glanced at them; the whole pack was staring at the door like children denied access to the garden on a sunny day. "I don't pretend to know how or what they think. But I admire Chastel for what he is able to do with them. I never thought I would feel safer with wolves by my side, but I do! I'm going to take a walk around the outside of the house. I'll be back in a few minutes."

The rest of the afternoon was quiet. Devin took the time to return again to the pages of The Bishop's Book. No one disturbed him for hours until Madame Aucoin sent up a tray with his dinner. The food grew cold on the plate as he tinkered with one formula after another to make the under-lined scripture speak to him of something more than its original intent. Nothing worked.

He was still at it when Gaspard came to bed. They barely spoke. He found some more candles and continued late into the night, finally crawling into bed when the words began to blur on the page and his head began to droop with sleep.

CHAPTER 28

Chocolate and Memories

Devin missed breakfast by several hours and came downstairs to find Angelique, still in high spirits, in the sitting room. She looked up from the table where she sat with Gaspard and gave Devin a stunning smile. "Gaspard is teaching me how to play cards!"

"Is he now?" Devin said, laying a hand on Gaspard's shoulder. "I hope you aren't playing for money."

"Neither of us has any money," Gaspard said cheerfully. "We are playing for chocolates."

"Chocolates?" Devin asked. "I may join you if you'll loan me the buy-in."

Gaspard frowned as though thinking very hard. "I'll take a chance on you," he said, extending three squares neatly wrapped in paper. "Just don't handle them too much. The chocolate melts easily and then we have to eat our earnings."

Angelique giggled merrily as she popped one chocolate in her mouth and arranged her remaining chocolates in a small stack. Madame Aucoin beamed at them from the fireside, her knitting on her lap, the cat sleeping blissfully at her feet. Devin smiled. Here they were on the brink of war, and yet yesterday and today had each held a shining moment that he would remember always, and it wasn't even time for lunch! How important it was to enjoy these extraordinary times when they came. No one ever knew what the rest of the day might bring.

He sat down on the floor and stroked the cat, feeling the rhythmic vibration of a purr start beneath his hand. For a moment, he stared at the empty fireplace, swept clean of gray wood ashes left from cooler summer nights. The conversation around the card game formed a pleasant backdrop. It was so nice to see both Gaspard and Angelique carefree for a moment. Gaspard had been talking, not a day ago, about assassinating his father. Now he was gobbling chocolate and giggling like a child. But then, his friend had always been like that, changeable as the wind.

A hand touched Devin's shoulder gently. "What dark thoughts are swirling in that head of yours?" Madame Aucoin asked.

He shook his head, suppressing any attempt to explain, and turned to look at her. "Thank you for dinner last night."

"From what I heard you didn't eat very much of it," she said with a smile. "You just moved it around on your plate. Surely, you know that every mother is wise to that technique!"

He laughed. "I tend to forget everything else when I'm studying. I've been spending a great deal of time with The Bishop's Book."

"That's what Gaspard told me," Madame Aucoin said. "My son was much the same. He would search for an answer and simply ignore everything else until he found it."

Devin nodded. "Finding what your son felt was so important in that book is like trying to find a needle in a haystack. I have no idea who underlined the passages or what kind of information he was trying to pass on. There are so many marked passages and no way to sort them or discover if there is a pattern there. I'll admit I'm frustrated by my lack of progress. I can't help but think there must have been some sort of key that has been lost." He rearranged his knees so he was facing her directly. "Madame, I hate to ask, but were there any personal effects returned to you after François died?"

She pressed her lips together and he wished he hadn't brought the subject up. Leave it to him to ruin their pleasant leisurely morning! Her momentary expression of pain vanished and Madame Aucoin was, as always, the gracious lady. "Just one thing, dear," she said, reaching into her pocket. He heard the beads clinking together before he saw them. "This is François' rosary; I carry it everywhere with me." She extended the polished beads with a sad smile. "Would you like to see it?"

"Yes, please," he said, reaching to take them. He let the beads slide through his fingers and pool on his palm. Even as a child, he had discovered that various rosaries felt different. His mother's had small silver beads webbed with an intricate design but they felt cold and hollow. His father's rosary had solid silver beads, dull with use, but they, too, were cool to the touch. François' were dark-green stone with a simple silver crucifix. The beads were smooth and polished, and glimpses of reddish stone lay swirled within the layers of green.

He held his breath for a moment and reached into his own pocket and held out his rosary beads to Madame

Aucoin. Her expression must have mirrored his own as the beads trickled into her hand. Her face lighted in soft surprise. "How on earth?" she asked.

He shrugged, extremely touched. "I don't know. I never cared for the silver rosaries my parents had, although my mother bought me one as a present when I was little. You might have thought I would have enjoyed using it out of sentiment but it always seemed cold to me. I didn't like the way the beads felt in my hand.

"One day, I walked past Marcus's room. The door was open and he was standing holding his rosary in his hand. One of his fellow officers had just been killed and though I doubt he'd ever admit it, they were very close. I was just a child and instead of concentrating on his grief and his need to be alone, I asked him where his beads had come from. He told me they were made in his family's hometown in Sorrento. He held the rosary out to me and I remember he said, 'They are a poor man's rosary, just stones worn smooth by time and water and strung on twine.'

"I told him I thought they were beautiful and he laughed. He promised to get a stone rosary for me the next time he went to Sorrento. And he did. He didn't make a production of it; I just found the rosary on my bed one afternoon when I was at lessons. When I ran downstairs to thank him, he claimed he hadn't been back to Sorrento since we talked and he hadn't put them in my room. I always thought he was teasing me, because where else would it have come from? No one else even knew that I wanted a rosary like that. But he did warn me to keep it in my pocket and use the silver rosary when I was in church with my mother. He thought it might hurt her feelings if I didn't. But I've always carried this one with me."

Devin handed François' rosary back to Madame Aucoin to compare the two of them. The crucifix on Devin's was lead; François' was silver but the stones were almost identical. Both were dark green swirled with red veins. They might have been made by the same craftsman.

Madame Aucoin gave a little cry of excitement. "Devin, do you know that François' first cross was lead, also? It broke when he dropped it on the stone tiles in the entrance hall at the chateau. I had it replaced for him with this silver one. He had several rosaries but this was always his favorite. I asked him where he got it once and he just smiled and said, "From a man who will someday change the world."

"Who was that?" Devin asked in surprise.

Madame Aucoin hesitated a moment. "Your father, Devin, the Chancellor Elite of Llisé."

CHAPTER 29

More Bad News

"I didn't realize they were friends," Devin said in surprise.

"François was a member of Council. They certainly met formally but I believe they had cultivated a personal friendship, too. François trusted him and I'm sure that is why he chose to take The Bishop's Book to him. I never believed that it was your father's men that had him killed, Devin."

"Apparently you did not convey that to Jules," Devin murmured.

"Jules anticipated an ambush. He begged François not to go. He still wrestles with guilt over having left my son with only four guards to protect him. I think he desperately needs someone else to blame and somehow it eases his conscience to blame your father," said Madame Aucoin.

"Well, considering the men were dressed as government troops, it was an obvious assumption," Devin admitted. "But Jules needs to remember that he was acting on your son's orders. Had he stayed and the book had fallen into the wrong hands, he would have had more to feel guilty about. Or he would be dead and at that point guilt wouldn't matter, would it?"

Madame Aucoin cocked her head to one side. "I've always wondered about that, whether we are still burdened by all our sins of commission and omission after death."

Devin leaned back and stretched his legs. "I've decided to just do the best I can and not worry about it."

She laughed and handed his rosary back. "An admirable goal, dear. What had you hoped to find when you asked me if I had received any of François' personal effects?"

Devin slipped the rosary into his pocket. "I hoped there might be a key to The Bishop's Book. Some cryptic letters scribbled on a piece of paper, perhaps. Surely, François knew there was a chance that the book would be intercepted."

"That's why he primed Jules to run and take the book with him."

"But Jules might have been captured and then the book would have been lost."

"So the key couldn't travel with the book," Madame Aucoin pointed out. "They must have kept the book and key separately. Could it have been in one of the letters that François sent your father?'

"Possibly," Devin admitted. "But if he did send it in a letter, there was always the danger that it might be intercepted. François' letters to my father should all be in Coreé. If this involves a high-level conspiracy, I think my father kept the information about The Bishop's Book completely to himself. Even Marcus knew nothing about it when I asked him."

"Marcus may have chosen to keep what he knew to himself, Devin. Didn't you tell me he was your father's personal bodyguard before he was yours? I imagine he will return to that position when you are back in Coreé. That makes his allegiance to your father paramount. I'm sure he feels there are some things that it would be better for you not to know."

"I'm sure he does," Devin agreed. "The subject has come up before. He won't even tell me what his orders are concerning me. I sometimes think that he may have been told to kill me rather than allow me to be captured."

"Surely, not!" Madame Aucoin gasped, her cheeks flushed.

"It's just a theory," Devin replied. "I shouldn't have put it into words."

"No, you shouldn't have," Marcus said quietly from the doorway. He crossed the room and stood over Devin. "Would it help you to know that your father has authorized me to use any means necessary to return you safely home to Coreé?"

"Yes," Devin said, rising to his feet. "It would." He stood shifting uneasily from one foot to another. "I wasn't being critical, Marcus; I simply wish I knew more than I do about the political forces that drive this government. I have spent several years immersed in the Archives, but that has never prepared me to deal with the events that are threatening to throw the provinces and Coreé into armed conflict right now."

Marcus raised the newspaper he had in his hand. "There is more bad news from Coreé. Several provinces are refusing to ship goods to the capital at all."

Devin closed his eyes. That was devastating news! Coreé was the capital of both Llisé and the province of Viénne. It was a center of learning and home to all of the government offices and those who ran its many branches. Viénne boasted of beautiful, extravagant homes for its Council members

213

and the noblemen who came as frequent winter visitors from their provincial chateaus and castles. But the province of Viénne wasn't noted for exportable products. The jewelry produced by its expert silver- and goldsmiths was highly sought after, but only by the rich. Specialty bakeries, restaurants, chocolatiers, tailors, and dressmakers lined the business district of Coreé. Everything manufactured there catered to the tastes of the affluent and powerful but depended on the provinces for any of the raw materials they used.

Viénne produced no food at all on its own land, although its earth was probably the most fertile in the Empire. The Danzig's floodwaters brought rich silt every spring to line its banks. Viénne lay protected and secure, bordered by the Danzig on the east, the mountains to the north and west, and the Chancellor's own province, Sorrento, to the south. Now, cut off from the provinces that provided everything from fresh vegetables to meat and wine, its citizens would soon face starvation at the hands of the very people Coreé claimed to control.

Devin shook his head. "This is disturbing, Marcus, really disturbing."

Marcus laid the newspaper on the table. "I agree. It seems we have Forneaux's group stirring up trouble: killing bards and terrorizing small villages; and the real government is being blamed for it. It is designed to make some provinces turn against Coreé and your father. I truly believe Forneaux plans a takeover, Devin. He is trying to make your father appear incompetent to deal with the situation that he, himself, has created. I think he plans to depose him and then step into the Chancellor's position."

"It's an elected position, Marcus!" Devin protested.

"Surely, my father has some Council members that will support him."

"It would be interesting to see which provinces have been targeted," Gaspard said, laying his cards on the table. "I would bet they are the ones that have Councilmen that have traditionally supported your father. The Councilmen with viewpoints contrary to the Chancellor's are already in my father's pocket."

"That was well thought out," Devin replied. He wasn't used to Gaspard providing such level-headed advice. "How can we document that?"

"I think Jules could obtain that information," Madame Aucoin said.

"Thank you," Devin said. "That would be very helpful. First, we need to find out what is happening to the people who have disappeared from these villages. I think that is the most terrifying aspect of this for the provincial people – that and the loss of their bards."

Devin paced back and forth. "Marcus, was there anything odd at all about Lac Dupré once the villagers disappeared? I noticed the farm animals were left behind but the pets were gone, even Armand's orange-striped cat."

"That's true enough," Marcus agreed. "Chastel had his men round up the sheep and cattle and drive them into his paddocks."

"A nice little dividend for Chastel," Gaspard commented.

"Chastel has become a wanted man because he helped us," Devin pointed out. "I believe he rounded up that livestock to protect it."

"From wolves?" Gaspard asked with a laugh. At Devin's expression he quickly added, "I was only joking."

"If your theory is right, Gaspard, then Lac Dupré becomes

the exception to the rule," Devin continued, ignoring Gaspard's outburst. "Forneaux believed that Chastel was his friend and supporter. There was no reason to target Lac Dupré."

"Except that you were there," Marcus reminded him. "Lac Dupré may have been targeted simply because had he been successful in killing you and Gaspard, there would have been no need to continue the violence any further. When that failed, he made it look like that was the first of many such incidents."

"How many more are there?" Devin asked.

"Rumor has it that the residents of both Obernai and Albi have vanished," Marcus said.

Devin turned around. "Madame Aucoin, do you have a map of Llisé?"

"Of course, there are maps in the study across the hall," she answered. "They are rolled tightly and tied with string in the corner by the window."

"I'll get them," Angelique offered.

As soon as she left the table, Gaspard swept the cards into a pile and deposited them in a red velvet box in the drawer of the side table. The chocolates he dumped into a candy dish and pushed to the side, after pocketing several.

"Those will melt in your pocket," Devin pointed out. "You might as well eat them."

Angelique returned almost immediately and handed three maps to Devin. The first one proved to be only of Arcadia and Devin gave it to Gaspard to reroll. The next map illustrated all of Llisé and he spread it out on the table and used books to hold down the corners. He marked the villages that had been emptied of their residents with the wrapped chocolates that Gaspard offered him from his pocket.

"All the villages are in the northern provinces!" Marcus said. "First Ombria and then these two towns in Arcadia."

"Two villages in one province?" Gaspard asked. "What is the point in that?"

"To make it appear random?" suggested Madame Aucoin.

"It's hardly random," Devin said. "One village is in east Arcadia, the other is in the west. All of these sites follow the path of the monoliths that stretch across the northern provinces of Llisé."

Gaspard leaned forward. "You're joking?"

"I'm not joking. I think that is very significant," Devin answered tensely. "They are working their way toward something."

"Or away from it," Marcus suggested.

Devin shook his head. "I don't think so. I wish Armand hadn't left with Chastel. I could use his expertise right now."

"On what?" Marcus asked doubtfully.

Devin stopped before he said too much. Armand had shared information with him that he had promised never to reveal. "He would know what these villages held in common," he answered. "Perhaps this is all about similarities, not differences."

"You can send for him," Marcus suggested.

Chastel's gray wolf sauntered into the sitting room as though it had been summoned and sat at Devin's feet, looking up. For just an instant, Devin had the strangest spark of recognition. It was gone a moment later as the wolf lay down with its head on its paws.

Marcus looked at him strangely. "What's the matter?"

"Nothing ... I just thought ..." Devin shook his head. "Never mind."

"What were you saying about the villages following the

path of the standing stones?" Madame Aucoin asked.

Devin pointed to the map. "Well, they do. It's as though they are working their way west but following that route. I have no idea why."

"But you think Armand might?" she replied.

Devin was certain that Armand would know why, and the reason chilled him to the bone. Even the death of Perouse's Master Bard fit the alarming pattern that seemed to be evolving right before his eyes. If by chance René Forneaux's men had extracted the location where the written records of the Chronicles were kept from one of the dying bards, they would have been instructed to destroy them. They had only Tirolien to cross before they reached the western coast of Llisé. Devin would have to choose between saving his Chronicles and stabilizing his father's government. It was a position he did not want to be in. "Yes," he said finally. "I think I need to send for Armand."

The wolf at his feet jumped up and nudged his hand. Without even consulting the others, Devin walked to the front door with the wolf at his heels. He knelt beside it, putting one hand in the ruff on each side of its head. Again, he had that distinct feeling of recognition, almost as though he were speaking to another human being. "Find Chastel and Armand and bring them back!" he said.

The wolf whined and scratched at the door. Devin opened it and the wolf was off like a shot through the ferns in the garden and then bounded into the trees, a blur of gray against the dark green of the forest. Devin stood a moment on the doorstep, hearing its movement long after he could see the powerful body leaping over rocks and fallen logs. He turned to see Marcus standing behind him.

"What's worrying you?" he asked.

Devin shrugged. "Nothing, I just think that Armand may be able to understand this better than you and I can," he offered lamely.

"It's more than that," Marcus answered. "You're on edge. I can feel it from here. What did you see on that map that disturbed you?"

Devin grabbed for the only explanation that might seem logical to Marcus. "Do you remember the ballad about Terre Sainté? Supposedly, the standing stones lead the way back to Terre Sainté, the place where all the people of Llisé came from. What if Forneaux plans to use that location in his campaign against the government?"

"You'll have to try better than that," Marcus said. "Besides, what possible political significance could it have? No one has ever found it before, have they?"

"No," Devin admitted.

"What makes you think they could find it now?" Marcus demanded.

"They are following the stones. Perhaps they have information that we don't have," Devin said. He didn't lie well and Marcus knew deception when he heard it.

"Even if they did find Terre Sainté, there would be people living there now, so I don't understand how that would help Forneaux's position," Marcus said. "What aren't you telling me?"

Devin clenched his hands together. "Something terrible is going to happen if Forneaux's men reach the western coast of Llisé," Devin said. "That's all that I can tell you, Marcus."

CHAPTER 30

Plots and Politics

Devin paced in front of the dining-room window most of the afternoon, his eyes on the garden, waiting for Chastel and Armand to appear. Both Angelique and Gaspard tried to tempt him to play cards but he declined. Problems crowded his brain, one after another, twisting into an impossible tangle. He needed to have time to think, to sort this mess into some kind of logical order. It was like trying to solve a puzzle when all of the key pieces were missing.

He had never claimed to have his brothers' political shrewdness; his talent lay in memorization and cataloguing. This current situation required a different type of thinking, an ability to foresee the impact of an action on all of the parties involved. He doubted that either Marcus or Jules had that aptitude either. They were trained in military maneuvers, not diplomacy. They needed both Chastel and Armand to craft a solution and make it work.

It was almost dark when the three remaining wolves in the hall leaped to their feet and ran to the front door, claws clicking on the tiled floor. Devin went after them. Marcus, as always, took anyone demanding entry as a threat. He pushed Devin back through the dining-room doorway and pulled out his pistol.

"It's Chastel," Devin reassured him. "Just look at the wolves. They know he's coming."

The wolves were whining and pawing at the door in greeting – not growling – but it didn't seem to relieve Marcus's concern. "Just stay put until we're sure," he instructed Devin.

Devin felt tired and gritty as though he, too, had traveled a long way to come here. His head ached with the task that faced them. There could be no more huddling in safety while the rest of Llisé went up in flames. They had to choose whether to light the spark themselves or devise a way to quench the flames that someone else was fueling. And the choice had to be made soon.

Moments later Chastel came striding across the garden. Armand followed, his pace slower and less sure. Four wolves surrounded them but the small grey wolf matched its pace to Armand's.

"God!" Devin whispered out loud.

Marcus whirled to look at him. "What's the matter now?" he demanded.

Devin shook his head. "Nothing," he said quickly.

"Well, keep your thoughts to yourself!" Marcus growled. "Don't send me chasing after daydreams when there are enough credible threats here to keep ten men busy!"

Devin read in the tense lines of Marcus's face that he was well aware that their world was inevitably blowing up around them. His orders had not covered this and if anyone in this group longed for Coreé and direct orders from the Chancellor, it was Marcus.

Then Chastel and Armand and the wolves were at the door and there was a great deal of whining and tail sniffing in the hall. Armand pulled himself away from the mass of tails and noses and looked at Devin. "So, was it Chastel or me that you needed?"

"You," Devin admitted. "Well, both of you really. I'm sorry to have disrupted your trip. I discovered something on the map that I think you should see."

They shed their coats and supplies into the hands of servants and walked into the sitting room bringing the scent of wolf, pine, and the north wind with them. Chastel sent the wolves to the kitchen and the chaos diminished considerably. Eight full-grown wolves made the sitting room feel like a barn.

"I'll ask for an early supper," Madame Aucoin said, excusing herself. "Angelique, will you come with me, dear?"

Devin saw Angelique's eyes go from her grandmother to the men clustered around the map on the table. "I'd rather stay, *Grandmère*. I want to hear what Monsieur Chastel and Armand have to say."

Madame Aucoin hesitated a moment and then bent her head as she left the room. It didn't disguise the smile on her face.

Devin bent over the map and explained the position of the villages where the disappearances had occurred. Armand immediately saw the significance of their locations in respect to the standing stones. Devin could see it in his eyes and the way he clutched his cane fiercely, more like a cudgel than a device for support. He hoped that Armand might explain why it was such a dangerous route, but he said nothing, and Devin dared not break a trust by saying anything himself.

Devin was well aware that there were two very different problems that needed addressing and ached for Armand to be frank with the group. If they concentrated their strength on shoring up the Chancellor's position, they doomed the Master Bards' written legacy to destruction. He was anxious to get Armand alone but could think of no tactful way of doing it.

Chastel tapped a finger on the map. "I find it interesting that none of the incidents have happened in the southern provinces. Is this all deception to cover their real intention – to kill Devin and Gaspard?"

"Hardly," Marcus answered, "Because they are moving farther away from us all the time. Here we are, hiding away from them, and they seem totally unconcerned whether we have been captured or not. Or they may assume we were all killed in that rock fall."

"I can't believe Forneaux would give up so easily," Chastel remarked. "If either Devin or Gaspard returns to the capital safely then everything he has done will be exposed."

"What if there are two groups?" Devin asked. "Marcus, you implied that there might be more than one when the men who were holding Gaspard attacked us. It doesn't mean that Gaspard's father isn't still the one in charge, but why couldn't he have assigned different tasks to different groups of men?"

"He certainly could have," Marcus agreed. "But that makes our task even more difficult."

"How many men could he have at his disposal?" Gaspard asked.

Marcus shrugged. "None of us knows that or how long he has been planning this. At first, I imagined he had collected a select inner circle of Councilmen who supported him, but military maneuvers that decimate villages imply amassed forces. I assume they are all wearing government uniforms. It will be difficult to identify Forneaux's men from the Chancellor's. It's a clever way to instill terror because no one will know who to trust."

"Marcus, the men who took Gaspard were not wearing government uniforms. They were wearing Forneaux's household colors," Devin reminded him.

Angelique ducked under Chastel's elbow and stood in the curve of his arm, centering herself in the discussion. "So the men searching for Gaspard and Devin may still be out there somewhere?"

"I believe they have to be," Chastel answered. "Marcus is correct in saying that should any of us reach Coreé alive, they will be able to identify Forneaux as the orchestrator of this plan. He would be crazy to allow us to go free and I don't think he is crazy."

"I wouldn't be too sure of that," Marcus said. "There has only been one Chancellor who has been deposed in the last thousand years. Elections by Council were supposed to eliminate any chance of that happening again."

"And if I remember, it takes a 75 per cent vote from Council to depose a Chancellor," Gaspard said. "I can't believe my father has that many other Councilmen who would support him in this."

Chastel stood quietly for a moment stroking one dark eyebrow. "There is more than one way to eliminate a Chancellor, my friends. Devin, wasn't there an attempt on your father's life shortly after you left for Ombria?"

Devin went still. How foolish could he be to think that particular attempt had been an isolated incident by a deranged madman? "That was one of Forneaux's lackeys?"

"We have no way of knowing that, Devin," Chastel said.

"Forneaux is smart enough to make sure the trail doesn't lead back to him. And the shooter in Council Chambers may very well have been some lunatic, but considering everything else that's going on right now, I think that is highly unlikely."

Armand cleared his throat. "Devin, you told me that there were discrepancies between the official records in the Archives and the oral Chronicles. Who else did you tell?"

"I only told you and Marcus," Devin said.

"You didn't tell Gaspard?" Armand asked.

Gaspard's head shot up. "I knew nothing about it, and even if I had, I wouldn't have mentioned it to my father!"

"I'm only asking," Armand replied. "Even if you had told your father, under normal circumstances there would have been nothing wrong with that. I'm only trying to understand your father's motivation."

"Power has always been my father's only motivation," Gaspard said. "He was perfectly content with Vincent Roché as Chancellor until Roché began to have his own ideas about how things should be done. My father saw himself losing influence and began to think he needed to rein Roché in. There is his motivation. I'm proud neither of it nor of him."

"I'm sure your father also knew the archival records and the Chronicles wouldn't agree, Gaspard," Devin said. "The discrepancies were bound to come out. He tried to get you to stay home. When that failed he threatened you that if you didn't come back, he'd disinherit you. I don't believe that murdering you was his first choice."

Something like gratitude crossed Gaspard's face. Perhaps Devin had just made opposing René Forneaux harder, but it was better than having Gaspard go to his grave convinced his father hated him.

Marcus stared at Devin in disbelief. "This is no time for sugar-coating reality. Whatever Forneaux's initial motives may have been, Devin, he intends to kill both you and his son. I think that you need to keep that foremost in your mind."

"So, do you know how to fix this mess?" Devin demanded. "Because I don't! Things just keep getting worse and I wonder what this little group of us can possibly do to make a difference."

"Remaining level-headed would be a plus," Marcus chided him. "We are missing a great many of the facts and that makes decisions very difficult to make. Perhaps we would do better to simply plan René Forneaux's assassination. Without him at the helm, the whole movement would lose its momentum."

"Well, that leaves out you, or me, or Gaspard. We are all equally recognizable in Coreé. Would you send Armand, or Jules or Chastel?" Devin snapped. "Because there are only six of us!"

"You are wrong," said Angelique. "We are seven! You could send me."

CHAPTER 31

Impasse

"That," Jules said, "I would never allow. I failed your father but I will not fail you."

Angelique faced him with determination. "I failed my father, too, Jules. Please allow me this opportunity to vindicate myself."

"You are not an assassin," Marcus said gently. "This requires someone who can kill without compunction and still act quickly enough to save his own life."

Angelique's chin rose, her face deadly serious. "If you think I cannot kill this man, then you would be wrong. He tricked me into revealing information that led to the deaths of everyone in my family. *Monsieur*, I would kill him in a heartbeat."

For a moment no one spoke. Armand took a step forward and put his arm around her shoulder. "You must think of your grandmother. It would break her heart to lose you. You are all she has left, child. Do you realize the aching emptiness there is in being the last of your line? It is more important for you to stay here with her than to go to Coreé. Allow the men to talk about it."

"Who has the greater right, *monsieur*?" she asked. "Only Jules holds second place. The honor should be mine!"

"Death is never honorable, Angelique," Devin said. "Taking a man's life, even a man you hate, is never easy. You will wake up screaming in the dark for years to come."

"I wake up screaming now, Devin," she said. "Besides, all of you are convinced that I won't survive anyway." She moved toward Gaspard, changing moods at a moment's notice. Suddenly a temptress and seductress, she planted a finger playfully on his lapel. "Tell me, *monsieur*, does your father like the ladies, too?"

Gaspard took her hand roughly in his, drawing it down to her side. "Any affection I have shown you, Angelique, has been sincere. Did you think we were playing courting games? I'm truly sorry if I ever gave that impression."

Angelique did not appear hurt. "I am simply demonstrating that a woman can get closer to a man much more easily than any of you can. No one would suspect me. I could take a ship to Coreé, play the part of someone's visiting niece or granddaughter, arrange an invitation to a party, and introduce myself to Monsieur Forneaux. Surely, one of you can give me a knife and teach me how to use it swiftly and quietly."

Madame Aucoin appeared in the doorway.

Conversation stopped abruptly. Gaspard dropped Angelique's hand and took a step backward.

"I'm sorry," she said. "I didn't mean to interrupt, but dinner is served."

Chastel recovered first. "Of course, thank you. Armand and I are starving." He faked a yawn behind a cupped hand. "I think we may need to go to bed early, too. I'm exhausted."

Devin exhaled and unclenched his hands. How much had

Madame Aucoin heard of their conversation and how could they deter Angelique from going with them?

The men seemed to have very little to discuss at dinner. If it hadn't been for Angelique chattering happily with her grandmother about some of the new fabrics they had looked at, the only sound would have been the clink of cutlery against fine porcelain plates. Devin watched Angelique's animated expression, wondering how he could reconcile her carefree demeanor with the young woman who had just volunteered to kill René Forneaux herself a few minutes before. Chastel had given them the perfect excuse to retire early and meet upstairs to continue their discussion and yet Devin desperately needed to speak to both Armand and Chastel alone.

He let Gaspard refill his wine glass twice and by the end of the third glass, he had a headache and Angelique's plan was beginning to seem plausible. She was right. She and Jules wouldn't be recognized. They could travel to Coreé, murder Forneaux, and make a quick exit. Madame Aucoin could actually go along to legitimize the trip and Devin, Armand, Chastel, and Marcus could travel to the western side of the continent and try to save the written records of the Chronicles. Except they couldn't do that because Devin had sworn to Armand that he wouldn't tell anyone that there were any written records. He closed his eyes and rested his head on his hand.

"Too much wine?" Gaspard asked cheerfully. "Or not enough?"

"Too many problems," Devin replied. "I can't see how this can all be resolved."

"Perhaps it can't," Chastel said quietly from Devin's other side. "But we will try to do what we can."

Devin turned his head to look at him, still supporting it on his hand. "What are you saying?"

"I'm saying that the six of us can't fix everything that's wrong. That's impossible. I think it's best to concentrate on one thing that can be accomplished." Chastel lowered his voice further. "If Forneaux's assassination will stabilize the government then we must find a way to do that."

"The people best qualified to do that would have the most trouble getting anywhere near Forneaux," Devin hissed.

"Then we must consider less conventional means," Chastel replied from behind his napkin.

"Angelique?" Gaspard said in surprise.

"Not necessarily," Chastel murmured.

Marcus frowned at them from across the table. He put his hand down on the table more forcefully than was necessary. "This isn't the place to discuss this!" he muttered. "Wait until later when everyone else is asleep."

"I'm afraid I may be asleep then, too," Devin said.

Madame Aucoin hushed Angelique with a gentle hand on her shoulder. "Is something the matter?" she asked, her fork poised daintily to choose a piece of fruit from her salad bowl.

"Devin has a headache," Gaspard replied helpfully.

"It has been a rather stressful day," said Madame Aucoin. "Perhaps you should go upstairs and lie down."

"My thought exactly," said Chastel. "I think we should all have an early night."

Devin stood up and pushed his chair under the table. "Would you be so kind as to excuse me now, *madame*?"

"Of course, my dear," she said. "Please let me know if you need anything,"

Devin left his napkin on his chair and started up the stairs. Behind him, Angelique's footsteps rang out on the steps. He didn't turn around but she caught his arm when he reached the hall upstairs. "I know what you are doing!" she said, her voice low and angry. "You men think that you will squeeze me out of any plans you make. I have more right, Devin Roché, to kill René Forneaux than you do!"

Devin turned to face her. "You have more reason to hate him, Angelique. You do not have more right to kill him."

She stood for a moment looking puzzled. "It is always words with you! You simply twist them around until they say what you want them to mean."

"I've had good training," Devin said. "That's what diplomats do and I was raised by one of the best."

"Can't you understand?" she begged. "I want this."

"Do you want him dead or do you want to kill him?" Devin said. "Those are two very different things."

She clenched her hands. "There you go with your words again!" she protested. "You are right. I do want him dead. But I would find a great deal of satisfaction in killing him myself."

"No one wants you to have to do that," Devin said, trying to keep his voice level. "Do you realize that the person who kills Forneaux will probably be killed, too, or at the very least thrown into prison?"

"I have very little to live for," she said quietly.

"What do you mean?" he asked in frustration. "You have more to live for now than you have had in the past twelve years. Your grandmother adores you."

"My grandmother is wonderful but she is very old," she whispered. "What will I do when she is gone? Live alone in this huge house? My ghosts have followed me here, too. I thought I'd left them behind but I didn't." She shook her head. "No, I never want to live alone again."

Devin was at a loss for words. "Maybe you'll meet a nice young man and ..."

She cut him off. "Do you mean Gaspard? Even I know the woman who marries him will never have his full attention. He can be sweet and funny but I can't see him as my husband or anyone else's."

"I wasn't speaking of Gaspard," Devin replied. "Although, I think you do him an injustice. I'm sure your grandmother intends to introduce you to her friends at parties. You might be surprised by the number of choices you have."

She looked at him, her eyes wild, like some half-tamed animal. "Don't you understand? I don't belong here. I belong among the ashes of my family. My life stopped when I was four years old, Devin. I would gladly spend what is left of it on bringing René Forneaux to justice."

CHAPTER 32

Counsel

The stair creaked and both of them jumped. They turned to see Chastel standing just a few steps below them. Devin exhaled in relief and leaned back against the railing. If anyone could talk sense into Angelique, perhaps he could.

Chastel mounted the last three stairs leisurely, as though he hadn't just heard his friend's youngest daughter vow to kill his murderer. "It seems we have all been telling tales to get out of your grandmother's dinner party," he said quietly. "She'll think we didn't care for the lamb."

Angelique looked at him uneasily, her hands still clenched. "What excuse did you give for not finishing your dinner?"

Chastel leaned against the opposite railing across from Devin, his body emanating calm. "I couldn't help but hear your conversation and I assume some of the others may have, too." He reached out a hand. "I think you are distressed unnecessarily, Angelique. We haven't come up with any plan yet and until the details are worked out no one will be designated as an assassin."

Devin saw her shoulders relax visibly. "I'm not to be

excluded," she insisted. "Not just because I'm a woman. No one has been hurt more by Forneaux than I have."

"On that we are agreed," Chastel said.

"I have a right to be included in the deliberations," she added.

"I will see to it," Chastel answered. "Why don't you go to bed now? We'll talk about it tomorrow."

The wildness was gone; Angelique simply looked weary and small. "Do you promise me?" she asked.

"Yes," Chastel said, stepping forward to kiss her on the forehead. "Sweet dreams, my dear."

He and Devin watched her walk down the hall to her room in silence. She turned for one final glance and opened her bedroom door and went inside.

Chastel took Devin's arm and steered him toward his room, closing the door before he spoke. "One crisis averted," he said as he sat down gracefully on the arm of one of the chairs in Devin's room.

Devin shook his head. "I didn't know what to say to her. She was so insistent. No argument I presented made any difference."

Chastel nodded at a bottle of wine that Gaspard had left on the table. "Do you mind?" he asked, picking up one of the glasses.

"Not at all," Devin said, sinking into the other chair.

Chastel gestured with the bottle. "Would you like some?"

"No, thank you," Devin replied. "How did you do that? How were you able to reason with her when I could not?"

"I didn't reason with her," Chastel said, returning with his glass and sitting down. "I agreed with everything she said."

Devin made a sound of disgust. "I don't understand."

"You tried to talk to her as though she is an adult, Devin. She's a four year old in an adult's body."

"Well, I hope you can work the same magic when it comes time to decide what to do."

Chastel laughed. "She remembers me as an authority figure. I told her to go to bed and she went." He wagged his fingers. "There was no magic involved."

"Speaking of magic," Devin said, "I wanted to ask you about your gray wolf."

"Which one?" Chastel asked, swirling the contents of his glass. "They all are various shades of gray."

"The one you left with me while you were away. The wolf I sent to bring you back," Devin said. He cleared his throat. "It's not just a wolf, is it?"

Chastel looked at him steadily. "That is certainly what it appears to be."

Devin's heart was pounding in his chest. "There's something different about its eyes. I can see the intelligence there. It's almost ..." he stopped, afraid to put his thoughts into words.

Chastel looked at him over the rim of his wine glass. "Almost what?"

Devin backed off, wishing Chastel would be more open with him. "I don't know. How long have you had her?"

"Not long," Chastel replied. "She arrived the night that Gaspard was kidnapped and the townspeople disappeared. She was not part of my pack but they welcomed her."

Devin leaned forward. "Is it possible she is not just a wolf?"

"What else would she be?" Chastel asked obscurely.

"You know what I mean," Devin protested. "Is it possible that she could be Jeanette?"

Chastel put his wine glass down. "My God, Devin, this is complicated."

"Could it be Jeanette?" Devin repeated.

"If it was Jeanette," Chastel said, "then I'm not sure the part of her that made her human exists anymore." He held up a hand. "Please don't ask me to explain because I can't. I can only tell you what might have happened. Maybe the night the soldiers came to the village, Adrian sent Jeanette off alone, hoping she would reach her grandparents safely. Maybe she was chased by wolves in the Forêt of Halatte, and she was so terrified that she changed into a wolf herself. Then somehow she found her way back to me. Jeanette has Chastel blood; just as her father does. It's possible it saved her life. But if she did become a wolf, she hasn't been able to change back into human form."

"Why not?" Devin asked.

"Devin, this is all supposition. I have nothing to base this on except some vague suspicion that you have relayed to me. I honestly don't know if she did change into a wolf," Chastel repeated. "If she did, maybe she was just too frightened to become human again. A wolf has power. Men fear them. Perhaps that appealed to Jeanette more than being a terrified young girl." He paused for a sip of wine before he continued. "Look, I'm only speculating. I don't understand this either. Perhaps the wolf form might seem safer to her now."

"Didn't you wonder at all when she came to you the night Gaspard was kidnapped?" Devin asked.

Chastel hesitated before speaking again. "I will admit that the timing seemed strange."

Devin looked at the carpet. Chastel seemed loath to confirm what Devin already suspected in his heart. He had been almost certain this evening when she returned with Armand, matching her pace to Armand's. But he had never dreamed it was possible to become a wolf and not change back. God, she must be so frightened.

"Devin," Chastel said after a minute, "what made you even ask me?"

"I …" One hand went involuntarily to his chest. "I saw something in her eyes while she was here. There was some kind of recognition like I was speaking to another person. The first time it happened I thought maybe you had brought your physician with you, but then he doesn't change does he?"

"No, he doesn't," Chastel said.

"Then I realized that the feeling I got from her was feminine and sad. I don't know why I didn't notice until now. Does Armand know?"

"Know what?" Chastel answered. "We don't know anything for certain. And I'll ask you to promise to keep your suspicions to yourself. I think that would be better, don't you?"

Devin made a hopeless gesture. "Isn't it crueler to let Armand believe that she's dead?"

"Devin, listen to me. She may be dead," Chastel warned. "Please don't complicate the situation any further by bringing this up with Armand."

Devin felt vaguely sick at his stomach. "I certainly have no experience in these matters. Has someone ever turned into a wolf and not been able to change back again?"

Chastel tapped his chest. "Certainly no one I have heard of personally."

"Has it happened to anyone?"

"Devin, I have no idea. Have you forgotten that my family

237

doesn't speak of this? The Chastel curse is a shameful thing – we didn't even discuss it among ourselves. I told you my father never even mentioned it to me. I assumed the curse had skipped his generation until I saw his name on the wall in the hallway."

Devin ran a hand through his hair. "I'm sorry. You have to realize how foreign this is to me."

"And I can only tell you my own experience," Chastel said. "And it's not as though we can go to anyone for advice."

"When you took Armand into the woods, was he able to change?"

Chastel shook his head. "He tries too hard. He thinks it should be like learning the Chronicles – if he practices often enough he will be transformed. I tried to tell him that it has to just happen but he wouldn't listen. He charged through the woods like a bull, leaping over branches and holes. I think he's made his leg much worse with the effort of trying to run with my wolves."

"Did you see the little gray wolf walked him back tonight?"

"I did. I noticed it although I don't believe he did. If what you suspect is true, I think the realization might be too much for him to bear. Allow him to hope that Jeanette will come back to him someday." He glanced at Devin. "I would advise you to do the same. What we have said here is only speculation. You may be entirely wrong. Don't let this tear you up emotionally. If you want to hold out hope for Jeanette, that is your business, but perhaps this is a good time for you to move on, as well."

CHAPTER 33

Fathers and Sons

A few minutes after Chastel left, Gaspard swaggered in, surprisingly sober. He took off his jacket and swung it carelessly over the seat of a chair and then sat on it.

"So have you solved the Empire's problems?" he asked, propping his feet precariously on the end of the table.

"I'm afraid I haven't made any progress at all," Devin replied.

"I was thinking about what Angelique said earlier. Maybe she's right. She has the least chance of being recognized in Coreé and the greatest likelihood of getting close to my father without raising suspicions."

Devin stood up. "God, Gaspard! How can you do that?"

"Do what?" Gaspard replied, unbuttoning the neck of his shirt.

"Talk about your father's assassination as though it were nothing," Devin said in disgust.

Gaspard's posture never changed. "Whatever hopes I had of having a father that loved me are long gone. Even as a child, I simply tried to stay out of his way to avoid incur-

239

ring his anger. Now, he's hurting other people and trying to bring the whole damn government down, as well." He gave Devin a bright smile. "So, what do you think about Angelique?"

"I think," said Devin, "that there is something inherently wrong about asking a sixteen-year-old woman to murder someone."

"And yet choosing her makes an odd sort of sense," Gaspard replied logically. "The only other person who might be able to go to Coreé without being recognized is Jules. And anyone would spot him as someone's bodyguard at a party and he would never be allowed near my father."

"Surely there are people that can be hired to do such things," Devin said.

Gaspard grinned. "None that I know personally but I'm sure that Jules or Marcus might know such people."

"Where is Marcus?" Devin asked.

Gaspard reached for the wine bottle on the table. "I believe he and Jules are in the study downstairs."

"That doesn't bode well," Devin remarked. "I wonder what plan they are hatching without us. I want to speak to Armand. Did he come up?"

"He followed me up the stairs. He's probably in his room. Shall I come with you?"

Devin stood up. "It's a personal matter. I'll be back in a few minutes."

Gaspard cheerfully poured a glass of wine. "Take your time. If you're not back by the time I finish this bottle, I may have to go find another. If I've passed out on the floor, please don't step on me if the candles are out."

Devin rolled his eyes. "I'll do my best."

The hallway was blessedly empty. He'd been afraid he

would run into Chastel or Madame Aucoin but all the bedroom doors were closed. He walked quietly down to Armand's door and knocked softly. When he heard no invitation to enter, he opened the door a crack to see Armand standing at the window staring out into the dark.

"Do you normally just walk into people's rooms without invitation?" Armand grumbled.

Devin slipped in and closed the door behind him. "I'm sorry to disturb you, Armand."

Armand turned slowly, his face weary. "It's been a disturbing night, Monsieur Roché." He limped to a chair and sat down stiffly. "Do you plan to make it more so?"

"I've been waiting to talk to you about the map and the route the soldiers seem to be taking," Devin began. "I couldn't tell anyone else why it's been troubling me."

Armand motioned to the other chair. "Sit down. I haven't the strength to come up with strategies tonight but obviously something must be done."

"You and I are the only two who realize what their destination must be," Devin said. "How can the two of us stand against a troop of government soldiers?"

"We can't," Armand said. "This isn't a war that can be won by force. We must reach Terre Sainté before they do. The records must be removed and safeguarded elsewhere."

"But they are already ahead of us," Devin pointed out.

"Then we need to move quickly."

"Chastel and the others are planning René Forneaux's assassination," Devin said. "Is this something you and I can accomplish alone?"

"Marcus won't let you go alone," Armand remarked. "Even if we set out tonight, he and my brother would find us and it would only call unwanted attention to our mission."

"So what are you proposing?" Devin asked warily.

"Tomorrow I plan to tell Marcus and my brother about the records."

"But you can't, Armand. You made me swear on my life not to tell anyone!"

"Believe me, I will make them swear not to reveal it either. The world has changed, Devin, in just this short bit of time. They are both honorable men. I know Chastel will go with me but I don't know if Marcus will allow you to go. There are too many troubles in this Empire and not enough men to fight them. The situation with René Forneaux must be resolved, too. If Marcus decides you are better off in Coreé or left here safely in hiding, then I must abide by his wishes."

"Marcus can be convinced, Armand, and if he can't I will go with you myself," Devin said.

"I cannot ask you to do that," Armand said. "This was never your fight. You became involved on a whim."

"It was never a whim, Armand," Devin insisted. "It was an attempt to reconcile the archival records with your Chronicles. If we can present the truth to Council, it could change everything."

"Devin, you will never have a chance to hear all the Chronicles, let alone learn them. You are two months into your journey and you have only learned Ombria's Chronicles. If the written Chronicles are destroyed, you have nothing." Armand threw his hands to his sides. "If the people of the provinces lose their history, we have nothing."

"Is there a chance that the soldiers don't know what they are searching for?" Devin asked.

"It's possible, but I think there is a chance they don't know where to hunt," Armand said. "Somehow they found out that the western coast is important but it is a large area to cover. If we can arrive ahead of them, we can hide the records."

"Where?"

Armand sat down wearily. "It would be ideal to bring them back here, but I don't know that we can."

Devin paced. "Why do you call the repository Terre Sainté?"

Armand shrugged. "It marks our beginnings. The oldest stories come from the provinces along the coast. It seemed appropriate to name the place where they were safeguarded for our mother country."

"Maybe the soldiers will think the stories are actually stored in Terre Sainté. No one has attempted to cross that sea and survived. The soldiers would be gone and we wouldn't have to worry about them anymore."

"More would follow, Devin. Initially I hoped they didn't know that the Chronicles existed in written form. But someone must have told them, or they found a repository under the floor of some Bardic Hall."

Devin thought of Shérif Picoté's and Adrian's ravaged bodies. If the murdered bards had been tortured before their deaths, it was understandable that they might have revealed information they had promised to keep secret. He didn't trust his own fortitude in such a situation.

"We have very little time," Armand murmured.

"Then we should leave tonight," Devin suggested. "I can get my things together."

Armand shook his head. "We need to speak to Marcus and Chastel first."

Devin stood up. "I'm sure they aren't asleep. Let me go and get them."

Armand grabbed his arm. "I cannot go tonight, Devin. I am too tired. It is hard to imagine, when you are young, what old age does to you. What I want to do and what I am able to do are two very different things. I can't leave on this trip without resting first."

"I'm sorry," Devin said. "I should have realized."

Armand looked at Devin. "Did my brother tell you I was a complete failure at shape-changing?"

"He only said that you and he needed more time together," Devin answered.

Armand laughed. "Always the diplomat. I'm sure your father could use your talents to shore up his government right now. Perhaps I'm wrong to try to involve you in saving these documents. What difference will they make, I wonder?"

"If all of the Master Bards were alive to keep retelling the stories, it really wouldn't matter, but already so many of you have been killed. Even you have lost your apprentice."

Armand's voice became sterner. "I believe you promised to hold that position until either you or I can train a replacement."

Devin turned to look at him. "Are Master Bards always men?" he asked.

"Always," Armand replied.

"Is there any way to contact the living Master Bards?" Devin asked.

"And tell them what?"

"Tell them," Devin said, "to train women as apprentices just for a few years. If these soldiers are looking for men who are Master Bards, they would overlook women entirely."

"There isn't time for that," Armand answered. "I'm not discounting your idea, because it might have had merit if we had started a few years ago. But once a Master Bard is established his identity is known. Whether a man or woman serves in that position, they would be vulnerable."

"Will we leave tomorrow?" Devin asked.

"Some of us will," Armand replied. "Now go to bed and let me rest. If you have never tried running with wolves through the forest, you cannot imagine how my knees hurt."

"I'm sorry," Devin said. "Is there something I can do to help you?"

Armand pointed at the door. "Leave! I find my mind works best while I am asleep. Sometimes our Holy Father sends me a resolution when I am completely still and cannot interrupt him. Hopefully, I'll have more to tell you in the morning. Now go! Just because you are young doesn't mean you don't need sleep, too."

Devin smiled. "Good night, Armand."

CHAPTER 34

Secrets

Devin almost expected Armand to have disappeared during the night, but when he entered the dining room, he heard Armand's cane tapping down the stairs behind him. Devin hadn't slept very much at all. He wanted desperately to go with Armand but he was concerned that Marcus would veto the trip. Something involving the Chronicles would not be high priority for Marcus.

Even Gaspard had come down on time to eat breakfast with them. Chastel greeted everyone, made appropriate complimentary comments about the food, and engaged Madame Aucoin in a discussion of the many varieties of wildflowers that covered the mountain range outside the window.

The rest of them, except for Gaspard, picked distractedly at their raspberry muffins, sausages, and eggs, anticipating the discussion that would come after breakfast. Everyone wondered who would be included in the team assigned to go to Coreé.

Only Devin and Armand knew a second team was also necessary, but their purpose could not be discussed with everyone else. Devin opened The Bishop's Book and leafed through it as he ate. His mother insisted it was bad manners to read at the table but even she had grown used to him having his nose in a book at meals. Somehow, he knew that his hostess would be lenient also.

Madame Aucoin laid her butter knife gently on her plate. "I want you to know, gentlemen, that I am aware that there are secrets being kept in this house. I know that some of them are impossible to share and I respect that, but allow me to make it clear that any dangerous mission you are intent on undertaking may not include my granddaughter without my permission."

The room was absolutely silent for a moment before Angelique exerted her independence. "*Grandmère*, I actually have a chance to avenge Papa's death and the deaths of everyone else in my family. If these good men see fit to allow me to accompany me, I want to go."

Chastel's silken voice exuded calm as his eyes met Devin's over the table. "I don't believe we have decided on a plan yet, ladies. Would you like to meet with us after breakfast to discuss it?"

"I would!" Angelique answered.

"We'll see," said Madame Aucoin.

Jules flushed an angry red. "You will not subject Angelique to harm. She has lived a hard enough life already. There is no need to put her life in danger when she is finally safe at last."

"And yet," said Gaspard, popping the last of a muffin into his mouth, "you and Angelique may be the best suited to carry out the work that needs to be done in Coreé."

"Are you referring to the death of a certain Council member?" Madame Aucoin asked.

"Yes, *madame*, I was," Gaspard replied.

Madame Aucoin raised her eyebrows. "You would send a girl to murder your father?"

"I would prefer not to, but the current circumstances call for desperate measures. No one but Angelique and Jules are able to get close to him without being recognized."

"*Grandmère*, maybe this is why I met these men. Maybe this is my chance to make a difference in this world," Angelique cried.

"Or maybe this will end your life before it has even started and our family will die out forever," Madame Aucoin said quietly. "Angelique, after all your father did to protect you, would you throw that away to become a murderer? Do you think that is what he would want? Will that become the Aucoin legacy?"

Chastel got up and closed the huge, arched dining room doors. "I see no reason to adjourn for our meeting. Since everyone seems to be involved," Chastel said smoothly, "let us define our goals and come up with a plan."

Devin looked at Armand who sat silently sipping his coffee. "There is another matter," Devin said. "One that has a bearing on …"

"Monsieur Roché," Armand said quietly, "we will discuss it later."

Devin stopped. So that was how it was to be. Armand intended to allow the business with Forneaux to take precedence. Whoever was left might be asked to help him, or perhaps he was just belligerent enough to try to save the records alone. And that, Devin decided, was something that he would never allow to happen. Wherever Armand went, he would follow him with or without Marcus's permission.

The discussion went on around Devin, a steady buzz from

which he only gathered a few words now and then. They talked about professional sharpshooters and Forneaux's security force, which had already become massive before Gaspard left Coreé. The conversation went around and around and always came back to Angelique and Jules. Tears ran down Madame Aucoin's face as she dabbed futilely at them with a handkerchief.

"Please don't ask her to do this," she murmured. "She is the only family I have."

Devin ran a hand across his forehead. "What if we wait?" he said. "What if we put a plan in place but we delay it until Forneaux does something that is publicly reckless?"

"Like having the Chancellor shot?" Marcus snapped. "God, Devin, what are you thinking?"

Devin took a deep breath before answering. "I am thinking that at the moment, most people know nothing about what Forneaux has done in the provinces. Right now they not only venerate Forneaux, but also empathize with him as a man who has lost his son and heir to 'savage' provincials.

"There is no one who can identify Angelique except Jules. No one will believe she is François Aucoin's youngest daughter, who supposedly died twelve years ago. If she murders Forneaux, people will assume that she, too, is a 'savage' provincial who dared to breach the security of Coreé. If Angelique isn't killed immediately, she will be tried and hanged for murder and Forneaux will become a martyr."

Devin's hand fell onto the cover of The Bishop's Book. "I don't believe this book came to us by chance. Maybe there is still something here that …"

Gaspard stood up angrily. "Forget the damn book, Dev!"

He yanked it out of Devin's hand and threw it over the table where it smashed against the wall behind Angelique. "How many nights have you wasted poring over that thing? You have found nothing – absolutely nothing!"

Devin stood up with the idea of retrieving the book but Gaspard grabbed him by the lapels of his jacket. "Do you realize how difficult this is for me? Planning the execution of my own father? Sure, I've tried to pretend it doesn't matter, but it does. How do you think I feel knowing his blood runs in my veins? Does that predict the kind of man I will become?"

Devin shook his head. "No, Gaspard, it doesn't. You aren't like him at all."

Gaspard tilted his head. "So I am not a liar or a thief? Come on, Dev, you know me better than anyone else does. Can you actually stand here and claim I have never been guilty of those crimes as long as you have known me?"

"It's not the same," Devin protested. "It's not the same, at all. Why are you so angry at me?"

"Everything can't be solved with words, Monsieur Roché!" Gaspard shouted, his cheeks flaming. "If it is necessary to kill my father, then by God, let's be done with it."

Devin gently removed Gaspard's hands from his jacket, hoping he would calm down. How completely out of character this meal had become. No personal matters were ever discussed at meals in upper-class families in Viénne.

No one said anything for a moment. Angelique stood up quietly and bent to pick up the book behind her. The spine was broken and half the cover was torn off. She brought it to Devin as though it was some fragile bird with a broken wing. She laid it in his hands, her fingers gently teasing a brown parchment from beneath its cover. "Devin," she

250

whispered, unfolding the parchment. "Look! This is a map. But I don't understand the language."

He laid the book on the table and carefully took the map from her hands. "It's in Latin," he said before reading it aloud. "For the Resettlement of Peasants in Danger in the Northern Provinces of Llisé."

Devin sat down abruptly. "My God, do you know what this is?" His eyes sought Armand's. "The people of Rameau weren't killed. The church relocated them through a series of tunnels to another village miles away. It's all here on the map. They saved every man, woman and child. They lived, Armand! They lived! And maybe the residents of Lac Dupré are alive, too! Maybe that's why there was no mass grave. Do you remember that the church door stood open when we went back in the morning and the floor was covered with leaves? People must have tracked them in as they escaped. The entrance to the tunnel was inside the church." He passed the map to Armand, his hands shaking. "This changes everything!"

"Perhaps I better ask for another pot of coffee," said Madame Aucoin.

CHAPTER 35

Hope

"Jeanette may still be alive!" Armand gasped, the lines in his face easing. He crossed himself and kissed the map. "My sweet Lord, this is all I have asked for."

Devin walked around the table to lean over Armand's shoulder. "The caves and tunnels crisscross this entire region. I wonder if Comte Aucoin's escape route was part of this older system.

"The people of Rameau disappeared years ago," Armand said. "Our Chronicles blamed the government for their mass murder."

"And our Archives claimed they died of disease," Devin murmured. "Each entity was trying to find an explanation for the disappearance of hundreds of men, women, and children and neither of us was right."

Chastel leaned an elbow on the table at Armand's side. "At some point the church stepped in to protect its people. Perhaps this time, Picoté and Adrian stayed behind to make certain everyone else was safe."

"And lost their own lives because of it," Marcus said.

"I didn't give Picoté enough credit," Devin remarked. "He truly did have the villagers' best interests at heart."

Gaspard grinned maliciously. "It was just you he hated, Dev."

Devin gestured. "Perhaps he had reason. I turned his quiet little village upside down and cost him his own life plus the lives of three of his residents."

"This is so different from what we have always learned," Jules said. "From the time we were children, we have been taught that the government was always the root of all evil." He glanced at Madame Aucoin. "Not the Aucoin family, *madame*, but even your servants fear those in charge in Coreé."

"With good reason," Angelique said. "Forneaux still killed my family."

Gaspard rested his head on his hand. "But he did not kill the villagers of Lac Dupré. At least, there are a few less lives to hold against him. Not that it matters. He still heads a group that intends to overthrow the Chancellor."

Chastel straightened up. "I was thinking about what you said earlier, Devin. With the information from this map we have even less to hold against Forneaux. Perhaps we should wait. If we make him a martyr, more people may flock to his cause. We may damage your father's position without meaning to."

"He needs to be punished!" Angelique interjected.

"Wouldn't it be better to gather the incriminating information we have against him and put him on trial for his crimes?" Devin asked calmly. "I know that you think that killing him yourself will allow you to avenge your father's death but I'm not sure that is right."

"Right for whom?" Angelique snapped. "You cannot know what I feel."

Madame Aucoin rose to fold Angelique in her arms. "He can imagine it, my darling. He is trying to protect you. Do not lower yourself to Forneaux's standards."

Angelique shook off her grandmother's attention. "I think I'll take a walk," she said.

Jules rose immediately. "And it will be my honor to attend you."

"Would you care for a third party?" Gaspard asked as he stood up. "You needn't watch your words with me."

Angelique reached out and took his hand.

After the three of them left Madame Aucoin stood up too, bringing the men to their feet. "I think there may be other things you wish to discuss. Please consider this room private until you finish. I will see that you are undisturbed. The servants will clear the table when you are finished."

Armand sat down first, his eyes going over the map as though within its folds lay the solution to all their problems. "Do you remember how the livestock was left wandering around after the villagers disappeared from Lac Dupré but the cats and dogs had vanished?" He tapped the map. "It makes sense, no? People took their pets with them. I can see Jeanette dragging that old scruffy orange cat with her, so he wouldn't come to any harm." His eyes filled with tears. "God bless Gaspard for throwing this book against the wall."

Chastel patted his brother's shoulder. "What is this other problem Devin spoke about?"

Armand visibly pulled himself together. "I ask you and Marcus not to share this information with anyone," he said, "for I have vowed to keep it secret under pain of death. It is imperative to tell someone now because we need help."

"We?" Chastel asked.

"Monsieur Roché already knows," Armand said. He folded the map and patted it gently with his hand. "The Master Bards of Llisé have been outwitting the government for a long time. First of all, each Master Bard teaches his apprentice how to read and write. Any additions to the Chronicles in a Master Bard's lifetime are recorded and placed under a stone in the floor of his Bardic Hall. It is a different stone in every hall and that information is passed on, too. When a Master Bard dies, the papers carrying any new stories are sewn into the new Master Bard's cloak. They are taken to a place we called Terre Sainté on the western coast of Llisé. Don't confuse it with the Terre Sainté that we sing about in the Chronicles. We named it that because it holds the history of our people from the very beginning. There is a complete record of all the Chronicles there – sort of like Monsieur Roché's Archives – only not so grand, I am sure. When Monsieur Roché looked at your map, he noticed that the places where villagers had vanished followed the line of the standing stones. We feel that Forneaux's men are traveling that way because they assume that the Terre Sainté we sing about is the same one where the records are stored."

"And yet this map indicates that those villagers may have been saved in advance by the church," Chastel pointed out. "They may never have been in danger at all."

"No, but the Master Bards and the records are in danger," Armand said. "If word came that soldiers were marching toward any individual town, the church may have taken steps to evacuate the people before they arrived. We need to stop Forneaux's men and relocate the records if they are ever to remain safe."

"How can we help?" Chastel asked.

"I'd like all of you to go with me. I hope there won't be fighting but we need help moving the records. I don't believe that Monsieur Roché and I will be able to do it without help."

"You and Devin?" Marcus asked, raising his eyebrows. "You would have taken the Chancellor's son, without asking me?"

"We would have left in the dead of night to evade you," Devin teased, "and changed our names and dyed our hair."

"This is serious," Marcus answered. "How can I justify our participation in this?"

"Because it uncovers another part of Forneaux's plot," Devin said.

"Devin, we aren't here to uncover nefarious plots," Marcus warned. "This isn't something your father requires of you."

"And yet no one is in a better position at the moment!" Devin said. "Some of the things we suspected of Forneaux aren't true but he is still trying to undermine my father's rule. If those records are destroyed we have no way of proving some of the awful things that have been done in the government's name."

Marcus sat glowering without saying a word.

Chastel pushed his chair back and folded his hands in his lap. "Perhaps this is one of those things that no one is ever prepared to do. It is thrust upon us and either we rise to the challenge or we spend the rest of our lives regretting our cowardice."

Devin tried to avoid smiling. Chastel's remark was perfect.

Marcus's chest puffed up. "I am charged with returning the Chancellor's son home alive. As much as I would like to help, that is my first responsibility and this new plan runs counter to my original orders."

Devin leaned forward. "Marcus, when I began learning the Chronicles, I became one of a brotherhood of bards. I owe them my allegiance, too. In this instance, I would be serving both my fellow bards and my father."

Marcus closed his eyes. "You could gild acorns and convince people that they fell from heaven! Don't try your rhetoric on me! No matter what you say, this seems in direct conflict with your father's orders and you will have a very difficult time convincing me to let you go."

"Would it make a difference if I told you that I intend to go with or without you?" Devin answered quietly.

Marcus bowed his head and ran both his hands through his hair. "I suspected as much all along."

"When should we leave?" Chastel asked cheerfully.

"Tonight or tomorrow at the latest," Armand said. "I suspect those villages have been evacuated in anticipation of Forneaux's men. They have several days' head start on us."

"What of Gaspard and the others?" Marcus asked.

"The larger the group, the greater the chance of being caught," Armand said. "Besides, I think Jules and Gaspard should have a plan in place to eliminate René Forneaux should our group fail."

"What do you mean by 'fail'?" Marcus growled.

Armand looked him straight in the eye. "We may all be killed, Marcus. That is a very real possibility."

Chastel grinned and raised his right hand. "I'm in. Who else is?"

Devin raised his hand, too. "I am."

Marcus raised his hand slowly. "Wherever Devin goes, I am bound to follow."

"You won't regret it," Devin said, excitement rising at this opportunity to do something meaningful instead of just waiting.

CHAPTER 36

Travelers

They left at dawn. Jules escorted them for the first few hours through a convoluted series of underground caves that, oddly enough, began in the wine cellar. The Aucoins seemed to have made the best use of terrain, just as the churches had.

"You surely don't bring Madame Aucoin to town this way," Devin asked, swiping at a cobweb stuck in his hair.

"No, I do not," Jules replied.

Devin expected some further explanation but Jules remained silent. At last they came out near the top of a cliff, where the cave had undercut the ground above. The ravine below them dropped hundreds of feet into a wide river.

"So are we going up or down?" Devin asked playfully.

Both Marcus and Jules scowled. "Up," Jules said. He climbed uphill, very nimbly skirting the opening of the cave as though he'd done it hundreds of times before.

Jules threw a rope down to Armand, who went up next. He tied it around his waist, as Jules pulled him up, his bad leg dragging painfully. Devin eschewed the rope when Jules threw it down to him. He placed his feet carefully, wary of his footholds before he put any weight on them. He reached the top almost as quickly as Jules had, which seemed to annoy Jules further. Marcus came up last.

Jules pointed to a small rise behind them. "Beyond that high spot there is a deer path. If you follow it downhill you will come to a road. Follow it west to Ceret. You should reach it by nightfall."

"I can take us from there," Marcus replied.

Jules inclined his head. "Good luck."

"Jules," Devin said. "Why did you pick the most arduous route to leave La Paix? I know you don't bring back supplies from the village this way."

"The secrets of the Aucoin family belong only to them," Jules replied obscurely.

Devin's jaw clenched. "Well, explain to me how we are supposed to retrieve Gaspard and the wolves when we are done? I personally couldn't navigate that system of caves again without your help."

"That was the whole idea," Jules said. When no one responded he reached into his pocket. "Here, I almost forgot." He handed Marcus a gold button with a falcon imprinted on it. "Present this at Madame Aucoin's house in town. Her servants will make you welcome and alert me that you are there."

"So we can climb down that cliff again?" asked Armand.

"We'll see," Jules replied. "Her house is number 31 on the Rue de St. James in Amiens. Don't write it down; just remember it."

With that he was gone, down over the side of the cliff so quickly that Devin thought he had fallen. Devin leaned over and saw only the edge of his sleeve disappear back into the maze of caves in the mountain below them.

They found the deer path easily. Worn deeply into the curve of the mountain, they followed it down to a narrow road below. It was deeply rutted by hand carts and oxen carrying heavier loads. Bordered by fragrant evergreens, the road always led them within the sound of water. Small streams ran into larger ones, tiny waterfalls trickled over mossy stones. Tangled tree roots gripped the mountain slopes, where blue and white wildflowers dotted the open spaces. Devin thought of the artificial fountains and regimented gardens at home and wondered whether living in Coreé would ever satisfy him in the future. He began to question his decision to work in the Archives, spending day after day without seeing sunlight or feeling wind against his face.

"I wonder how much time that little detour cost us?" Armand said angrily.

"More time than we could spare," Chastel replied, "but at least we're on our way now."

"Jules just wants us to know that he is in charge," Marcus said. "It will take more than our return of his precious Angelique to become his confidant."

"We hardly allowed him to become ours either," Devin reminded him. "First we announced that we had to leave on a mission that we could share with no one else in the household. And we left him with eight wolves and Gaspard!"

Devin jumped to the middle of the road to avoid a deep rut. "Do you think Gaspard is angry that we didn't take him with us?"

"He'll get over it!" Marcus growled.

"He thinks you don't trust him," Chastel whispered from behind him.

Devin dropped back to walk with him, leaving Marcus and Armand ahead of them. "That's what I'm afraid of."

"I'm joking," Chastel replied with a laugh. "Gaspard has realized from the beginning that there were things about the Chronicles that you couldn't share. Besides, this will give him some uninterrupted time with Angelique. I think he really cares for her."

"Gaspard has always cared for every girl that took his eye," Devin observed.

"Perhaps 'cared for' gives the wrong impression," Chastel answered.

"Well, love is too strong a word," Devin said. "Gaspard is reckless and selfish and Angelique is ..."

"Unstable?" Chastel asked.

"Frankly, yes."

"How could she be otherwise?" Chastel said. "I'm surprised she is still alive. Can you imagine the skills it took just for her to live?"

"I've been trying not to," Devin replied. "Unlike Gaspard's designs on her, when I first met her, I would have liked to take her home to my mother. After six boys she would be delighted to have a girl to fuss over."

Chastel batted at an overhanging branch. "Don't misjudge Gaspard. He's not quite the bad boy he seems."

Devin turned around and walked backwards, so he could face him. "You're telling me?" he said tapping his chest. "I can't even remember a time when he and I weren't friends. Part of his persona is an act; part of it's real. Even I can't tell the difference sometimes."

"Watch where you're walking!" Chastel warned.

Devin heard a squish and looked down at his boot. "Shit!"

"Horse shit," said Marcus.

"Thank you," Devin remarked, scraping his boot with a stick, "for your expert identification."

"Peasants don't own horses, Devin!" Marcus said, pushing him into the trees. "Get off the damn road! This is fresh and it means men on horseback are only a few miles ahead of us. They may be behind us, too."

All of them scuttled like beetles into the densely wooded area beyond the road. They stood, completely silent, and waited. Nothing disturbed the forest but the whisper of wind in the pines, the chatter of squirrels above their heads, and the sweet gurgle of a small stream that paralleled the road. The silence stretched on and on and finally Marcus waved them forward.

His voice was hushed. "From now on one of us needs to keep an eye on the road ahead and someone else needs to watch behind us."

"I'll walk backwards," Devin volunteered. "I've already wrecked my boots. There's no sense in anyone else doing the same."

Marcus leaned toward Devin's ear. "And no more talking. I want to hear what is coming toward us and what is traveling behind us. Is that clear?"

Devin silently gave him a mock salute. He may have been going to his death on this journey but somehow he felt elated, invincible and brave this morning, and he wasn't going to allow anyone to dampen his spirits.

They reached Ceret by dusk. It was a small desolate gathering of homes and shops. Candles burned in a few of the windows and music and laughter floated out of a tavern at the entrance to town.

"We don't dare go in together," Marcus said. "Those same horsemen we saw signs of earlier may have stopped here for the night."

"So which of us is the least recognizable?" Marcus asked.

"Not Armand," Devin said. "And probably not Chastel either."

"Well, don't think you are going!" Marcus snapped.

"Then I guess that leaves you," Devin answered. "Where shall we meet you?"

Marcus glanced around the small settlement. "Here is safe as anywhere. Go off the road and rest. I'll see what I can find out."

"Some food would be appreciated," Devin called after him.

Devin and Chastel helped Armand get settled. Devin unbuckled his pack and dropped it on the ground. He lay back, clasping his hands behind his head. It was amazing how comfortable pine needles could feel after a day of walking.

"I hope I can do this," Armand spoke into the dark. "So much depends on me and I am not sure I am capable of it anymore."

"You have help," Devin answered. "Have you thought, at all, about where we can move the records?"

Armand's voice sounded weary. "First, I thought of one of the churches but these caves seem endless, so maybe there is way to hide them there. After this is over, every Master Bard will need to be told that the location has changed. I don't see myself traipsing the Empire to inform everyone."

Devin took a deep breath. "Maybe I can do that. It was always my intention to visit every province."

"But your Archives ..." Armand protested.

"Maybe I can do both," Devin said.

"A man who tries to do two things well, succeeds at neither," Chastel said quietly. "We have all changed on this journey, Devin. Think hard about where your heart lies."

"My true heart is missing at the moment," Devin said, thinking of Jeanette.

"But safe," Armand murmured as he fell asleep. "Thank God, she's safe."

"God, I hope he is right," Chastel whispered when Armand began snoring rhythmically.

Devin thought of the small gray wolf. No one could have convinced him three months ago that a man could become a wolf and still have the ability to turn back into a man again. He simply prayed that Jeanette wasn't trapped inside a wolf's body with no idea how to get out.

Marcus was gone a very long time. Finally, Devin heard unsteady footsteps approaching. He sat up just as Marcus slumped down beside him, smelling of tobacco and beer. "We need to move farther from the road," he said. "There were horsemen asking about any strangers who might have passed through the village earlier. There were only two of them, Devin. It's a worry that we might be passing up help without knowing it. I would imagine your father will comb these provinces until he finds you or your body."

"That thought is both reassuring and disturbing," Devin replied.

"Where do you want us to move?" Chastel said. "The farther we are from town, the more danger we are in from wolves."

As though to punctuate his sentence, a single howl broke the silence followed by a chorus of others. "I never thought I would say this, but I miss your wolves," Devin said wistfully.

"It would have been impossible to travel through towns with them at our heels," Chastel pointed out. "Where shall we move, Marcus? Armand's sound asleep."

"There's a church at the other end of town," Marcus answered. "We'll walk quietly behind the tavern and the shops. The shops are all closed for the night. No one should see us or hear us."

"Unless they are looking for a group of strangers," Devin remarked ironically. He dropped a hand on Armand's shoulder. "Armand, we have to go somewhere safe for the night. Can you get up?"

Both Devin and Chastel helped pull him to his feet. "It's not far," Devin whispered.

They cut behind the tavern just as a back door opened. Each of them froze, sliding back around the corner and flattening themselves against the wall of the building. The contents of a bucket of wash water came flying through the doorway and splattered on the dirt. There was raucous laughter and joking about who could throw the water the farthest and a second bucket of water joined the first. When the third bucket preceded the water through the door, banging and rolling through the yard, someone, presumably in charge, yelled a string of expletives. The bucket was retrieved and the door slammed shut. They waited in the shadows for a few moments before crossing the wet ground directly behind the tavern.

The shops were indeed closed, but many of the shop-keepers lived above their places of business. Candlelight shone from two of the second-story windows. Armand was steadier on his feet now but occasionally his cane snapped a twig or stick. A dog began to bark in one shop and then another.

"Hurry," Marcus advised. "The church is only a little further away."

With that a dog raced around the side of one of the

buildings, snarling. "Go," Chastel said. Marcus hustled Armand away but Devin turned for an instant to watch. There was no transformation as he had hoped but Chastel simply stood and faced the hound. The dog took one look at his face in the light of the waning moon and whirled around and ran whining back to the house. Chastel raced to catch up with the rest of them.

The church was situated at the edge of town. It was a simple stone structure that had seen better days. Ivy covered most of the walls and Devin suspected its sturdy vines played a large part in holding the old building together. The church backed against the evergreens of the forest. In front, a forlorn cemetery sheltered the scattered graves of village loved ones, the stones tilting in the moonlight. A few scattered leaves blew across the stone steps as they crept up to the front door. Marcus tried the front door and it was open. Devin gave a sigh of relief. Breaking into a church seemed wrong on so many levels.

CHAPTER 37

Hallowed Walls

Marcus closed the door quietly behind them and they had a moment to look around. The old stone walls seemed to emanate peace. The waning moon gave enough light through the tall windows to see the layout of the sanctuary. The pews were simple pine benches with low backs. The sanctuary was ancient but it smelled cared for. There were whiffs of beeswax and the floor had been recently scrubbed.

Marcus circled the walls looking for additional doors or rooms where the priest might be living. He finally returned to them. "Everything seems safe and even those confounded dogs have quieted down. I suggest you sleep while you can."

The floor was stone so Devin took one of the pews on the side toward the center aisle. He bunched up the pack he was carrying and buttoned his jacket. "It's cool for June," he observed.

"That's because it's the end of July," Marcus said. "Next week it will be August. August evenings are cold in the mountains. By September there will be snow. We need to conduct our business and return to Madame Aucoin's."

"July?" Devin asked. "How could I possibly have lost so much time?"

Armand was sitting on the pew in front of Devin. "Time takes on its own dimension when you are running for your life. Be grateful that we have somewhere safe to return to."

"I am," Devin said. Arranging his backpack for a pillow, he lay down. "Armand, is it possible that La Paix might be a good place to store your records?"

"It would be a matter of housing the chickens in a fox's den. The purpose of recording the Chronicles was to keep them safe from the rich, the Councilmen's families ..."

Devin interrupted him. "People like me."

Armand nodded. "In any normal situation, yes, but you've proven your honesty and trustworthiness."

"And Madame Aucoin hasn't?" Devin asked.

"Not yet," Armand answered. "I didn't tell her where we were going. I'd rather she didn't know. She hasn't been exactly forthcoming about some of her own secrets. Believe me, it just wouldn't work." Lifting his bad leg, he lay back on the bench. "I am not one to talk. I have already broken so many rules that I swore to uphold as a Master Bard. I guess I am the one who is unreliable."

"Go to sleep," Chastel instructed. "Thank heavens tomorrow is Thursday and there shouldn't be a morning service to worry about."

Everyone settled down but Devin couldn't sleep. His hand slipped into his pocket and pulled out his rosary. He fingered the tiny second cross he had attached to it. Maybe it was the archivist in him but last night before he went to bed, he decided to mend The Bishop's Book. He had meant what he said when he told Angelique that it hurt him physically to see a book in such poor condition. He went downstairs and borrowed some glue and wood from Jules to mend the battered binding.

He cut a piece of thin wood the thickness of heavy paper to firm up the spine itself. When he tried to slide it into place he kept hitting something at the bottom. He turned the book upside down and out tumbled a number of tiny, thin crosses hidden away in the spine of the book. They were metal and almost paper thin. He considered putting them back where he found them but something made him hesitate. He took one and used a wire to attach it next to the crucifix on his rosary. At a glance it was barely noticeable. If he was searched he prayed that no one would take a second look at his stone rosary with two battered crosses. He took the handful of other crosses and carefully put them back in their hiding place. By shortening the piece of wood for the spine, the crosses were accommodated and no one was the wiser. Last he straightened the end papers, gluing and smoothing them over the inside of the old cover. He piled several other books on top of the Bible to weigh it down while the glue dried.

Devin closed his eyes, falling into a series of brief and violent dreams of capture and torture. He woke sweating and then shivering in the cold sanctuary. Just as he began to fall asleep again, he felt someone lay a hand on his head. He made no attempt to turn and see who it was. The sensation was warm and comforting. He felt safe and loved for the first time in months. It was like coming home, but better somehow, and he hoped he would always remember the sensation.

He wakened to the smell of coffee and sat up so quickly that his backpack went crashing onto the floor. A kindly priest stood in front of them, a pot of coffee in one hand

and a plate of some kind of sliced sweet bread in the other. "Please, please," he apologized. "I'm so sorry to have wakened you. You see, the funeral committee meets here at nine o'clock and I didn't want them to come in and find you."

"We'll leave immediately," Marcus said, coming to his feet.

"But you don't want to be seen?" the priest asked.

"That would be preferable," Marcus said.

Devin's hand touched the little cross on his rosary and something made him take it out and hold it where the priest could see it.

"Oh, I see," he said, his rounded face suddenly very sober. "Come with me right away and make sure you haven't left anything here that might indicate that you spent the night."

They gathered their supplies quickly and followed him behind the altar. He rolled up an ornamental rug and exposed the floor, paved with large flagstones. "It's this one," he said hurriedly, scuffing his foot against the one he had indicated. "Are you able to pry it up? It's so heavy, I can't lift it alone anymore."

Devin and Marcus upended the stone, revealing a staircase that curved down under the sanctuary. "There are lanterns along the way," the priest instructed. He lifted one of the candles from the altar and handed it to Devin. Chastel retrieved the first lantern and lighted it, just as the sound of voices could be heard outside.

"We have some questions ..." Devin began.

"I will be glad to answer them later," the priest replied. "Please go now."

They slipped down the staircase and Chastel and Marcus fitted the stone back into place, just as a surprisingly cheerful funeral committee entered the sanctuary, happy to partake

271

of the priest's baked goods and coffee. They heard the rug go down with a flop, hiding their refuge.

Marcus herded them back further in the tunnels where their voices couldn't be easily overheard. He grabbed Devin's arm roughly. "What, in the name of God, did you just do?"

Devin held the rosary out to him. "I found about a dozen of these tiny crosses inside the spine of The Bishop's Book when I went to mend it. I wondered if they were a token of safe passage into the tunnels, so I wired one to my rosary. For this system to work, priests had to be able to identify people in need of sanctuary. I imagine each priest had a few crosses because surely every church isn't connected directly to the tunnel system."

"You might have told me first," Marcus blustered. "That was a dangerous thing to do. You had no idea what that signified."

"As I said, I found it hidden inside The Bishop's Book. It had to be connected to the map. It's a cross," Devin pointed out. "What possible difficulty could it cause?"

"It cost our dear Savior his life, Devin," Armand said. "Marcus just wants you to be vigilant."

"The system makes sense though," Chastel said. "As you said, every church can't be connected by the tunnels."

"Although keep in mind," Devin said, "often the church is the first building when a new community springs up. Perhaps that was all part of a master plan. It's scary when you think about it. For centuries there has been this shadow government and for just as long the church has been protecting its people from it. It's difficult to believe that the church has been battling evil that the rest of us never knew existed. While I love the Archives, it makes me question everything they contain."

"A few days ago you were advocating their methodical preservation of the truth," Armand reminded him.

"That's the thing," Devin said in frustration. "Whose truth is it? My father noticed the errors around the same time I did."

Chastel sat down on a rock. "It's quite feat to keep a clandestine organization intact for hundreds of years without the Chancellors being aware of it."

"Perhaps some Chancellors were a part it," Marcus said. "Others were elected because of their ability to be swayed by their counselors and others took office because of their popularity with the people."

"How much does my father know, Marcus? Does he have good people to advise him or is he surrounded by advocates from this other organization?" Devin asked.

Marcus shook his head. "I can't tell you, Devin. As far as I know it is something that he has only become aware of in the last year. I believe he only shared that with you and me. He has your brothers' confidence, but he may not have felt he could tell them until he had proof."

"Proof which we were to find," Devin said. "Now I can't even get a message to him safely and he thinks I'm dead. Who are these people? What do they want?"

"Power," Chastel remarked calmly. "The status quo – they intend to keep the provincials ignorant and voiceless and make money on the backs of the poor."

"That's all?" Devin replied.

Chastel raised his voice. "That is the whole structure of Llisé! Those with power and money make all the decisions and those who do the work have no voice. It's no little thing, Devin. Some men have a great deal to lose should the system ever change."

"And thousands have a great deal to gain," Devin said. "But if this system has roots that are hundreds of years old, how do we kill it or at least stop it from poisoning all the generations to come?"

Chastel shrugged. "I don't know. You know my views on politics. I try to remain friends with everyone and keep my mouth shut. Why do you think I don't have a house in Coreé?"

"But you'll help us?" Devin asked.

Chastel glanced at Armand and Marcus. He bowed to Devin with an extravagant flourish. "I would say I am deeply committed to your cause, Monsieur Roché."

CHAPTER 38

Honor Among Thieves

It was another hour before they heard someone knock on the stone above. Marcus and Chastel raised the stone, half afraid that they might be faced by soldiers, but it was only the little priest. They scrambled out, brushing dirt from their feet for fear of marring the floor.

"I didn't even ask your name," Devin said, holding out his hand in greeting.

"Father Michael," the priest said.

Marcus interceded quickly. "You'll forgive us if we don't share ours."

"Of course," Father Michael said. "We don't ask questions but I understand that you may have some. Where do you need to go? Do you have a destination in mind or should I choose one?"

"To Tirolien," Armand answered, "as close to Calais as possible."

Father Michael shook his head. "That's a long way. The tunnels could take you the entire way but I don't recommend it. The directions would be complicated and if you take a wrong turn you could very easily become lost. I don't have anyone to send with you. It would actually be shorter above ground."

Devin nodded. He hadn't expected to reach their destination underground but at least now he knew how the system worked and how someone could escape. Father Michael was already giving them directions to make their way overland but he also suggested that the Church of St. Bastian in Calais would be able to direct them into the tunnels again should they decide to come back.

"Thank you for your help," Devin said, slipping a donation in the Poor Box.

"I cannot let you leave without food," protested the priest. He handed them the remains of the sweet bread and some sort of very long preserved sausage. Marcus clasped it to him like an old friend. "If you leave on the far side of the church and go into the woods, no one will see you," he advised. "You can parallel the road from there."

They left silently like thieves, drifting into the forest like lingering mist, and were gone. Marcus wouldn't allow them to eat until they were several miles away from Ceret, despite Armand's moaning about being hungry. At last, close to noon they found a small clearing with a stream and sat down to eat.

"Fresh water is a bonus," Devin pointed.

Chastel pulled a bottle from inside his jacket. "Wine is better!"

"Where did you get that?" Devin hissed.

"There were lots of them at the church," Chastel remarked. "They won't miss one."

"That's communion wine!" Devin snapped. "What sort of men will Father Michael think we are?"

"Thirsty men," Chastel replied, pulling the cork.

"Let it go," Marcus advised Devin. "We can't take it back now."

"It's stealing," Devin said, "and from a church, no less. What does that say about us?"

"It says nothing about us," Armand replied, "only Chastel, and he doesn't seem to care."

"You are absolutely right!" Chastel replied, taking a swig from the bottle. "Any of you sinners are welcome to share with me."

When Devin glared at him, Chastel laughed. "For God's sake, Devin, I didn't steal it! I asked Father Michael if I could buy one and he simply said to make a donation to the Poor Box. I thought you knew me better than that. It was a joke!"

"Well, why didn't you just say so?" Devin said irritably. "I thought on this trip I wouldn't have to deal with Gaspard's antics, but it seems you are just as bad."

"Why don't I teach you an Arcadian story while we're eating?" Armand suggested quietly.

Devin sat down beside him. "I'd like that. I've been thinking about the Master Bard of Tirolien. Does he have an apprentice?"

"He did have," Armand answered. "He has been with him two years now but I've heard he's young, skittish as a colt. He'll be no help to Dariel Moreau if there is trouble. He'd be the first one to run."

"Then I pray we reach Dariel before they do," Devin said.

"As do I," Armand answered. He sat back, touching his fingers together and then drawing them apart as though he planned to pull magic out of thin air. And then suddenly he did. There were lavender flowers in both of Armand's hands where there had been nothing before. The flowers grew wild and profusely in sunny patches, clinging to the rocky ground with tenacious wiry roots.

"How did you do that?" Devin gasped.

Armand looked exceptionally pleased with his sleight of hand. "Ah, it is my job to teach you Arcadia's Chronicle, not magic, Monsieur Roché. That, you will have to learn for yourself." He smiled a self-satisfied smile and began.

"My story concerns a little girl named Lavender. Her mother had passed away when she was just a child and her father, who was a rich man, showed his affection for her by providing her with everything she could possibly want.

"One night after dinner as they sat by the fire together, Lavender said, 'Oh Father, someday I would love to have a pony so I could ride through the mountains with you.'

"Her father stroked his beard, pleased that she wanted to spend even more time with him and asked her what color pony she would like. Lavender snuggled against his chest and said, 'I want a pony that is as white as the mountain mist.'

"So, on her eighth birthday her father bought her a beautiful white pony with a long curling tail and mane. Lavender called the pony Mist and she rode him everywhere. One night there was a terrible storm and Mist was left out in the pasture by an inexperienced stable boy. Terrified by the lightning and thunder, Mist jumped the fence and ran away. Lavender looked for him everywhere. She walked for miles through the mountains searching for any sign of him. Occasionally, she would catch sight of his beautiful tail or glimpse his glorious white mane.

"Finally her father offered to buy her another pony but Lavender didn't want it. Even as a young woman she roamed the mountains, still looking for her beautiful white pony. And that is why these beautiful flowers are called Lavender. They cover the mountain slopes, marking Lavender's footprints where she searched for her pony and in the early morning, you can see the wisps of Mist's tail rising in the fog in the mountain valleys."

Armand paused, gauging the effect it had on Devin. "Some bards add that Lavender died slipping into a mountain ravine, but I don't."

Devin said, "I didn't know that we were granted any leeway in how these stories conclude."

Armand shrugged. "For some reason latitude is common in the Arcadian Chronicle – I have no idea why. There are even a few stories that are basically unfinished, allowing the audience to choose the ending. Some bards tell one of those stories at the end of their performance to hold the audience in place well after the presentation's assigned time to conclude. They love hearing the listeners debate all of the possibilities and choose an ending."

"Well, I'm glad you didn't kill Lavender off at the end of the story," Devin said. "When I tell it, I will repeat it exactly like yours. There are too many stories that end in gloom and doom. We don't need another one."

"As a bard you have the right to end this story where I did or you may continue and finish it at a more morbid point," Armand said with smile. "But keep in mind that many of these people have very little experience with happy endings. Their lives are hard: they die young, their babies die at birth, their mothers die in childbirth, and often fathers die trying to protect their families from wolves or God

279

knows what else. A story that ends badly is no more than they have come to expect."

"Still, there is something to be said for hope," Devin remarked. "I think it would be good to end your tales with a story that promised peace and something better to come."

"In most cases, you'd have to make it up," Armand said. "Is that allowed?"

"If you make it quite clear from the beginning that this is a story you have created yourself to share with them. It may or may not be well received. You would have to judge the audience. People gather to hear the Chronicle because not only is it their history but it is cathartic. It gives them an acceptable place to cry for all the losses they have experienced in their lives and it gives them strength to go on the next day."

Devin thought of Armand's grandmother and her tears over the story about the two small girls killed by wolves. "That is so sad," he murmured.

"That's life in the provinces, Monsieur Roché. Why should a bard leave people hoping for something that may never come true?"

As if they had signaled that they were finished, Marcus stood up and had them pack up their things. Chastel placed the empty wine bottle strategically under a tree with a grin. Perhaps this was the side of himself that he showed to Gaspard. If so, Devin could see why they got along so well.

They tramped through the forest, occasionally rejoining the road when they needed to cross a bridge. The weather was glorious, sunny during the day and cool and clear at night. Devin thought of his original itinerary and how foolish it was of him to think he could visit a province a month and still have time to travel and learn their Chronicles.

Madame Aucoin had packed food for them – things that would travel well like apples, cheese, and hard crusty bread. They hoarded it, setting it aside for times when they were unable to pick up food along the way.

Armand seemed to grow stronger with the constant walking each day. He was limping less and he seemed much happier than he had been since Jeanette disappeared. No doubt, the map they'd found in The Bishop's Book had given him hope, which was exactly the point Devin had tried to make with Armand about his storytelling. A story that ended in hope could turn someone's life around.

They stopped one night by a standing stone. Its solidity made Devin feel safe, almost as though the stone itself provided protection to anyone within its sphere. They had stayed back from the road far enough that Marcus allowed them to build a small fire for the two rabbits that Chastel graciously caught. It was already dark by the time the rabbits were skinned and placed on a spit. Soon the smell of roasting meat made their mouths water and Devin sliced bread to use to soak up the meat juices. Chastel walked down to the stream for fresh water.

Devin and Armand sat together, the warmth and glow of the flames splashing across their faces and on the brush that surrounded them. It was almost as though they had created a small sanctuary in the center of the woods and Devin thought it would be hard to move on in the morning.

The first hint of trouble was a gentle rustle in the bushes behind him and Devin turned to see two bright eyes glowing in the brush. He didn't move or look away but he called out quietly to Marcus. "There is an animal behind me."

Marcus pulled his pistol as a low growl sounded from Devin's side of the encampment. A flying mass of teeth and fur leaped at Devin. Marcus fired but missed and Devin went down, struggling with a huge wolf that seemed intent on ripping his throat out. He planted a hand deep in the fur on each side of the wolf's neck, and locked his elbows, hoping to hold it off.

He wasn't certain what happened next. A second wolf hit the first one from the side, rolling it off Devin and close to where the fire burned brightly. The first wolf yelped and howled but the second wolf wrestled with it, rolling it ever closer to the fire until the animal screamed in pain. Then he let it go and it raced off into the brush.

Devin stood up and turned to face the wolf that had saved him. "Thank God, Chastel," he said shakily.

Marcus stood staring, his pistol still on target as though unsure of whether he could trust their rescuer, just as Chastel arrived running. He stopped dead at the campsite, his eyes going from Devin to the wolf. He assessed the scene quickly. Just as Devin realized that Armand was the only one missing, Chastel dropped to his knees in front of the wolf.

"Armand?" he said quietly. "It's all right. The danger's over."

Chastel walked toward him slowly, picking up Armand's scattered clothes and taking them into the bushes. He talked, constantly coaxing Armand to follow. At last, he did. His grey tail disappeared into the brush as Chastel continued to encourage him.

Devin slumped down on the ground, his breath ragged. Marcus crossed on the opposite side of the fire and stood beside him, the pistol still drawn. "It wasn't ... it wasn't Chastel," Devin stuttered.

"Apparently not," Marcus said, his eyes on the bushes. "Are you hurt?"

"No," Devin answered. "I don't think so, but I would have been dead if it hadn't been for ..." He stopped short as Chastel emerged from the bushes with Armand at his side.

"Are you all right, Devin?" Chastel asked.

"Yes," Devin said. "I don't know quite what to say except thank you, Armand."

Armand had an elated expression on his face that turned into a huge grin. "I did it, Chastel! I did it! I never even thought about it! It just happened. I saw Monsieur Roché go down and I was a wolf – all teeth and claws – and I knocked the other wolf off and rolled him close to the fire. I believe I even singed a few of his hairs!"

Chastel seemed more subdued. "I'm glad you were able to shape-change, brother, but just remember that when you are a wolf, you become one with them. Don't put yourself in a position where you are fighting your own kind."

"Monsieur Roché is my own kind!" Armand blustered. "My God, what do you mean? That I should have become a wolf and participated in the killing of my friend?"

In a calm, soothing voice Chastel continued: "Not at all, Armand. Sit down, please, while I explain."

Armand lowered himself to the ground near Devin, his face still flushed with exhilaration. He had no apparent pain or stiffness because of his leg.

"Perhaps I've studied wolves more than the rest of my family," Chastel began, his voice always diplomatic. "I've discovered that you have to operate within certain constraints when you become a wolf. You want to be one of them – not a threat to them. In this case, you could have made it known that Devin was your property. The other wolf would probably have backed down."

283

"Frankly," Devin said, his voice still shaking, "there wasn't time, Chastel. I was on the ground with the wolf on top of me. If Armand hadn't acted when he did, I'd be dead right now. Marcus couldn't get a clear shot without hitting me."

"I wasn't certain how events had transpired," Chastel answered.

"He's right," Marcus concurred. "With them both twisting and turning, I was afraid to take a shot. I think Armand took the only option that he could."

Chastel nodded and gave him a guarded smile. "You are to be congratulated then. You saved our Chancellor's son's life."

"To be honest," Armand said, avoiding Devin's eyes, "my only thought was that if we find my darling Jeanette, how could I ever tell her that I allowed the man she loved to be killed by wolves and I did nothing to stop it?"

Devin swallowed. He had expected to have to fight Armand every step of the way if he ever tried to marry Jeanette. He had made a point of not talking about her where Armand could hear, because there was no reason to antagonize him further. How unexpected it was to find out that Armand had apparently come to accept their relationship. Perhaps Devin had nothing more to anticipate at this point but the usual mild animosity between father and son-in-law. He just prayed that Jeanette was still alive and safe.

"Thank you, Armand," Devin said. "I would never have been able to do the same for you."

Armand placed a hand on his knee. "Each of us has our talents. Believe me, my friend, that would be a terrible way to die. I'm glad you're all right." He seemed calmer now, less on the defensive, and he turned to Chastel. "Tell me more about this wolf. Will he come back tonight?"

Chastel settled himself by the fire. "I don't really know a great deal about him. He was obviously hunting alone tonight – not with a pack. He had no other wolf to come to his aid. And believe it or not, he wouldn't have attacked anyone if he'd had clear access to the meat. Devin happened to be between him and a meal and he attacked him to eliminate the competition."

Devin gave a shaky laugh. "I would have shared."

CHAPTER 39

Calais

On the fourth day, they crossed the border into Tirolien. Armand described it as a long skinny province with its head in the mountains and its feet in the sea. The terrain changed into soft, green foothills and even at two days' distance they could smell the salty wind off the sea.

In the past few days, they had fallen into an easy pattern. At first, Armand lagged behind the others but his first change into a wolf brought about another transformation, as well. He seemed more self-assured, his steps were faster and steadier. Even though he'd had to leave his cloak behind at La Paix, it was as though it still swirled around his shoulders, a badge of honor that had become part of his very being. Once again he was Ombria's Master Bard!

The ground sloped gently downward. It was easy walking and they made good time with the sun warming their backs in the morning and the fresh sea wind in their faces. They still tried to avoid the main road as they neared Calais but it became more and more difficult. At least, wolves seemed to no longer be a problem.

"Where will we stay once we reach Calais?" Devin asked, since sleeping beside the road was not an option anymore.

"At the Bardic Hall," Armand answered. "I haven't seen Moreau for several years but I know we will be welcome there."

Marcus shifted his pack, extracting a knife to conceal in his belt. "Calais is a seaport. It's likely to be crawling with soldiers. From what you've told me, we need to get this friend of yours out of the Hall and somewhere safe. I don't think staying at the Hall is an option."

Armand had been silent about his plans once they found Dariel Moreau. "Can we take him back to La Paix?" Devin asked. "Surely, he would be safe there."

Chastel shook his head. "We can hardly ask that of Madame Aucoin. She is concerned with security herself. How can we allow her home to become a camp for refugees?"

"It would be interesting though," Devin said. "Can you imagine all the Master Bards gathered in one place? I would love to have the opportunity to study their various styles and the way their personalities affect their storytelling. It would be a wonderful experience!"

"One I doubt you'll ever have in this current political climate," Chastel said soberly. "A gathering like that requires a peaceful atmosphere and a government that equates storytelling and oral history with the arts."

"Apples, gentlemen?" a woman called from the side of the road. She had a basket of green summer apples hanging from her elbow. She stepped forward rubbing an apple vigorously on her tattered striped skirt and then on her dirty sleeve. She held it out to Devin. "They were picked today."

"No, thank you," Devin responded but she scampered

into the road in front of him, her large breasts almost slipping the confines of her low-cut dress. "First of the season, sir," she said, ignoring his refusal.

"No, thank you," Devin said again.

"No, thank you, says he!" she taunted, hoping someone would listen. "Does he have babes to feed? A husband who can't find work?"

Devin sighed and slid his hand in his pocket, looking for coins.

"Don't!" Marcus warned, firmly grabbing Devin's arm and pulling him along.

"You don't care, do you? None of you care for the likes of me and my wee babes!" the woman yelled after them. Her well-thrown apple cracked Devin in the back of the head.

Marcus spun around, snatched the blade from his belt and held it at her throat. "You, my lady," he said in a voice like steel. "Go home for the day or I will take you to the *shérif* myself."

"You can't tell me what to do!" she whined. "A poor girl has to make her money."

"Go, now!" Marcus said. "Or you will be sorry you got up this morning."

The woman brushed at her dirty skirts as though contact with Marcus had made her feel filthy and paraded down an alley to the left without another word.

"Welcome to Calais," Armand said, "the City by the Sea!"

"The City of Sluts," Chastel remarked coolly. "I've never seen a city with more prostitutes."

"She wasn't a prostitute," Devin protested. "She was selling food to feed her family."

"Couldn't you smell the alcohol on her breath and see

the flask stuffed in her apron pocket?" Marcus instructed Devin. "She wasn't trying to make money to feed her children; she wanted to buy another bottle for herself. If we are hailed by a vendor again, man or woman, keep your eyes straight ahead and don't speak."

Devin rubbed the knot on his head from the flying apple. "I'm sorry. I had no idea. Why did you say you would take her to the *shérif*, Marcus? We can't afford to run into any of the *militaire* today."

"She wasn't about to push it to that extent," Chastel said. "She hoped to shame you into giving her money. I'm sure she has been in and out of jail many times before and may be again before nightfall."

"And, if by any chance she was stationed here to be on the lookout for us, my threat to take her to the *shérif* hopefully would have convinced her that we were not who she was looking for," Marcus added.

"This is a seaport town and the docks will be watched in case you might be trying to catch a ship back home to Coreé, Devin," Armand said. "Let's find the Bardic Hall as quickly as possible and get out of here."

"Would it have been better to come at night?" Devin asked.

"Thieves and wanted men use the night to shelter them. Ordinary men who have nothing to hide travel by day," Chastel commented cheerfully. "Try to look ordinary, Monsieur Roché, to avoid having any more fruits or vegetables thrown at you."

"Little Calais is over there," Armand said, pointing to a cluster of houses clinging to the side of a hill. At its center, but above the level of the houses, stood a rather impressive-looking stone building, not unlike a church. "It's quite a climb through a warren of back streets but the Hall is really extraordinary."

"Let's get on with it," Chastel murmured. "None of us is getting any younger."

They wound their way up the hill under Armand's impressive guidance. Devin realized Armand had a wonderful memory not only for storytelling but for directions as well. There was no hesitation in his steps, no fear that they might have taken the wrong one of dozens of alleys and streets. By late afternoon, they stood high above Calais, the sea wind blowing their damp hair from their foreheads. The view here was unrestricted, providing a breathtaking view of the ocean stretching to the horizon.

"Pick up the pace, Monsieur Roché," Armand urged. "There's no time to admire the view."

The Bardic Hall faced the sea, its stone walls well cared for, the stone steps scrubbed clean. Bright flowers bloomed in window boxes with ivy dangling down. But the area around the Hall was deserted. No vendors sold their wares, no children played in the streets. Devin had an empty feeling in the pit of his stomach that had nothing to do with not having eaten since this morning. Armand walked up to the front door and rang the bell. He waited and rang twice more but no one answered it.

"Perhaps I should go in first," Armand suggested. "He knows me."

"Marcus, something is very wrong," Devin murmured to his bodyguard.

"Since when have you gone all psychic on me?" Marcus demanded, his eyes on Armand.

"I just have a bad feeling about this. Let me go in with him," Devin insisted.

Marcus nodded. "We'll all go. Although, you know this may be a trap."

Armand went straight to the kitchen but Devin smelled blood as soon as he entered the front hall. He turned the knob on the door to the left and entered the performance hall. Two men lay motionless on the floor.

"God," Devin murmured. He stepped back only to bump into Marcus' reassuring bulk. He'd seen enough to know that both men were dead. He didn't want to know the details. Armand came in the door behind them. He made a short pained noise and then pulled Devin against him to walk over and examine the bodies.

Moreau had been beaten. His apprentice lay dead from a single knife wound to the chest, his arms spread wide on the floor, as though he had toppled over backwards in surprise. Moreau had curled into a pathetic ball, trying to shield his vital organs from the blows of his assailants. Armand gently turned him on his back, uncovering Moreau's left hand clenched beneath him.

Devin dropped to his knees beside him and gingerly opened Moreau's fingers, uncovering the familiar symbol from the monoliths. "Armand," he said softly. "He drew the symbol for Terre Sainté on his palm in his own blood."

Armand collapsed, bending forward at the waist, his forehead bowed against Moreau's chest, and sobbed. No one spoke for a moment, allowing him his moment of grief.

Finally, Marcus broke the silence. "We need to leave, Armand. If these bodies haven't already been discovered then they will be soon. The last thing we need is to be arrested for murder."

Armand straightened, his face wet with tears. "May I borrow your knife, Marcus?"

Marcus handed it over and Armand counted flagstones in the floor from the left wall of the performance hall to where they met the stage. He shoved the blade of the knife downward, loosening a stone and tipping it up on one side. Chastel went to help him, gripping the stone and pulling it up and out on to the floor. Armand reached reverent fingers down to lift the papers out that lay inside. But he had no cloak in which to conceal them and handed them to Devin, who stuffed them hastily into the front of his jacket. Chastel checked the area beneath the stone and slid it back into place.

Devin walked across the floor several times, shifting dust with his boots into the perimeter around the stone. Marcus stepped forward and gently rearranged Moreau as they had found him on the performance hall floor. Spitting on his wadded-up handkerchief, Devin wiped the bloody sign of Terre Sainté off Moreau's hand. They started to leave when they heard voices outside.

"In here," Armand whispered. He grabbed Devin and yanked him toward the fireplace, motioning everyone else to follow them. He bent and fumbled near the hearth until it swung up suddenly like a door. "Jump," Armand said, shoving Devin down into the darkness first.

Devin landed on his feet in a space just large enough for two or three people to stand. He flattened himself against the back wall as Chastel and Armand followed. Marcus jumped down last, helping Armand to latch the hearth back in place. They were packed together so tightly, Devin doubted that any of them could turn around or sit down.

The place was dark, musty, and smelled of centuries of old wood smoke that had seeped into the very stone of the building. Devin smothered a cough against his shoulder. He could see nothing except for a tiny sliver of light marking the rectangle where the hearth had slipped back into place.

Above them, some women came into the room. Their cheerful conversation turned suddenly to gasping and weeping. Their grief was almost palpable. They didn't seem to think of calling the authorities – or perhaps they did, but those trapped below them had no way of knowing that. Their sobbing wore on and on until Devin felt like joining them.

Devin felt for the wall behind him, trying to give Marcus more room. He wanted to sit down in the dirt or ashes or whatever lay on the floor but there was absolutely no space to move around. The wall was rough stone, much like the exterior of the building. Had Armand had a safe hole like this in his performance hall? Was every Bardic Hall built with one? Just how much had Armand shared with Devin and how much had he kept hidden?

There is so much death, Devin thought. Moreau had done nothing but share in spreading the history of his people and now he was dead – not only dead but beaten as well. Was this Gaspard's father's work? Or was someone else behind it? Armand was one of the few northern bards left alive and Devin wondered how long they could keep him that way!

CHAPTER 40

Hidden

The afternoon dragged. The room above them seemed always full of people; a steady procession of feet walked the scene of Moreau's murder. Devin had a sobering thought. Perhaps they would lay Moreau out in the performance hall where he died. God, it was even possible that the funeral might be held there to accommodate the number of people that would want to show their respect for him.

Finally, the noise above them died down. Devin would never have believed it was possible but a change in the air made him certain it was evening. He was deathly tired of standing and he had at least a dozen questions he wanted to ask Armand. The enforced silence was wearing thin. Above them, the door to the performance hall was shut and locked.

A single pair of shoes tapped its way across the floor and stood in front of the hearth. Surely, it wasn't cold enough for a fire? Someone fumbled with the latches on the hearth but Armand and Chastel pulled down on them to keep the hearth from opening. The person above them knelt on the floor and pressed close to the crack between the floor and the stone.

"There is no one here but me," said a woman's voice. "You need to get away while you can. The soldiers will be back."

Marcus looked at Armand and neither of them moved.

"I'm Elsbeth, Dariel's wife. I know that you didn't kill him and I also know that one of you is a Master Bard, or you wouldn't know about the safe hole. Please release the latches so I can help you."

Armand exhaled audibly and nodded to Marcus. Armand released one latch and Chastel released the other. When the hearth opened up they all blinked in the light of dozens of candles.

"Let me help you," Elsbeth said. She was a big woman with broad shoulders. She reached a work-hardened hand down to Devin because he was the lightest and Marcus boosted him up onto the floor. Devin helped Armand up and then Chastel boosted Marcus while Armand and Devin pulled him up. Marcus turned and pulled Chastel up by both hands.

"Elsbeth," Armand said. "Do you remember me? I'm Armand Vielle, Master Bard of Ombria."

She went into his arms, laid her head against his shoulder and stayed that way for a long time. When she stepped back she touched Armand's face. "I'm glad they haven't found you yet. Why are you here? It's not safe for you in Calais. There are soldiers everywhere."

"We suspected they would try to kill Dariel next. We came hoping to save him," Armand said. "That sounds so pathetic because we didn't arrive in time to help him, at all. I am so sorry, Elsbeth."

Elsbeth shrugged. "I was at the market. I stopped to talk with some of the other women by the fountain. Had I returned a few minutes sooner I might have saved him myself."

"No, my dear," Armand answered kindly. "We would have lost you as well." He gestured at the two coffins surrounded by candles of every size. "What was Dariel's apprentice's name?"

"Absolon Colbert," Elsbeth said. "He has been with us for about three years."

Devin knew what Armand was thinking. Had the apprentice been new, it was possible that he had been planted by Forneaux's men. Three years was a long time to lie in wait for the proper time to betray your superior.

She continued. "Dariel knew that they were systematically killing the Master Bards. He thought his time was short." She faltered then, tears running down her face. "Do you think they killed Dariel first or Absolon?"

Armand hesitated. "I think they wanted information from your husband which he wouldn't give them. Absolon must have supplied it but they killed them both anyway."

She nodded, dabbing at her eyes with her apron. "I remember when being a Master Bard was the most honorable profession a man could have in the provinces. Now they slaughter you like dogs. What is it, Armand? What information do you have that the government wants?"

Armand took her hands in his. "Nothing you need ever worry about again, Elsbeth."

She looked uneasily at the locked door behind her. "It's important that you are able to leave here safely. Where will you go?"

"We have one more task to complete," Armand said.

"With God's help we can salvage something from this reign of terror."

She leaned forward and whispered, "Did you take his papers?"

"I have them," Armand said.

"Then you must go now. It's getting late but people have been stopping all afternoon and evening to bring food and say goodbye to Dariel. Everyone loved him."

"With good reason," Armand said, motioning them forward. "May we use the kitchen door?"

"Of course. Do you need food to take with you? There is more than I will ever eat." She led them past the two pine boxes set up on wooden trestles. Moreau's face still bore the ravages of his attackers; his apprentice merely appeared to be asleep.

Devin, personally, couldn't foresee a time when he wanted to eat again.

"We'll be fine," Marcus said. "Be safe, please."

Devin turned at the door. "I've been wondering how you knew we were hidden under the hearth?"

She smiled. "Your dusty footprints. Didn't your mother ever teach you to wipe your shoes when you come inside?'

"She did," Devin answered with a bow. "I have not been as careful in the provinces. Thank you for reminding me."

She opened the back door and checked her little garden, which was so much like Jeanette's. She kissed Armand and they walked out into the darkened streets of Little Calais.

"Don't talk," Marcus warned them all. "Armand, take us out of this town as quickly as possible."

They ducked into alleys and crossed half a dozen back streets. It was later than Devin initially thought. There were very few people about; here and there a dog barked or prowled the alleys looking for scraps of food. They passed two lovers pressed against the wall of a house, their arms locked around each other. Devin recognized the woman's red-striped skirt, hanging down in dirty tatters; her companion had his head down and his back to anyone passing by. Devin grabbed Marcus's arm and inclined his head. They maintained their pace as they walked past the couple but Marcus made an abrupt left turn into the next alley and raced to the end. Armand skidded halfway down, almost fell, and then limped valiantly to try to keep up with them. Devin took his arm as they made another rapid left turn and then another until they came back out at the intersection where the woman and her lover had been standing. The couple had gone but they heard running feet in the distance. Apparently, she had been commissioned to watch for them and it was only Marcus's quick thinking that had saved them from capture. They crossed the street quietly. Leaving the last few houses of Little Calais behind, they headed up along a hedgerow that concealed them as they fled back to the forests of Tirolien.

The moon hadn't risen and without its light they couldn't move very quickly. Armand was in no shape to travel, at all. He groaned with every step as he limped through the tall grass that snagged at his boots. Marcus took the lead while Armand gave him instructions. At first, he led them along some open fields and at last they reached the forest again. It seemed as though they walked for hours, Devin thought, but he could hardly complain when Armand limped doggedly along beside him with no complaints. How different might this escape have been if they had been able to save Moreau and his wife? There would have been a sense of euphoria and a hope that they had finally bested Forneaux's men.

At last, when the sky began to lighten, first to pink and then to gold, Marcus stopped in a grove of young evergreens where the ground was covered with brush.

"We'll stop here," Marcus announced. "I'm exhausted and I'm sure all of you are, too. Let's sit and eat and we can sleep for a while here under the brush. No casual pursuer will find us here."

Devin helped Armand to the ground. "What happened back there when you almost fell?" he asked.

Armand shook his head angrily. "I wrenched my bad knee. I'll be lucky if I can walk tomorrow."

Marcus and Chastel exchanged a look.

"Don't be so pessimistic," Devin said cheerfully. "How can I make you more comfortable?"

"The day I'll be comfortable, is the day I'll be dead," Armand grumbled.

Devin elevated Armand's knee on his pack and then dropped where he was, totally oblivious to the sticks and rocks that poked him in the back. The last day seemed nightmarish in retrospect and he had an awful feeling that the world was about to become much crueler and darker before they saw the light.

CHAPTER 41

Changes of Plans

Devin woke just after noon. He lay for a moment just soaking up the sun's warmth until he became aware of the whispered debate going on a few yards away from him.

"They are probably already hours ahead of us," Chastel said reasonably. "There may be nothing left to save once we arrive."

Devin sat up and moved away quietly from Armand, who was still sleeping, and sat down beside Chastel and Marcus. "What's the problem?" he asked, looking at their grim faces.

"We think that if the sign on Moreau's hand meant that either he or his apprentice revealed the location of Terre Sainté, then the records may already be destroyed. Forneaux's men could be hours ahead of us, Devin. There will be nothing left to save when we get there," Marcus whispered.

"If nothing else, we owe it to Armand to try, Chastel," Devin said. "This is Llisé's legacy, too, not just the legacy of the provinces. We are the only ones in a position to save it."

"Then why didn't you get up sooner?" Chastel joked.

"I was tired," Devin responded.

"My point exactly," Marcus said. "These men ahead of us have probably been in Tirolien for several days. They are starting off fresh and we are all exhausted."

"I'm not exhausted," Devin replied. "And I'll bet Chastel isn't either."

"Don't put words in my mouth," Chastel replied. "I could do with a good night's sleep, just like everyone else. The point is, Moreau is already dead and we were extremely fortunate to escape with Armand still alive. If we continue we will surely lose the Chronicles and maybe Armand, as well. We need to return to La Paix, where he will be safe."

"We can't accomplish anything by staying safe!" Devin said. "And Armand would be the first to agree with me."

"Consider this from our point of view, Devin," Chastel argued. "You and Armand are vitally important to this Empire. Are the Chronicles worth having both of you lose your lives?"

Devin didn't answer. "If we intend to beat these men to Terre Sainté, why are we sitting here arguing about it?" Devin asked. He glanced around. "Let's wake up Armand."

"No," Chastel answered, blocking Devin from going to Armand. "Let him sleep. He hurt his bad leg again last night, Devin. He's not going to be able to travel quickly."

"Then let Marcus and me go and you stay with Armand," Devin suggested.

"He'll never agree to that," Marcus said. "And I'm not certain I will either."

"Please understand this," Devin begged. "Not only are these records vital to the identity and self-esteem of the provincial people, but also, with the written Chronicles in hand, we can bring Forneaux down. This isn't some scavenger hunt to pass the time."

Devin jumped up. "What if we went now?" he said. "What if we left right this very minute?"

"Do you know the way?" Marcus asked.

Devin nodded. "Armand told me, in case something happened to him."

Marcus looked at Chastel. "If we go, Chastel," he said softly, "can you get Armand back to La Paix?"

Chastel exhaled. "I will do my best. There are no guarantees."

Devin removed Moreau's papers from his jacket and handed them to Chastel. "Take these with you. At least, if we are captured, Tirolien's Chronicle will be safe."

"If for any reason we should have to shape-change, Devin, they would be safer with you. I can't carry any baggage as a wolf."

"Well, I guess that's true," Devin said. He ripped the lining on his jacket and slid the papers up under his left arm.

Chastel handed them half the cheese that was left. Its surface was moist and slimy but it was better than nothing.

Devin shook Chastel's hand, suddenly terrified that he might never see either Armand or Chastel again. Chastel gave him a bear hug. "We'll see you at La Paix in a week and plan our takeover of the evil Shadow Government. Go now, before Armand wakens, please." Devin reached into his pocket and pulled out his rosary with the tiny extra cross. "Take this. You'll need it if you have to use the tunnels."

Marcus held out the brass button that Jules had given him. "You'll need this, too, to get back to La Paix."

"Then how will you and Marcus get back?" Chastel asked.

Devin laughed. "We'll rely on our charm and good looks! Slide the button on the wire with the cross. Can you put it around your neck so that it will stay on if you have to shape-change?"

"If nothing else I'll put it in my mouth. I'm sorry to take your rosary."

"It was a gift," called Devin as he and Marcus started out over the fields. "I expect it back!"

The first step of Armand's directions was simple enough: follow the line of the forest to the north-east coast beyond Calais. Marcus and Devin set off before noon. The terrain sloped downhill and the walking was relatively easily even without a road to follow. Occasionally, deer paths headed in the same direction that they needed to go. When the path was clear ahead, both of them ran to make up some time.

There was exhilaration in running. It made Devin feel free and unencumbered by the myriad problems that troubled his mind. In his heart, he knew that Chastel was probably right. Their chances of saving the documents now were slim. Only a miracle would save them and miracles were in short supply. The people who wanted to destroy them were so much closer to them geographically. Maybe they had always had an idea that the repository lay in this part of Llisé. Perhaps they only needed a bard who was driven to confess the exact location through pain and suffering.

Devin stopped abruptly as Marcus threw out his arm in front of him. "Someone's coming," Marcus whispered, grabbing Devin's arm and yanking him down an embankment; they rolled into a patch of brambles.

They lay flat, faces hidden against the ground, wedged under a bush whose thorns stabbed at them from every direction. Devin held his breath, listening for the sounds of voices, but heard only the rush of hooves instead. Sneaking a peek, he saw six deer racing down the path they had just been traveling.

"Something scared them," Marcus hissed. "Stay down and wait."

But though they remained hidden for at least a half an hour, nothing more appeared on the path above them. "Better safe than sorry," Marcus growled, climbing back up the slope.

"Wolves?" Devin asked.

"I don't think so," Marcus answered. "Wolves are relentless. They wouldn't have let that herd go. It may even have been something as simple as a flock of crows that scared them, but then the question remains: What scared the crows?"

"I've been wondering about Moreau," Devin said as they walked. "Did he seem to be the type of man who would have given up the location of Terre Sainté under torture?"

Marcus gave him a look. "No man ever knows how he will react to torture. Don't judge something that you know nothing about."

Devin shook his head. "I'm not judging at all. It's just that four other Master Bards died without disclosing its location."

"As I remember, none of them were tortured," Marcus replied. "Lucien Reynard was shot, Remi Maigny died in a fall, Phillippe Duvoison was poisoned, and Gautier Beau Chère drowned when his ship was scuttled."

"Adrian was beaten," Devin reminded him.

"I believe that Adrian was beaten so he would disclose Armand's location. If you remember, Armand didn't go to hear your final performance at Chastel's that last night. He stayed at the hall because he was so upset about Lucien Reynard's death. It was only later, when Forneaux's men came looking for Gaspard, that Armand went out to the chateau. Perhaps they expected him to still be at the Bardic Hall when they took Adrian."

"I guess I have put the causes of their deaths out of my mind," Devin said. "Moreau's death, I will never forget. But doesn't it seem stranger still to you that Moreau was beaten?"

"He was closest to where the Chronicles were," Marcus speculated. "Maybe they assumed that only he knew their exact location."

"I remember that you thought Jeanette might still be alive because we found Adrian beaten to death. You said that Forneaux's men would have beaten her first to get Adrian to talk."

"I still believe that," Marcus answered.

"Then why was Moreau beaten to death? Why didn't they start with his apprentice in the hope that Moreau would break at seeing him in pain?"

"They must have assumed that his apprentice didn't know the information. When Absolon tried to stop them from beating Moreau by blurting out the location, perhaps they simply killed him, too." Marcus stopped. "Devin, does any of this really matter? You've chosen your path; put everything else out of your head and concentrate on that."

"I suppose you are right," Devin said. He wondered if he would ever be able to understand the cruelty that one man could show to another. Moreau's performance hall would be forever indelibly etched in his brain. As hard as he tried, that scene overshadowed everything at the moment. The men they were dealing with were not reasonable men.

They were trained assassins. There would be no talking his way out of death should they meet over Llisé's Chronicles.

They continued without incident as the sun set behind the hill to their right. The sunset's fiery rays shooting through the trunks of the evergreens lent a spectacular end to the day. But they weren't in sight of water yet and their steps were slowing.

"How late do you plan to travel?" Devin asked, as the evening air cooled and filled the ravine where they walked.

"You are the one obsessed with reaching Terre Sainté," Marcus said. "It's your call."

"I think we should stop at dark," Devin said. "It's too hard to judge distance once the sun is down."

"The others probably set out from Calais and traveled right along the coast," Marcus pointed out. "Do you realize how fast a horse can travel compared to a man?"

"No, actually I don't," Devin answered.

Marcus laughed. "I don't either. I just don't want you to be disappointed if we reach the repository and everything is gone." He stopped and turned to look at him. "And dear God, Devin, I don't want to lose you. Your father will never forgive me if I do, and I could never forgive myself."

CHAPTER 42

Night Musings

Twilight didn't linger. Night came down with the suddenness of a dark curtain and Marcus tucked them in for the evening under an overhanging rock overlooking a small stream. The sound of water over stone was soothing but the subsequent swirling tendrils of mist rising from the water were unnerving. Normally they would have reminded Devin of Lavender's beautiful white pony, but tonight he saw only ghosts and assassins in the mist.

For the first time in several weeks Devin missed the safety and predictability of the Archives. If only he hadn't made a point of looking for consistency in the records he filed. In most cases he wasn't required or even encouraged to read the files he handled, and yet he had intentionally made a point of building up his own file of incidents that seemed questionable. At first it seemed strange that the reports often came from the same men or offices inside the government and it wasn't long before a pattern emerged. After a while, he could almost feel a file that had discrepancies before he even opened it. He'd left a list of them in his room at home in the center of a rolled-up green carpet that his mother seldom used. There was a second list in the Archives where only he could find it. He should have told his father before he left Coreé.

Somehow all of that research had led to where he was this evening: sitting with an empty belly in a forest in Tirolien, hunted by assassins and wondering if maybe tonight was his last night on earth. He fumbled for the comfort of his rosary, forgetting that he had passed it on to Chastel.

"Here," Marcus said, offering him his. "You use it much more than I do."

Devin shook his head. "We both may be dead by tomorrow night. Keep your rosary. You may need it."

"I don't," Marcus replied and dropped it into Devin's hand.

The cool, familiar stones slipped through Devin's fingers. The sizes of the stones were not all quite the same as the ones on his rosary but the type of rock was. It was as though touching them grounded him in Sorrento, the province his father's family had come from. "Thank you," he murmured.

They shared the last bit of greasy cheese that Chastel had sent with them and longed for more. The water from the stream was clear and cold and both of them drank and drank.

"Water fills an empty belly," Marcus announced. "They told us that in training. It works, too. You just have to piss a lot."

Devin laughed. "That's good to remember."

"Are you scared?" Marcus asked after a moment.

Devin nodded.

"Do you have a plan to rescue these documents once we reach Terre Sainté?"

"No," Devin said, shaking his head. "I thought somehow that either the Chronicles would be gone and we wouldn't have to save them, or they would be there and we could."

Marcus raised his eyebrows. "How many are there?"

"I don't even know. I should have asked. If every province but Viénne stores them there, then there must be quite a lot."

"More than we can carry?"

Devin nodded. "Probably."

"So, we'll need a wagon," Marcus stated. "Getting out of here with a wagon will be tough. We'll need produce or some kind of goods to cover the manuscripts with, or we'll be spotted before we go a mile."

Devin put his hand to his forehead. "This is a really bad idea, isn't it?"

"We'll work it out," Marcus said reasonably. "I used to have contacts in Calais. I could have gotten us a squad of men, a wagon, horses, and guards to take us back to La Paix safely. Now I don't know who I can trust. Where are all these manuscripts going?"

"I don't even know," Devin answered, appalled at his own ignorance. "Armand suggested the tunnels."

Marcus laughed. "I am not giving you any points as a strategist, Devin."

"We also left Jules and Gaspard completely up in the air," Devin added.

"No, we didn't. I told Jules that if we weren't back in a month, he could proceed with René Forneaux's assassination," Marcus replied.

Devin turned to look at him. "Even if the best plan involves Angelique?"

"The best plan does involve Angelique, even though none

of us wants to admit it. I left it entirely up to Jules. What he decides to do is his business."

Devin crossed his legs and leaned against the dense mossy side of the rock behind him. "Chastel said we can't fix everything."

"He's right."

"But if we succeed at this, we will have made a difference in the world, won't we?" Devin asked. "All I want, Marcus, is to leave this place a little better because I was here."

"Don't get all soppy on me. You're not going to die tomorrow," Marcus said. "Trust me. Now, shut up and go to sleep."

CHAPTER 43

The Last Day

Devin wakened to the drip of a steady rain from the overhang above them. It was still dark. Marcus sat next to him, a pistol across his lap. "How long ago did this start?" he asked.

"About an hour ago," Marcus said. "I'm surprised the thunder didn't waken you."

Devin rearranged himself to avoid the drips. "What time is it?"

"Around midnight," Marcus said.

"Let me watch while you sleep," Devin offered.

"Can you stay awake?" Marcus asked.

"I'll waken you if I can't," Devin said. "You need to sleep, too."

Marcus passed him his pistol. "It's not cocked. Do you remember how to do that?"

Devin nodded. "I do."

Marcus crossed his arms and closed his eyes. Devin sat and stared into the dark. He hoped that Chastel and Armand were somewhere dry tonight. The rain wasn't cold but it did nothing to improve his dismal mood. He wondered briefly what Marcus would say if he decided to forget the whole thing. Could they even retreat in safety? And would Armand hate him forever if they did?

He discarded that idea and watched lightning flicker over the mountain tops, giving trees and branches a macabre look. The thunder echoed on and on through the valleys and down to the sea. He imagined that in the rush of water from the stream and torrents of rain falling he could hear the waves crashing on the shore in the midst of the storm. If Armand had a plan to save the Chronicles, he hadn't shared it. Perhaps he, too, had hoped for divine inspiration at the last moment.

It was a long lonely night, with his thoughts skittering from one thing to another. He wished now that he'd had the opportunity to write to his parents or at the very least send them a message that he was all right. But then, after tomorrow maybe that would be a lie. Perhaps it was better not to get their hopes up. Instead of providing his father with eyes and ears in the provinces, he'd gotten himself into trouble in the first month and things had gone from bad to worse. Now the information that they had gathered along with all the Chronicles would probably be lost, as well.

He glanced at Marcus snoring peacefully. Despite Devin's initial doubts about Marcus's loyalty, his bodyguard had been with him every step of the way, even this last step, which might cost them both their lives. If Marcus died tomorrow protecting him, it would just be the loss of another life to add to the growing total that he was responsible for. God, had he known what awaited him in the provinces, he'd have heeded his father's advice and stayed home.

Devin was extremely thankful for the sunrise. The storm was over and the sun rose in nearly cloudless skies. The torrential rain had swollen their little stream into a raging torrent. The leaves and branches were spangled with glittering raindrops. Somewhere, he suspected there might have been a rainbow in the skies above the forest's canopy as the sun made its appearance just as the rain was ending.

Marcus woke up with a start. "You didn't need to let me sleep all night!" he protested. "Weren't you tired?"

"I was too tired to sleep," Devin replied. "It's as though I have a dozen rabbits racing around in my brain and every one of them wants a carrot."

"Too bad we couldn't fry one of those rabbits for breakfast," Marcus said wistfully. "Even our stream is pretty mucky this morning. It's a good thing I saved some water last night."

"Then I guess we might as well have a drink and be off," Devin said. "There isn't time to mourn our breakfast."

The road began to slope down to the sea. The trees became less dense and grassy spaces began to dot the forest around them. A brisk wind made the evergreens pelt them with their remaining raindrops as they walked. By noon, they could see the ocean below them. The waves thundered onto the shore, leaving muddy foam to mark their passage as they retreated back into the water again.

"Where do we go now?" Marcus asked.

"We follow the beach to the north until we come to a part that's very rocky. There is supposed to be some kind of a stone tower," Devin said.

"Well, that's a bit obvious!" Marcus blustered. "How do they expect to keep anything hidden if they put it in a stone tower that anyone can see?"

"It's not in the tower," Devin hissed. "That's just one of the landmarks we are to look for."

"Well, how was I to know?" Marcus snapped. "And then what?"

"We're to walk up the hill and into the forest. There is a little shepherd's hut," Devin said, "directly in line with the stone tower. It's built into the side of the hill near the top. Armand said it looks as though it's falling apart."

"And the Chronicles are in there?" Marcus asked in surprise.

"They are in a cave underneath it," Devin told him. "There's supposed to be a stairway hidden under the floor."

Marcus shook his head. "I hope you are right about this, Devin. It sounds like a God-damned trap."

"Armand gave me the instructions," Devin assured him, "and he has been here before."

"Armand was here when bards' lives weren't in danger," Marcus muttered.

From their viewpoint, the beach seemed to be deserted. There were no boats in the water because it was still too rough to go out after the storm. Waves crashed onto the beach, carrying wood and seaweed in the surf. The empty landscape did nothing to bolster Devin's confidence. The beach was too quiet and he had a nasty feeling in his gut that Forneaux's men had arrived before them. The top of the stone tower showed far down the beach ahead of them. Had it been an ordinary day, Devin would have liked to explore it. Today it seemed to be shouting "Danger! Danger! Stay away!" at them.

"This doesn't feel right," he said to Marcus.

"I feel that way, too," Marcus agreed. "Let's go back up into the woods."

"But, we need to ..." Devin began.

"We need to stay alive," Marcus said. "Follow me. We can always come back down later if I'm wrong. Try to act natural, as though you and I just decided to take a walk this morning with no destination in mind."

Devin stopped and looked at him. "Do you think they are already in the shepherd's hut?"

"I do," Marcus answered. "Let's pretend not to be interested and see what they do. Do you want a pistol? I have two."

Devin shook his head.

Marcus removed a knife from his belt. "At least take this."

Devin slid it into his belt. He thought of Angelique, so ready and willing to kill a man, and he wasn't certain that he actually could – not even to save his own life. "I still have Tirolien's Chronicle in my jacket," he said. "If they search me, they'll find it."

"We'll try to avoid that," Marcus said. "Is there any activity up the hill?"

Devin took a quick look. "None that I can see."

"They know what we want and they'll be willing to wait for us to come to them," Marcus said.

"What if they aren't here yet?" Devin asked, second-guessing his own intuition. Maybe the feelings he had were just about what they intended to do and had nothing to do with Forneaux's men being here at all.

"If they aren't there yet," Marcus replied, "we've lost nothing in trying this."

"How far do you intend to walk?"

"I want to go way up behind the shepherd's hut," Marcus said calmly. "If we have to wait them out for a couple of days, we will. I doubt they will have seen us yet; the tower is still a long way down the beach."

"Or maybe they don't care about us and they just want to destroy the Chronicles," Devin said. "Maybe we are just giving them extra time to do that."

"Trust me, Devin," Marcus said. "It's better to get an idea of who we are up against than to barge into a nest of hornets."

They turned up the hill and hiked back into the forest again. Devin felt more at ease almost immediately. The brush gave them cover and Marcus made him walk steadily higher until they had to duck between branches to even catch sight of the tower.

They continued to walk, twisting between the trees until they'd almost reached the top of the hill. "I'm hoping the hut is between us and the beach now. I don't suppose you have any idea how far up the hill it's supposed to be," Marcus whispered.

Devin shook his head. "Armand didn't say."

"Armand left out a lot of the important parts. I say we stay here for a while and see what happens below us," Marcus said, crouching down among the bushes, where he had a good view of the hill below them.

Devin sat down on his heels, as though that might give him a better chance of outrunning an assassin should the occasion occur, but the position was uncomfortable after a while. He sat down quietly on the damp ground next to Marcus. "Have you heard anything?" he asked.

"No, and I won't if you keep talking," Marcus answered.

"What if they aren't there? We've wasted a lot of time that we could have been using to save the Chronicles."

"They're there," Marcus hissed. "Now be quiet so they don't know that we are here."

"It's a little late for that," said a voice.

CHAPTER 44

Emile

Devin stood up so fast that he lost his footing and went down on one knee. Marcus had already drawn his pistol before he even turned around.

Two men in the uniforms of the *militaire* faced them. "Marcus," the taller one said. "We have finally caught up with you!"

"Emile," Marcus said calmly. "Whose side are you playing on today?"

"The winning side," Emile said with a smile. "I'm always on the winning side, my friend. Come down and join us." He gave Devin a mock bow. "You will enjoy this, Monsieur Roché. We've found this very primitive little archive, right in the middle of the forest, but I believe you knew it was here, didn't you?"

Devin said nothing. He turned and walked with them, surprised that Emile hadn't taken Marcus's pistol. He had a growing sense of dread with every step he took down the hillside.

The shepherd's hut was tucked up into the hill. Its roof

was the earth of the hillside. A few dozen stones slanted and curved to mark the doorway. The wooden door with its rounded top probably wouldn't close completely. It hung on rusted hinges, the bottoms of its boards scraped and splintered by years of being forced into place. It seemed pathetic that the Chronicles were stored in such a forlorn-looking building.

"I know what you are thinking," Emile said, beckoning to Devin. "But wait until you see the inside."

Marcus nodded for him to go ahead. There were two more men inside, lounging on the dirt floor. They stood at attention when Devin and Marcus came in but the action seemed almost comical, as though they mimicked the correct posture. Apparently, the floor only appeared to be dirt. A center stone had been brushed clean and pulled up from the floor and a set of carved serpentine steps went down into the ground.

"Amazing, no?" Emile said. "It is more amazing down below. Would you like you to see?"

Devin nodded, wondering if he had just signed his own death warrant. The darkness below reminded him of the safe hole in Moreau's performance hall. All Emile would need to do was slide the stone back over to close off the entrance and he would be trapped, starving to death among the provincial Chronicles.

Emile lit a torch. "Take this with you so you can see," he said cheerfully. "Marcus, would you like a torch, too, or is one enough?"

"I'll take one, too," Marcus answered. "I can't let Devin go down alone."

Emile grinned. "Of course not, I didn't expect you to."

Devin hesitated but Marcus put a hand on his shoulder. "Do you want me to go first?"

318

Devin shook his head. He took the torch from Emile's hand and bent to steady himself on the floor as he descended the stone stairway. He gasped when he reached the bottom. Armand had once compared this repository to the Archives and Devin could see why. The sheaves of paper were neatly packaged in fabric bags, embroidered with each province's emblem. The bags took up nearly two full walls and there was room for more. He slid one of Ombria's bags from the shelf, traced the wolf emblem that was exactly like the one embroidered on his cloak. How dare Coreé refer to the provincials as primitives? They had duplicated a simple archival system that worked just as well for them as it did for Coreé.

"It's amazing," Marcus said behind him.

Devin had forgotten he was even there; he was so entranced with the way the Chronicles were shelved. He laughed out loud. "I'll bet they are in alphabetical order, too!"

Marcus pushed him along to the shelves farthest from the stairway. "Emile is part of your father's guard, Devin. I've known him for years. He's cocky but he's always been loyal. I have no idea what is going on here."

"If he's one of my father's men, how would he know we were going to be here?" Devin said.

"I don't know, except that if Forneaux has been gathering information, surely your father has been, too. Did you think he would allow you to disappear without looking for you? He has lots more resources than Forneaux has."

"I don't know who to trust," Devin whispered.

Marcus sighed. "I'll admit I agree with you. Let's go back up. Maybe we can determine what's going on."

"Is everything all right down there?" Emile called, his head sprouting from the doorway above them.

"We're on our way up," Marcus answered, as he moved to the stairway.

He and Devin passed their torches to two of the men who were waiting. The hut felt incredibly crowded and Devin just wanted to go outside. He positioned himself near the door in case he had to run, his hand on the knife hilt in his belt.

"How do you happen to be here?" Marcus asked Emile. "It seems terribly convenient that you arrived right before we did."

"We had people stationed in Calais in case Devin tried to take a ship home. I believe you are acquainted with a young woman who threw an apple at you?" Emile said with a smirk at Devin. "She spotted you as soon as you came into the city. We thought we had you in Little Calais but Marcus eluded our agents."

"You were sent by the Chancellor?" Marcus asked.

Emile smiled. "I guess you weren't listening earlier, Marcus. I said I was playing for the winning side."

"Forneaux?" Marcus demanded, pulling his pistol from his belt.

"At the moment," Emile agreed. "We'll see how the wind blows. Put that thing away, Marcus. There are four men here with guns. Do you think you are going to be able to kill all of us before we are able to get to you and the boy?"

"I wasn't chosen to be the Chancellor's bodyguard because I run away from a fight," Marcus said, putting himself between Devin and the others.

"That's why Forneaux asked me to offer you a job," Emile said. "You could be incredibly helpful to the new regime."

"New regime!" Devin spat out. "My father is Chancellor Elite of Llisé. There will be no new regime!"

"I guess you haven't heard," Emile said. "Opposition to your father as Chancellor is growing daily. Forneaux is poised to gather up the reins of the government as soon as Roché is deposed."

"He can't be deposed without a vote of Council!" Devin snarled. "Chancellors are not so easily set aside!"

"Perhaps he will simply be shot by a disgruntled soldier," Emile replied with a grin. "I would volunteer for the job."

"You bastard!" Devin snapped angrily, stepping forward.

Marcus halted him with an arm across his chest.

Emile chuckled. "Your life will be short enough, Devin. Don't waste the few moments you have left on a lost cause." He gestured with his hand at the two soldiers who held the torches. "Set fire to this precious little archive, will you?"

"No," Devin yelled, struggling against Marcus. "Do you have any idea what you are doing? You can't simply destroy something like that!"

Emile smiled. "You'd be surprised. Paper burns very quickly."

The soldiers descended the staircase and were gone only a few moments before smoke billowed out the doorway in the floor.

"Maybe we should continue our discussion outside," Emile said calmly. "It's about to get very smoky in here."

"Damn you!" Devin yelled. "You are destroying the entire history of the provinces. What kind of man are you?"

"I'm a man who follows orders," Emile replied. He stood, backed by his four accomplices, two on his right and two on his left. "Christ, I gave you a few moments to admire them – I didn't have to do that. What more do you want from me?"

"Calm down," Marcus hissed at Devin. "You'll only make matters worse."

"Good advice," Emile said, "which brings us to our next order of business. Marcus Berringer, I am prepared to offer you the same position that you now hold – bodyguard to the Chancellor. The Chancellor may change but your position will not. You would be incredibly valuable to René Forneaux. You have information that no one else has." Emile shifted with a swagger and waved his gun in the air. "There is only one test that you must pass before you can take your new position. I will need you to kill the Chancellor's son, because if you don't, I will shoot you both where you stand."

Devin's mouth went dry. He backed away so that he and Marcus could make a run for it, but his bodyguard turned and looked directly at him. He cocked his pistol and aimed at Devin's head.

"I'm sorry, Devin," Marcus said. "I hoped it wouldn't come to this."

Acknowledgements

First of all, I want to thank my family: my husband, Dennie and my daughters Mollie and Elizabeth for their unswerving support and love! Please add a round of applause to my faithful proofreaders: Dennie, Elizabeth, and Cody Magill.

Special thanks goes to Veronica Pacella, Jackie Adams, and my SCBWI Critique Group who gave me the confidence to submit my manuscript and offered suggestions and encouragement.

I especially want to acknowledge Harper Voyager for the fantastic opportunity they gave me in publishing this fantasy series! I will never forget Natasha Bardon's phone call from London to tell me they would be "delighted" to publish *Among Wolves*. I have accomplished a livelong goal in seeing this series come to life on the printed page and no matter how many novels I write the *Wolves of Llisé* will remain forever set apart and special because it was the first! Thank you also to Lily Cooper who untiringly answers my questions and emails.

Grim Tidings, the second book in the *Wolves of Llisé*

series remains a tribute to the tradition of oral storytelling and the power of both the written and spoken word!